# THE

# SHIELD RING

# THE
# SHIELD RING

*Rosemary Sutcliff*

*Illustrated by*
*C. Walter Hodges*

New York

HENRY Z. WALCK, INC.

*First Edition 1956*
*Reprinted 1957, 1960*

*Printed in Great Britain by Richard Clay and Company, Ltd.,*
*Bungay, Suffolk*

For Crooky, who first put me on the
track of the Northmen in Cumberland,
and for Spencer, who helped me to
follow it up.

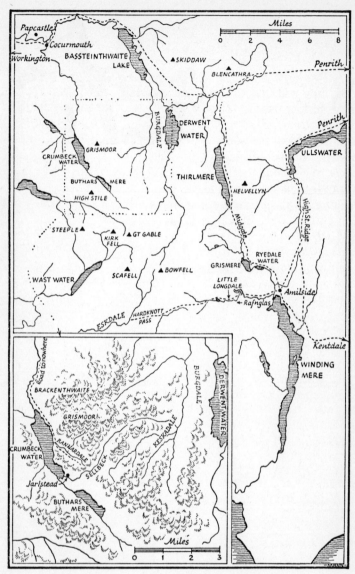

The Lake Land as it was in Jarl Buthar's day

## AUTHOR'S NOTE

SAVE FOR RANULF LE MESCHIN, I do not think that you will find the people of this story mentioned in any history book. Nevertheless, they were real people, though the trace of them and their long-drawn fight for freedom is in local tradition, not in written history; in old stories and the names of places, and the odd fact that Domesday Book, the Conqueror's great Survey of England, stops short at the foot of the Cumberland fells, and Lake Land finds no mention in it. Buttermere still bears the name of the Norse Jarl Buthar who made his stronghold there and from it held all Lake Land free of the Normans for thirty years. Aikin's How still looks down on Keskadale and the low ground toward Derwentwater, marking the place where Aikin the Beloved was laid, with his great sword Wave-flame in his hand and his hound Garm at his feet, after the last battle of all.

R. S.

# CONTENTS

# I

## THE PALE FLAME

THE THING HAPPENED with the appalling swiftness of a hawk swooping out of a quiet sky, on a day in late spring, when Frytha was not quite five.

She had been out about the sheep with Grim, who had been her father's shepherd in the old days before Norman William laid waste the North in payment for the massacre of his York garrison, and was now hind, ploughman and everything else as well; and they had made a wide cast through Garside Wood on the way home, to visit a flycatcher's nest that Grim had found for her. Five speckled eggs the nest had in it, faintly and wonderfully blue. Now they were on their way home in earnest; little black hairy Grim and Frytha with her kirtle kilted to her bare briar-scratched knees and her honey-brown hair full of twigs, hand in hand, in companionable silence, for Grim discouraged chatter in the woods; it drove things away, he said. And just ahead of them, Vigi the big black sheep-

I

dog, looking round every few moments to make sure that they were following. Vigi was as silent in the woods as his master, and never chased squirrels or ran yelping on the scent of the fallow deer, as more foolish dogs did.

They were late, for there had not really been time for such a roundabout way home. The last sunlight had flickered out among the tree-tops long since and as they came up the long slope toward the crest of the ridge, the day was fading fast and the woods growing shadowy about them. 'I shall ketch it from thy mother, bringing thee home at owl-hoot,' Grim said, grinning down at Frytha through the tangle of black hair that almost covered his face.

Frytha gave something between a gasp and a giggle by way of reply, for the slope was steep just there and full of pitfalls. She had an uneasy feeling on the edge of her mind that she also would ketch it from her mother, but most of her was still taken up with the flycatcher's nest, and in her heart she knew that a possible smacking was no more than a fair price to pay for the round perfection of the moss-lined nest and the magic of those five eggs; so tiny, and so blue under the darkness of the ivy leaves.

They were almost at the top of the ridge now, and the white tip of Vigi's tail waving plume-wise just in front of her was beginning to take on a faint shine of its own, as white flowers shine in the twilight. She climbed on, and on, her legs growing tired under her—and then all at once she knew that something, somewhere, was wrong.

All about her, the wood was uneasy. The little rustlings and flutterings of the woodland creatures had died away as though there were a storm coming. Vigi seemed to catch the strange unease at the same moment. He stopped in his tracks, his muzzle raised, the white star of his tail tip quivering downward. And when Frytha reached out to touch his back, she felt his coat rise under her palm, and snatched her hand away as though something had stung her.

'Grim!' She was suddenly frightened, too, as Vigi began to stalk forward on stiff legs. 'Grim, I don't like it!'

2

Grim said nothing, but his hand tightened over hers until it hurt her, and she had the feeling that his hairs were rising in the same way as Vigi's.

A distant confused sound of shouting came dipping toward them over the crest of the wooded ridge.

And then they were on the crest, among the crack-willow and whitethorn of the woodshore, staring down the long curve of ploughland and summer fallow toward the home steading.

There were many men down there, a dark flicker of men all round the house-place and among the byres, and a saffron flicker of torches, and in the instant that they checked there on the woodshore, something like a flower—a rose—of flame sprang out on the house-place roof, and spread and blurred, sending out wriggling threads of brightness through the dark thatch.

Next instant Grim had a hand on Vigi's collar, and the other round Frytha, scooping her up, sweeping both of them back into the shelter of the trees. 'Bide you here,' he said, setting her down among arching brambles between the roots of an ancient may tree, 'and bide you still, until I come again.' And to Vigi he said 'Keep!' as he did when he wanted him to hold a clump of sheep together. Then he was gone, slipping along the woodshore like a shadow, toward the place where the curving wind-break ran down toward the rick-garth.

Vigi lay down in front of Frytha, nose on paws, watching her with an unwinking gaze, as he would have watched a clump of sheep left in his charge, unmoving so long as they did not move. Frytha made no attempt to move. She sat where Grim had set her down, like a young hare frozen in the grass when a hawk hovers over, staring down through the brambles and tall-growing things of the woodshore. She saw the torches jigging to and fro; she saw the threads of fire spread and run together, until suddenly a sheet of flame leapt into the dusk, roaring up from the dry thatch. She heard cattle lowing and the frightened neighing of a horse, and saw the dark shapes of her father's kine against the fire, as men drove them past

3

toward the Lancaster road; and the shouting seemed to rise higher with the flames. The flames were pale and bright in the dusk. That was the thing that Frytha remembered ever afterward: the pale bright flame of burning thatch.

Behind her, Garside Wood began uneasily to make its night-time noises; bats flittered needle-squeaking overhead among the branches of the may tree, and the owls were crying, answering each other from tree to tree, and still Frytha sat frozen, waiting for Grim to come back. She was not afraid; she seemed to have gone through fear and come out the other side in a place where it was black and very cold. It seemed a long, long time that she waited, a whole night—many nights. And yet the dusk had not deepened to full dark when there was the faintest rustle among last year's leaves, and the ghost of a whine from Vigi, and Grim was crouching beside her breathing hard as though he had been running.

It seemed to Frytha that the shouting was coming nearer, but she could not see what was happening, because now Grim was between her and the open land. But she saw the sheet of flame leap higher yet, rimming the bramble leaves with fire behind the dark bulk of his head and shoulders as he looked back. 'That is thy home burning,' he said in a grating voice that did not sound like Grim at all. 'That is the Normans' work, and never thee forget it!'

Then he caught her up, and began to run again, deeper and deeper into the wood. Once or twice he checked to listen, craning his chin over one shoulder or the other, and Frytha, clinging to him without quite knowing why, could feel the life-thing in his chest, where he was holding her tight against it, thud-thud-thud, very fast, like the hoof-beats of a stampeding horse, somehow more frightening than the torchlight and the shouting behind them. And then at last there was no more torchlight and no more shouting; only the night sounds of the woodland, when Grim stopped to listen. Only the bark of a dog fox in the distance, and the little night wind among the trees.

After that there was a time that always seemed to Frytha,

4

looking back on it, to be a kind of cloud in which things came and went half seen and no more real than the things one dreams just before waking up. She thought that they went a long way, she and Grim and Vigi. There were days and nights in the cloud, and sometimes she walked until her legs gave out, but most often Grim carried her on his back or on his shoulder. Grim was very kind to her in this way, and spread his ragged cloak over her in the night time, when she lay curled against Vigi for warmth. But there did not seem to be any warmth in Vigi, no warmth anywhere. Sometimes there were things to eat—once Vigi caught a hare, and Grim cooked it in a fire that he lit from the little fire-stones he always carried with him; and once they robbed a hen's nest that they found in a ruined garth, and sucked the warm eggs. And Frytha ate whatever Grim gave her to eat, and lay down and got up, and walked or climbed on to his back to be carried, just as he told her; and never thought to ask, or even wonder, where they were going, because she never really understood that they were going anywhere, only that the world had fallen to pieces and that it was very cold among the ruins.

Then there began to be mountains: grey and dun and purple mountains with mist hanging among their high corries, that towered above the tangle of forest and marsh and great sky-reflecting lakes; mountains so high that the upward rush of them made her want to crawl under something and hide. There were men, too, though which came first, the men or the mountains, she never knew; but clearly they belonged to each other. And after the men came there was more food—flat cakes of barley bread that looked as hard as millstones; but when Grim broke a piece off one and gave it to her, it was soft and sweet under the hard crust as bread newly baked. Once there was a steading at the foot of a great sweep of moor, and warm milk in a little birchwood bowl, and a woman who was kind. Frytha thought that the woman would have had them stay, but Grim would not; and they pressed on again, and the men with them—but whether they were the same men she did not know.

The mountains began to come down all around them; either that or they were climbing up into the mountains, further and further up until the world of men was left behind and they came into another world that belonged to the great singing wind of the emptiness. And then they came down out of the emptiness, down and down and down, and there was a grey lake shore in the twilight, and little wavelets lapping on it.

And at last, when she had fallen half asleep in Grim's arms, bursting on her unawares out of the gathering dusk, there was a great hall full of firelight and torchlight and hounds and men and a roar of voices.

With Vigi at his heel, Grim carried her straight in, thrusting through the thronging men and hounds, toward a golden giant who turned in the High Seat, midway up the hall, to watch them coming; and bent and set her down on the giant's knee.

The giant put out an arm on which there were great golden rings twisted like serpents above the elbow, and crooked it about her lest she roll straight off again; and his eyes under their thick golden brows went thrusting from her to Grim and back. 'God's greeting to you, Stranger,' he said, in a voice that matched his huge size. 'What wind is it blows you and the bairn up here into Butharsdale?'

'A wind from Normandy, Jarl Buthar,' Grim said harshly.

'So. What roused the wind this time? Deer-stealing?'

'Some hungry fool robbed and slew a knight on the Lancaster road, half a moon since, and for that the whole countryside must pay wyrgeld in blood and burning. It is in my heart that my master knew who the robber was, and would not give him up. For that also there must be payment.'

A ragged muttering rose from the men along the walls, who had fallen silent to listen.

'The North has paid over much wyrgeld in blood and burning for Duke William's York garrison twenty summers ago,' said Jarl Buthar, as though half to himself. 'And so you fled up here into the mountains.'

6

'Aye, as many a one has done before.'

The Jarl nodded, pulling with his free hand at his golden beard. 'Aye, many and many a one; and none that was not heartily welcome.' He looked down at Frytha. 'Is the bairn yours?'

'Nay, I was her father's man, and his father's before him, in the days when the farm was rich before the wasting of the North, with as many serfs on the land as there are fingers on my two hands. Of late years there's been none but me.'

Frytha heard their voices going to and fro above her, but the words had no meaning. Just for a moment, as the light and the roar of voices broke over her, she had thought that she was going to wake up, and find herself in her own corner behind the bolster in the great box bed at home. But she had not woken up, and she was not in her own corner; she was in a place such as she had never seen before: a long firelit hall that must surely be greater than the great church at Lancaster where her father had taken her last Christmas-tide. Roof-trees rose out of the firelight into the dark beyond the drifting peat-reek overhead, like trees in the aisles of a forest, and everywhere there were men, crowding the benches along the shadowy walls, lounging with their legs outstretched among the hounds on the fern-deep floor, with the firelight flickering on their weapons and in their eyes. Her gaze scurried to and fro among them, searching frantically for faces that she knew, but they were all strange to her save Grim standing with a hand on Vigi's collar; and Grim and Vigi were part of the bad dream in which she was trapped, so that they could not help her now.

And then her darting, terrified gaze found another giant, sitting close at the golden giant's feet; a grey giant, this one, with nothing golden about him save the firelight on the strings of the harp he held on his knee. His mane of hair was striped and brindled grey and dark, with a great white wing in it so that it seemed to grin like a badger's striped mask in the fire-light; and long yellow teeth showed in the grey tangle of his beard as he smiled up at her, so that his face might have been the most frightening of all the faces there, but it made Frytha think of Bran, her father's old brindled wolfhound, who she had loved, and somehow that made it a thing to cling to.

'. . . I crept in under their noses for a closer look,' Grim was saying, 'but there wasn't naught to do but bring the bairn away.'

And suddenly the faces were closing in on Frytha, all eyes and teeth, and terrible because they were strange. She sat rigidly upright on the Jarl's knee, like a small proud figure carved in stone; but her wide terrified eyes were fixed on the grey giant's face like a cry for help. The grey giant laid down his harp and rose to his feet with a harsh exclamation. She did not hear what he said, nor what the golden giant answered, but strong arms caught her and swung her up, up and away out of the confusion and the terrible crowding faces.

Food was being brought for Grim and the mountain men who had come with him, and room and welcome made for them on the benches, as the grey giant carried Frytha high against his shoulder up the Jarl's Hearth Hall, and thrusting open a door at the end of it, into a place beyond.

Here there was softer, clearer light from a lamp, and women were gathered round the central hearth, combing and braiding their hair as Frytha's mother had used to do when she made ready for bed; and one of them, who was tall like a spear, with a cloud of pale hair round her head, rose from a cushioned bench as they entered, and came quickly through the rest, saying, 'Why, what is this that you bring us, Haethcyn?'

'A girl-bairn,' said the grey giant, 'a small, very spent girl-bairn, with a long road and a burned home behind her, my Lady Tordis. A shepherd has just brought her in from beyond Lancaster.'

'Her father?'

'Nay, you must ask of the Normans concerning her father, and all her kin,' the grey giant said meaningly.

The other women were exclaiming softly and bitterly as they crowded round. The one who was like a spear said:

8

'Give her to me,' and held out her arms. 'Signy, do you bring milk and warm it. . . . Ah, poor bairn, she's as light as a half-fledged tit.' She asked no more questions. She had seen many fugitives from the outer world here in this Norse settlement of the Cumberland Fells, but she sat down again beside the hearth, and held Frytha close on her lap, and called her by the soft cradle names that Frytha's mother had used.

Frytha sat as still and straight on the woman's knee as she had done on the Jarl's, not hearing the cradle names, and looked about her. The light of the low-set lamp scarcely reached to the walls, and the gloom seemed to move and deepen among the great carved kists and the furry animal darkness of bear and wolf skins piled upon the low benches; and there was something tall and skeleton-gaunt against the gable wall that might be a loom in the daytime, but was not quite a loom now, and a thing that glimmered pale behind the half open door of the huge box bed as though something were crouching there.

The women had gathered about the fire again, and Frytha's gaze scurried to and fro among them, searching as she had searched among the faces in the hall. They looked back at her kindly, but they were not her mother; and the grey giant had gone, and taken safety with him; and she had lost even Grim now. A very old woman sat by the fire spinning; her hair was like rough silver in the lamplight, but her brows were black as feathers from a raven's wing, and under them she peered at Frytha, half smiling, through the faint fronds of the peat smoke.

'That is Unna. She will be very kind to you,' said the woman like a spear, seeing whom Frytha was looking at. 'She was my nurse when I was smaller than you are now, and she was very kind to me.'

The girl called Signy had come back from somewhere, with a pipkin of milk, and as she stooped to set it over the fire, her shadow leapt up and swallowed half the chamber, as though she had spread dark wings. Panic began to whimper up in Frytha, tightening in her chest so that it was hard to breathe;

9

but the woman held her closer, and whispered, 'Na Na, you must not be afraid, Tita, there is nothing here to be afraid of. Soon you shall have some warm milk, and then you will sleep. You shall have a little straw pillow, and a dappled deerskin to keep you warm; and in the morning when you wake, the shadows will be gone—all gone, you will see.'

But she could not reach Frytha through the nightmare.

And then there was a faint rustling somewhere in the far shadows, like an animal gathering itself to spring; and with a little gasp, Frytha wrenched herself round to face it. Something was humping and upheaving in the darkness of a closet that yawned blackly in the far wall. One of the women laughed half in exasperation, but Frytha never heard her. She was watching the humping and upheaving in a fascinated horror that left no room for anything else.

But the thing that shook itself clear of the shadows and the dark piled skins was neither wolf nor ghost, but a boy. He stood in the closet doorway, shaking the black hair from his face, and stared at her. Frytha stared back. He was a year or two older than she was, a very dark boy—as dark as Grim—with a long cleft chin, and eyes as tawny-pale as peat water and as bright as a wild animal's. And something in his ruthlessly interested stare came piercing through the nightmare, and reached Frytha in the cold place where she was, so that all at once she drew a long breath, and let it go out softly, like a sigh.

'I heard things happening,' said the boy. 'What does the girl-bairn here?'

'You should be asleep,' one of the women began. 'The wolf out of the North Star will come and eat you if——'

But the woman like a spear said very quietly: 'No, Margrit, wait,' and her hold on Frytha grew lighter.

The boy completely ignored the interruption. 'Why does she look like that?' he demanded. 'Has somebody hurt her?'

'Somebody has hurt her, yes,' said the woman like a spear, and her touch on Frytha grew as light as a leaf.

Without knowing it, Frytha slid off her lap, and stood wavering a little with sheer weariness, then moved forward. At the same instant, the boy moved forward also. They squatted down in the rushes, and stared at each other, tense and wary, like two small wild things, each unsure whether the other is friend or enemy, or perhaps both; while the women watched, and from the great hall beyond the door came the sound of voices and harp music to fill the silence.

The girl Signy was making a soft nest of rugs on one of the sleeping-benches; and when that was done, she brought a little bowl of blue earthenware, and poured the warm milk into it, and brought a piece of bannock thick with butter, and gave them to Frytha.

For the first time the boy's eyes moved. He looked at the bannock, and put both hands over his stomach. 'I am hungry, too,' he said.

The old woman Unna gave a cackle of laughter. 'Never think to feed one puppy and fast another in the same basket!'

So Signy laughed too, and brought more buttered bannock and gave it to the boy, who took it without again turning his gaze from Frytha's face, and began to chew.

Frytha tried to eat her own bannock, but she was not hungry; and now that she was no longer afraid, she was growing desperately sleepy. Someone was coaxing her at least to drink the milk, and she managed to obey. Everything was turning hazy, and the warm milk seemed to make it hazier still; but even through the waves of sleep, she saw the pale bright eyes of the boy staring at her; and she stared back over the tilting rim of the bowl.

Then the voices were saying something about going to sleep, and somebody stooped over her as though to pick her up. But the boy swallowed his last mouthful of bannock with a gulp, and reaching out, caught hold of the tattered hem of her kirtle. 'Na Na,' he said. 'She must come in-by with me'; and then, speaking to Frytha herself for the first time, 'Come you.'

And wavering to her feet, unquestioningly, Frytha came, followed by the cackling laughter of the old woman by the fire. 'He is the Lordly One! The Lordly One! "Come you," says he, like as it might be the King of Norway!'

It was warm and dark under the skins in the closet, and Frytha and the boy burrowed together like a pair of puppies. She was too far gone in sleep to hear the women moving in the Bower, or the sea-surge of voices in the great hall where the men still sat; but she felt and heard when the boy rolled over against her shoulder, and whispered 'What is your name?'

'Frytha.'

'My name is Bjorn the Bear, and my father's name was Bjorn the Bear, but mostly people call me "Bear-cub" yet awhile,' said the boy, and flung an arm over her neck. 'I shall call you Fryth, but nobody else must. And nobody shall hurt you again, excepting me.'

And then the quiet and kindly waves of sleep broke over her.

## II

## THE HARP

A T FIRST FRYTHA found it hard to understand what
the people of the Jarlstead said to her, for though the
Norse tongue was close kin to the Saxon, there were
many differences between the two. But as time went by it
came more and more easily to her, until she could speak the
pure Norse with the Countess Tordis, and change to her old
tongue when chattering to Grim, without even noticing that
she was making the change at all.

And as her new tongue grew friendly and familiar, so little
by little her new life grew friendly and familiar also, and the
old one sank away into the distance behind her, so that in a
year or two, she often went whole days without once thinking
of it.

The Jarlstead was the centre of her world. The great
Hearth Hall where the fire never quite went out even in the
hottest weather, and where the High Seat was made from the
timbers of the Viking ship whose snarling figure-head, set high
and smoke-dimmed on the main house-beam now, had led the
Jarl's foreganger west-over-seas in the days of Harald Fairhair. The bower and byres and barns that clustered round

the Hall, the kale-garth and the apple-garth where the bee-skeps stood. That was the centre; and the rest of the world opened out from it little by little, like the petals opening slowly from the heart of a flower, until at last it took in the whole Dale, from the strong place at the foot of Crumbeck Water where the grain and cattle came in by night from all the Alverdale lowlands, to the little stone-built chapel at the head of Butharsmere, where Storri Sitricson went up every Sunday and rang the bell that hung from a rowan tree beside the porch, and preached the Word of God to all who came to hear.

There were other children in Frytha's world. Little round-about Gerd, whose father was Hakon Wall-eye, one of the Jarl's Chieftains, and Erland Ormeson, and Jon from the Millhouse, with his freckles and his small merry eyes and his taste for standing on his head. Gille Butharson, too, who would be Jarl one day after his father—but he was eleven, almost grown-up—and many more. A mingled pack of children and dogs, and always there was the boy Bjorn.

Bjorn's father had been one of the Jarl's household warriors, until he was killed in the fighting which was always a background to the life of the Dale; and his mother had died soon after he was born; and now he was foster-son to Haethcyn the huge grey harper, who had been his father's friend.

When Bjorn was seven, which was just half a year after Frytha came to the Dale, he went to sleep with the other boys in the lofts and byres around the Hearth Hall, and Frytha was left to sleep by herself in the little closet opening off the bower; and at first she was desolate with loneliness every night. But she did not cry, not even on the first night, when old Unna crept in to comfort her with a little hot apple, which somehow made it very hard to bear.

Everyone treated Unna with great respect because she had the Second Sight, and who knew what ill thing in the future she might foresee for anyone who annoyed her? She had come with the Lady Tordis from her old home in Barra and been nurse to the three bairns who had all died in the cradle before Gille came, and then nurse to Gille; but now that Gille was long past her nursing, she sat by the fire, spinning, always spinning, gossamer yarn such as few but she had the skill for, from the soft wool pulled from behind the ears of the little dark mountain sheep. A great spinner, old Unna, and a great teller of stories, wonderful stories, with a kind of twilight mystery about them, a gloom shot through with strange lights, like those that one could see sometimes raying across the northern sky in winter. Stories of seal women, and kingdoms under the sea, that she had brought with her from the Sudreys, the islands in the west; stories of trolls and ghosts and heroes, too; of the far north where there was no sun, but only frost and darkness, while deep down under the frozen earth burned great fires where the dwarf kind worked with gold and silver and iron, and wrought such weapons as only heroes might wield. 'Such swords as Wave-flame, that Ari Knudson carries,' said old Unna.

Frytha loved the stories that Unna told while the women spun and wove the wool of the last clipping. It would be a while and a while yet before Frytha would be old enough to learn to spin, but she fetched and carried for the others, and cut off loose ends where they told her to, so she was not idle. She began to help when the women baked and brewed; and she worked with the other children at harvest time in the little fields of barley and flax that clung to the lower slopes of the fells. They had fun in the harvest-fields, fun at seed-time, too, with the bird-scaring. But best of all were the times when she could slip away and run wild with Bjorn the Bear-cub.

With Bjorn, she scoured the fells like a goat, pushing further and further afield as her legs lengthened. They speared gold and silver char in the tails of the mountain pools; they rough-rode the shaggy half-wild ponies, and spent long days out on the hill sheep runs with Grim and Vigi, who lived in a little shepherd's hut far up the Sell Glen and helped to keep the Jarl's sheep. They slid and scrambled among the rocks, and explored the mountain streams, and lay hour-long on their stomachs among the heather, watching things.

On a spring day almost a year after Frytha came to the Dale, they were lying on their stomachs on the shoulder of Beacon Fell, high above Butharsmere. The year was still young, and the little wind blew chill through the long heather, smelling wonderfully of bog and thin sunshine, and a little of the snow that still dappled the north-eastern crests of the high fells; and all around them the curlews were crying, filling all the world with their wild bubbling music.

It was a curlew that they were watching now, a curlew at his mating flight, weaving, it seemed to Frytha, a kind of garland of flight round the place where his chosen mate must be, among the heather. He skimmed low over the ground, then suddenly swerved upward, up and up, hung a moment poised on quivering wings, and then came planing down, his wings arched back to show the white beneath, skimmed low again, and again leapt skyward. And all the while he was calling, calling; a lovely spiral of sound bubbling and rippling with delight. But his whole dance, undulating, floating, swerving, with always that flash of underwing silver on the downward swoop, was a dance of sheer delight.

To Frytha, watching entranced, it seemed all the more lovely because it had come unsought, like a shining gift dropped into their laps from nowhere. They had tried so often to get close to a curlew, without the least success ('wary as a curlew' people said, and with reason). And today they had been merely lying on their stomachs watching a beetle, when the wild sweet bubbling had risen from the fellside almost under their noses, and Bjorn had parted the heather very carefully and there he was, weaving his lovely garland of flight, now high in the air, now almost brushing the heather tops with his wings, so close that as he hung poised they could see the sunlight shining through the tips of his quivering pinions.

And then suddenly it was all over. The she curlew leapt up from the heather, and was away, sweeping right over their heads, and her mate after her, calling as he flew, and where they had been, there was nothing but the wind brushing along the fellside.

For a moment neither of the children moved, and then, with a little sigh for the magic that was over, Frytha sat up. Bjorn remained on his stomach, looking out through the parted tangle of last year's heather as though he were still watching the lovely ring-dance that was not there to watch any more.

'If I had my foster-father's harp, I could play that,' he said at last, still without moving.

Frytha looked at him, a little puzzled. She was often puzzled where Bjorn was concerned. 'How could you play the way a curlew bubbles?' she asked doubtfully, but willing to be convinced.

'Who wants to play the way it bubbles?' Bjorn said. He sat up, shaking the rough dark hair out of his eyes, and suddenly there was a flash of white intensity about him that startled Frytha. 'I could play all of it—the wings and the shining and the *liveness* and—and the being happy. I know just what it would sound like!'

Frytha said nothing, but because the curlew's mating flight had seemed to her like a garland, she was beginning to understand.

'Maybe you could get them to lend you the Hall harp,' she suggested.

Bjorn shook his head. 'The Hall harp would not be any good.'

'Why not?'

'The Hall harp makes a heavy sound—a smoky sound.' Bjorn said, fumbling for the words he wanted. 'You couldn't play wings on the Hall harp, and you couldn't make it shine. The Sweet-singer makes sounds that shine.'

Frytha nodded gravely. Haethcyn himself had told her that the Sweet-singer was not strung with twisted horse-hair, as the Northmen strung their harps, but with white bronze, in the Irish manner. That was what made the difference, she supposed. But Haethcyn had never been known to allow anyone else to touch his beloved harp. It lived in his hands by day, and at night it hung in its worn leather bag above his sleeping-bench; and when there was song and story-telling in the great hall on winter evenings, it was the Hall harp that passed from hand to hand as man after man took up the tale or gave his song for the general pleasure. Haethcyn's Sweet-singer was for no man's playing but his own.

'Maybe if you asked Haethcyn, and promised to be very careful?' she suggested at last, without much hope.

'He would not let me touch her,' Bjorn said. 'You know he wouldn't, Fryth.'

'You could ask,' she repeated stubbornly, persisting because though she did not understand the thing at all clearly, she felt very clearly indeed how much it mattered to Bjorn. 'It would not do any harm to ask.'

But Bjorn only shook his head again, and began to pull bits of heather to pieces, and she saw that it was one of those great and terrible things that the more you wanted, the more you could not ask, and that because Bjorn wanted so desperately, he would never be able to ask at all.

So she said no more, and presently they went home to supper.

Years and years afterwards, when she thought of that day, it always seemed to Frytha that it was the beginning of everything. If they had never watched the curlew weaving his lovely garland of flight, sooner or later something else would have wakened the harper in Bjorn, she knew that; but nevertheless, it was that day on Beacon Fell that the harper wakened, and so came all the things that happened after. . . . But at the time it was so swift in its coming and going—as swift as the curlew's flying shadow and as hard to lay hold of; and Bjorn never spoke of it again. And she had almost forgotten about it by the evening some months later, when they came up from the boat-strand with their noses full of the hot pitch reek of the boat-sheds in the sunshine, and found Haethcyn asleep on the guest-bench before the Hearth Hall doorway.

His head was bent on to his breast, his breath puffing in and out through his beard. The Sweet-singer lay on the bench beside him, and his hand, which had been on the carved front stay, had fallen away in sleep. It was still early for the evening home gathering, and there was nobody about save an old hound scratching for fleas beside the peat-stack.

Frytha had been half asleep herself as she walked, soaked through and through in sunshine, so that when Bjorn came to a sudden check beside the guest-bench, she bumped into him and woke herself up with a start. Haethcyn slept on, undisturbed by the slight scuffle. And all at once it seemed to Frytha that everything was very quiet. Bjorn stood quite still, looking down at his foster-father; looking down at the harp that lay beside him.

How beautiful it was! The woman's head, carved where the slender curve of the cross tree met the front stay, seemed to smile very faintly, as though at a secret nobody else knew. The evening sunlight ran like golden water on the strings as Frytha moved. Very slowly, as though they were being drawn, Bjorn's hands came out toward it.

'No!' Frytha whispered. 'No, Bjorn, you mustn't!'

He glanced at her, then away again, his mouth shut in a straight line. Then he went a deliberate step closer, and took the lovely thing in his brown brier-scratched hands, and lifted it carefully off the bench.

Not daring to protest again, Frytha watched him with caught breath, half dreading, half desperately hoping, that Haethcyn would wake up now, this instant, before it was too late.

Bjorn turned away, cradling the Sweet-singer in his arms; and still Haethcyn had not woken up. Steadily, looking neither to right nor left, Bjorn crossed the rough short grass to the gateway in the turf wall of the apple garth. And with something that was almost a sob of sheer fright, Frytha scurried after him. There was nothing she could do but keep close and share the storm when it broke; but she could do that, and she would.

In the midst of the garth, where the half-wild apples were pale green on the dipping branches, Bjorn sat him down on his heels, settling the Sweet-singer on his knee as he had so often seen his foster-father do. Frytha snatched a hurried glance over her shoulder, and saw the old harper still sleeping clear in view.

'Bjorn, he'll hear the harp and wake—and he can see us here!'

Bjorn looked up, and she saw that he was frightened—as frightened as she was. 'I can't take the Sweet-singer where he might wake, and not see her,' he said, and as though putting the fear aside, bent his head to help steady the harp, which was much too big to fit into the hollow of his shoulder as it did into Haethcyn's; and began softly and experimentally to finger the strings. He made a kind of wandering, hum-thrumming sound as though a wind blew through the strings, and then small clear twanging notes. But they were not the notes he wanted, though he tried again and again, frowning in the depth of his concentration.

Soon, despite her fears, Frytha was almost as engrossed as he was; and deep in search of the secret that would make the harp obey him, neither of them heard steps brushing through the long grass of the apple garth, until Haethcyn's great shadow fell across them.

It was Frytha who first woke to his coming, and looking up with a frightened gasp, saw him towering over them, with a bleak and smouldering wrath in his face that made her want to run. But she did not run, she only moved closer to Bjorn, who had scrambled to his feet and now stood holding the harp to his chest and looking up at his foster-father, very white and quite silent.

Haethcyn said in a voice that had sunk far down below its usual pitch. 'And what is it that you do with my harp, Bjorn Bjornson?'

'I try to play her,' Bjorn said steadily.

'So. And if the Hall harp was not good enough for you, that you must needs meddle with my Sweet-singer that no man handles save only me, could you not at least have asked my leave?'

Bjorn's pale bright eyes were fixed on the other's face. 'You would not have given it to me,' he said. He was not being impudent, simply stating a fact.

Haethcyn did not answer at once, but a faintly questioning look had begun to mingle with the wrath in his face. 'Tell me then, why had it to be my Sweet-singer?' he demanded at last.

'The Hall harp makes sounds that are smoky,' Bjorn said after a moment, 'and I wanted to make—something shining. This one makes shining sounds.' And then he added in a rush, 'But I cannot make her sing as I want her to.'

There was a long, long silence, and then, to Frytha's relief, suddenly Haethcyn smiled in his brindled beard, and sat down on the bench where the women came to spin sometimes in the heat of the day. 'It is none so easy to make a harp sing as you would have her; and there is much that you must learn before you can wake the singing,' he said. 'Give me back my Sweet-singer, and I will show you. . . .'

A long time later, as it seemed to Frytha, Haethcyn took back his harp yet again, and sat looking down at his fosterling with a slow half-smile narrowing his eyes. 'Aye,' he said in a reflecting rumble. 'It is in my heart that one day you will be a harper, for you have the music in you. And that, I am thinking, is a gift to you from your foremother out of Wales.'

"Did I have a foremother out of Wales?"

Haethcyn nodded. 'When Bjorn Sigurdson came west-over-seas from Stavanger with the Dragon ships—that was in the days of Harald Fairhair—he took to wife a woman of the people who ruled this land aforetime. Seemingly it was a fierce wooing, for she was of proud stock, and she yielded at last half unwillingly, but yield she did; and came to spin beside his new-lit hearth-fire over yonder among the Eskdale Falls. She was your foremother.'

'But why should it be her?' Bjorn asked, frowning. 'The music, I mean.'

'See now. Your Northern scald can weave you the bright word-patterns, and beat them out upon his harp-strings; he can retell the high far-off stories so that men's blood leaps to hear him; but he has not the music. It is the Saxon kind, and the Britons who were before the Saxon kind, who have the music.'

Frytha, puzzled and suddenly tired of being left out in the cold, came closer and put a hand friendlywise on the old man's knee. 'But there's you—and you have the music,' she pointed out.

Haethcyn turned to her, the smile broadening in his beard to show the long yellow dog-teeth. 'I? I am no Northman. Did you think that I was? I am of the Saxon kind, like you, small Frytha. I was for Harald of England at Stamford Bridge, not for Harald of Norway. I was for Harald of England at Hastings, half a moon later.'

To Frytha, the names of old battles meant little, but Bjorn, who had been lightly fingering the carved front stay of the harp as the old man held it, looked up quickly. 'I have heard men tell of that fight,' he said. 'I did not know that you were there, Fostri.'

'Aye, I was there.' Haethcyn bent his head as he spoke, parting the strong badger-grey hair with an exploring hand, and swept back the white wing from his forehead. 'See, I bear the mark of Hastings on me yet—and set there by one who was bed-and-board-fellow with me, aye, and friend beside, when I learned my letters like many another Saxon lad at Bec Abbey among the Norman kind. That is war, my bairns.'

And looking, the children saw the line of an old scar, silvery and puckered on the brown skin of his temple.

Then he let the white wing fall again. 'Nay, but we have wandered a long way from my Sweet-singer. Listen now, Bjorn Fosterling. You shall not touch her again without my leave; but I will teach you how to handle her as she deserves, that one day you may be a harper.'

## III

## THE SWORD

TWICE, THE CONQUERER had come North; once to
settle the matter of his York garrison, and once, while
the North was still bare and blackened from the first
time, when Earl Gospatric, sitting in his stronghold at
Carlisle, took to playing off the Scots and Normans against
each other for his own ends. That time he stayed longer, and
when he turned South again he left Ranulf Le Meschin, one of
his own knights, to hold Carlisle, with a younger brother
William to hold the levels of Coupland between the mountains and the sea. Coupland remained in Norman hands,
but by and by, when the Conquerer was dead, Gospatric's
son Dolfin came down with half Scotland baying at his heels,
and was sitting in Carlisle again before any man well knew
what wind was blowing.

And then, the third spring of Frytha's life in the Dale, the
next King William, who men called the Red, for more than
the colour of his hair, came North as his father had done before him, to clear the Scots out of Carlisle and make an
English frontier on the Solway, once and for all.

And on a day about the middle of cuckoo month, with the Red King and his host encamped at Kent Dale barely three days' march away, Frytha was in the armourer's shop, watching Anlaf the swordsmith at work. Bjorn was at archery practice with Erland and Jon and Ottar Edrikson and the rest. In a year or two Frytha would have begun archery practice herself, for the Jarl would have all the women of Lake Land able to swell the ranks of the War Host, if the need should come one day. But at the moment she had a strong feeling that she ought to be with Unna, sewing her seam under the old woman's watchful eye, which was why she had taken refuge with Anlaf in the armourer's shop.

Anlaf was very like the dwarfs in Unna's stories, a little dark man all shoulders and strong slender arms, with no legs to speak of, who looked at the world with his head slightly on one side and one eye screwed up, as though it were a sword-blade just coming up to the right heat for tempering. He was the best swordsmith in all Lake Land, and had once let Frytha watch when he was tempering a blade. It was an oddly exciting and beautiful thing to see Anlaf as he watched the heating blade in the forge flame, until the glowing, iridescent metal took on exactly the right colour and tint of colour; to see the swift movement as he caught the one perfect instant to plunge it into the trough of running water that led in from the beck, and hear the hiss like a thousand infuriated snakes and smell the cloud of throat-catching steam that rose from it. 'Three times,' said Anlaf. 'Three times to temper a sword-blade, once for the Father and once for the Son and once for the Holy Ghost; and that makes a blade that will not betray its man in battle.'

But Anlaf was not working on a new sword-blade now; he was sitting on the bench just inside the door, dealing strongly and delicately with a sprung rivet in the hilt of an old one, while the man whose sword it was went about the business of supplies which had brought him back from the War Host earlier that day.

Frytha watched fascinated. It was the first time that she

had had a near view of the great sword that Ari Knudson, the Grey Wolf, loved as Haethcyn loved his Sweet-singer. Wave-flame, she thought, that was a lovely name for a sword, and the sword was fitting to its name; such a one as the dwarf-wrought weapons of Unna's stories. The grey iron blade that the light rippled on as on running water, the hilt curiously twined with gold and silver wires that seemed to writhe dragon-like about the grip, the great ball of yellow amber, glowing like the sun, that formed the pummel. A wonderful sword.

It was hot in the smoke-blackened armourer's shop, and when the forge fire rose, the red light flooded all the place, and when it sank again, the shadows crowded everywhere, save here beside the door where the westering sunlight slanted in; and Frytha's ears were full of the busy ring of hammer on anvil, where Trond Thorkilson and his brother were at work. But the place was not so busy as it had been a while since, when the War Host was gathering and before it moved south. Sitting on the bench beside Anlaf, watching the work of his hands, Frytha was remembering the time of the Spring Host-ing, the ring of hammer on anvil that went on night and day, the reek of boiling glue from the fletcher's workshop, and all the women at work flighting arrows while the spring sowing got done as best it could between whiles; the sharpening of sword and axe-blade and the re-furbishing of worn battle-sarks, that had made the whole Dale buzz like a disturbed bee-skep. Exciting, that had been.

Now the Dale was very quiet, and there were scarcely any men left in it. It had happened every year, but somehow the stir had never been quite so stirring, nor the quiet that fol-lowed it quite so still, as this time—or else Frytha had not noticed it so clearly. She had always known about the fight-ing, of course; she had seen the red fires signalling from moun-tain-top to mountain-top through the dark; she had seen spent and wounded men come back from raids, and heard tell of others like Bjorn's father who did not come back at all. But the fighting had been away beyond the fells that made a rampart of safety round the Dale. And so it was exciting, but not quite real to her—not real and near as learning to sew, and Jon's tame otter, and the wild raspberries up the Sell Beck were real and near.

'Gille Butharson says that the Red King has brought a very great army with him from the south,' she said suddenly, kicking her heels. 'A great great greater army than there has ever come against us before. He says that there will be a very great holm-ganging this summer.'

Anlaf screwed his head round sideways and looked at her out of one eye as usual. 'It is in my heart that Gille Butharson speaks big words for a fourteen-year-old,' he said. 'But they do say that the Red King has come north to turn Dolfin Gospatricson and his Scots from Carlisle, and maybe not to have dealings with the Lake Land at all, this summer.'

'Gille will not like that,' Frytha said with decision. 'Gille has got his shield this hosting. He won't like it if there is not any battle.'

'There will be other holm-gangings in other summers, I'm thinking; maybe even enough for Gille Butharson,' Anlaf said shortly, turning Wave-flame on his leather-aproned knee to come at the other side of the hilt.

Frytha turned her attention to the world outside the door. It was a shining day; every leaf was a flake of green flame on the trees of the apple-garth, and there was a sheen of light on the grass; and the Sell Beck ran bright and swift and foam-streaked between the armourer's shop and the bakehouse below the mill, where all the bread for the War Host was baked in flat round bannocks that never got stale. The curve of water on the mill wheel was dark and smooth as glass, breaking into the foaming tumble of the tail-race, and the swallows were busy under the thatch.

'The swallows are building again under the mill house eaves,' she said.

Anlaf nodded without looking up from his work. 'Aye—swallows under the eaves there, ever since 'twas built.'

It was odd to think of the mill being built, of a time when

26

it had not been there at all and the swallows had not been able to make their nests under its brown broom-thatch. 'Do you remember it being built?' Frytha asked, faintly awed.

'Aye, I mind it like 'twas yesterday. Save for the armoury here, 'tis about the oldest building in the Dale—grinding barley, it were, when the Jarl was still sleeping under a striped ship's awning where the Hearth Hall stands now. *And* I mind Hrodney Svendson that built it—a big fat merry-looking karl that could put an arrow through a gore-crow's head at three hundred paces. He fell in the Normans' hands only the year after 'twas built.'

'What happened to him?'

'We didn't see him again to ask,' Anlaf said with grim simplicity.

Frytha was silent a moment, feeling sorry, and then, because feeling sorry was uncomfortable, she changed the conversation slightly. 'You must mind a lot,' she said, looking thoughtfully at Anlaf. He was certainly very old.

Anlaf grinned. 'I mind the Dale when there was naught here save a few herding huts for the men who kept the Jarl's sheep on the high summer pasture, any ways.'

'Tell about it.'

' 'Twas when Norman William laid waste all the North,' Anlaf said. 'You'll have heard tell of that, I'm thinking. There was burning over all the North, that year, and the folks as got away with their lives fled into the mountains for refuge. The Jarl was a youngling then, new wed and new settled in the hall of his fore-elders in Eskdale, but when he saw how the North went up in flames, up he comes here into the heart of the Fells, and most of us from the Eskdale settlement with him; and says he, "This is where we'll make our Shield Ring. 'Twill be a fine refuge for broken men, and a strong rallying point against the Norman kind," he says; and he sent out the Fiery Arrow in all directions, summoning the War Host together. And from all the mountain country and the lowlands between the Furness Sands and the Solway that have been ours since the Dragon keels came west-over-seas (and that

27

was before ever Rollo the Northman went Viking down through France, and Normandy came into being, let me tell you), the Northmen came in to the Hosting. And so, in a manner of speaking, we made our Shield Ring here, and from it we've held the Fells free of the Norman kind these twenty years and more. Aye, and we'll hold them another twenty, and another twenty after that, if needs be.'

Frytha remained silent, thinking long thoughts that she could not quite disentangle, partly about the pale flame that thatch makes when it burns, and partly about the Dale, and the things that she had only just begun to guess at, that were somehow behind the Dale. It was all rather too much for her, and she was glad when the tall figure of a man in war gear strode into the sunlit world framed in the doorway, heading for the mill house. She leaned forward to watch him, tall and grey and grim—wolf grey and wolf grim—and thought that he looked very alone. But even in the midst of all the Jarl's Chieftains, Ari Knudson had a way of always looking alone, save when Aikin, his foster son and the Jarl's young brother, was with him; and then the two of them had a comradeship that other people had not. Ari Knudson, the Grey Wolf, oldest and wiliest of those three leaders of the War Host who seemed to stand out from the rest as the three ancient birch trees above the mill dam stood out from their lesser fellows of the Sell Glen beyond them. The great golden Jarl himself, and the Grey Wolf, and Aikin, who men called The Beloved, with his odd gentleness and the sheen of a tempered blade about him. Three of them, standing together like the three great birch trees; but it was only between Ari and Aikin that there was that special togetherness.

'Ari Knudson has gone into the mill house,' she said. 'I expect he'll come for his sword soon.'

'Let him come when he chooses,' Anlaf said. 'For see, she is ready for him now,' and he breathed lovingly on the grey wave-sheeny blade and rubbed it up with a scrap of leather, and took up from the bench beside him the sheath of worn

28

grey wolf-skin cross-bound with leather strips which had once been crimson.

Then a shadow fell across the sunlit doorway; but it was not Ari Knudson. It was a small shadow, and it belonged to Bjorn, still carrying his bow. 'I thought maybe you'd be here,' he said. 'Unna has sent Margrit to look for you. She says you have not finished sewing your seam. Come away up the Beck before she finds you.'

And so a little later, having got safely and unseen across the log bridge and away behind the mill house into the mouth of the glen, the two of them were lying up in the curl of the Sell Beck under one of the three great birches that grew there. Soon their empty stomachs would send them home to supper, but in the meantime, safe from Unna and the officious Margrit, it was nice in the curl of the beck, with the birch leaves a rustling dazzle of palest sun-shot green overhead, and the swift water singing and swirling down to the sudden stillness of the mill pool. And Bjorn had pulled out his knife and begun to whittle a boat out of a bit of stick, with a thin shaving of silvery birch bark for a sail.

Frytha, not wanting to talk, lay in her favourite position, on her stomach, with her chin in her hands, sometimes watching Bjorn with his twig boat, sometimes staring down glen between the arching tangle of the wild raspberries. You could see most of the settlement from here, and the settlement could not see you, which made it a good place for going to cover. The wide tongue of the levels reaching out and away between its two lake shores was so green that it was almost yellow in the evening light—the shrill yellow of whin flowers—and the shadows of byre and barn lay cool upon it; while already, across the Dale, Gate Fell and Starling Dod, Red Pike and High Style were bloomed with smoky shadows. There were people about, people down at the boat-strand, where one of the grain boats had just come in. There was a woman spinning in a doorway, and a pig rooting in a garbage heap, and presently Ari Knudson crossed the bridge and disappeared into the armourer's shop. Frytha watched it all, and above the soft liquid rush of the mill wheel, she heard the *clang*-klink-klink, *clang*-klink-klink that told of Anlaf and Trond still at work mending old weapons and forging new ones.

'It is a kind of tune,' Bjorn said, as though she had spoken. 'The big sledge, and then Trond coming in with the hand hammer—like the longest and shortest strings of the Sweet-singer.' He made a final adjustment to the twig boat, and with infinite care slipped it into the water, where it ran smooth, well out from the bank. 'There she goes!'

The tiny vessel shook herself as though pleased to feel the water, and set out on her voyage as valiantly as ever the great long-ship whose figure-head now snarled from the house-beam of the Jarl's hall could have done. But a moment later, caught by a cross eddy, she was driving in toward a headland of tangled alder roots. Bjorn was already half up, ready to scramble down to the scene of disaster, but Frytha stayed him. 'No, look, Bjorn. She's shaking clear!' And even as they watched, the tiny craft spun round and slipped triumphantly free from the eddy, and was out round the headland, and running free. No longer a twig boat, but a Viking galley with the wind behind her.

They watched the silvery flake of the sail bobbing away down the beck until it was swept into the mill-pool and on toward the glassy rush of the leat, and they could not see it any more. Then Bjorn picked up another bit of stick and began all over again.

They were finding the exact place for the birch-bark sail when, above the rush of the mill wheel, they heard the brush-ing of someone coming up the beck side, and the faint ringing that link mail made when its wearer moved, and peering through the wild raspberry tangle, Frytha saw the Grey Wolf coming up toward them. 'It is Ari Knudson!' she whispered, and they froze like two wild things. But the brushing came on steadily, and the tangle parted, and Ari Knudson stepped out into the little clearing under the birch trees.

The old warrior stood dark and grim against the last sun-light that jinked on the shoulder-rings of his battle-sark and made a green-gold dazzle behind his bent head, resting both hands on the hilt of Wave-flame, and looking down at them.

'Ah, the shipwrights,' he said.

Frytha rolled over and bundled to her feet, feeling rather as though the tall head of Grismoor itself had unbent to speak to them friendly-wise. 'God's greeting to you,' she said respectfully and then, her mind leaping to Unna and the unfinished seam, 'how did you know that we were here? Is it that Anlaf told you? We don't show from the mill, do we?'

A sudden smile ran into the old man's eyes, deepening a thousand fine lines round them. 'If you should ever be hiding from the Normans, my bairns, do not you be sailing twig boats down the beck.'

'Oh,' said Frytha blankly.

He turned to Bjorn, who stood silently by, holding the little half-made boat in his hand. 'Let me see the one that you are making.'

Bjorn gave it to him, and he turned it over in his fingers, looking at it. 'Ah, yes. It was thus that I used to make my long-ships. . . . Out of iris buds, too. Do you ever make boats out of iris buds?' Then as Bjorn shook his head, he answered his own question half impatiently. 'Na, Na, of course not. There are irises in Eskdale, not here.'

'Do they sail well?' Bjorn asked.

'Aye, if they be made well. It must be nigh on fifty years since I made one—or this kind, either, for the matter of that. I wonder if I have lost the knack of it. . . .'

Bjorn picked out the best from among the bits of stick that he had collected, and held it out to him without a word, and his knife with it.

The old warrior looked at him in silence a moment; then, as on a sudden impulse, he took both stick and knife, and set to work, his big gaunt hands moving with surprising delicacy. 'I had a friend, one time, who made these things far better than ever I could do,' he said after a few moments, frowning over his work. 'But he had the gift of making things—boats

31

and puddle dams and birding bows—when we were boys, and then—bigger things. It was he that built the mill yonder. He was years in the South, among the Saxon kind, and being always interested in the making and the working of things, he brought back a useful knowledge of water-mills with him.'

'Anlaf the smith says the man who made the mill fell into the Normans' hands afterward, and nobody saw him ever again,' Frytha said, and then rather wished that she hadn't.

Ari Knudson's mouth set like a wolf-trap, but he went on carefully shaping the bows of his long ship. 'Aye,' he said at last, 'those who fall into the hands of Ranulf Le Meschin are not wont to be seen again by their own kind. The Normans have certain ungentle methods with captives who will not answer their questions.'

'Questions?—About the Dale?'

'Questions about the Dale.'

'But nobody has *ever* told them about the Dale, not yet,' Frytha said, almost as though she were defending someone.

'No, not yet.'

'How if they take somebody one day—who isn't brave enough?' Bjorn asked, half under his breath.

'I wonder,' Ari said seriously, looking down into the boy's face. 'They have taken more than one captive in the past twenty years. They cannot all have been brave men; but so far, none have betrayed their brothers.' He turned a little, the long ship still in his fingers, to look out across the valley, where the shadows of the far fells were creeping out to quench the gold. 'That is our Shield Ring, our last stronghold,' he said, 'not the barrier fells and the tottermoss between but something in the hearts of men.'

For the moment he seemed to have forgotten the two children who stood gazing up at him, and it was as though he spoke to himself, or to someone they could not see. Then he remembered them again, and the long-ship, and drawing to him a slender branch of the birch tree, made careful choice from it of a completely perfect leaf. 'This will serve for a sail,' he said, and made a tiny slit, and eased the leaf sail into it. Then he got down on to one knee, the rings of his mail jarring and chiming faintly as he moved, and while the children pressed up on either side to watch, bent and slipped the tiny craft carefully into the water.

'Now, are you seaworthy, or is the knack gone from me?' And then, as she slipped free on her voyage, his voice went up triumphantly, as Bjorn's might have done. 'There she goes! Sa ha! She rides the water like a gull!—a fine spring Viking down the Whale's Road!'

The main race of the water caught her as she sped forward and away, clearing the headland on which Bjorn's ship had so nearly come to grief; the birch-leaf sail with the sun behind it like a tiny tongue of green flame flickering down the beck. Once she was caught in the swirl of water round a stone but she shook herself clear, and went bobbing on, small and smaller down the beck, the green flame of her sail only a spark now; and Frytha shut her eyes because suddenly she did not want to see the valiant spark go out.

She heard the ring of Ari's battle-sark as he moved sharply beside her, and opened her eyes to see that the ship was gone; and a long-legged boy with hair the colour of barley straw was coming at a springing pace up the beck side.

'There's Gille,' she said, 'and he's in a hurry.'

Ari Knudson had risen to his feet. 'Here—I am up here,' he called.

Gille looked up and lengthened his stride. 'The Normans are out in force, by the road to Amilside,' he called. 'A runner has just come in from Longdale.'

Ari's hand went to the great sword at his side, in an instinctive movement. He glanced down at the children, the smile running again into his hard old face. 'Here is your knife again. God be with you; it was a fine spring Viking.'

Then he was striding down the beck to meet the newcomer. They came together, and Gille turned back beside him, his bare barley head tipped eagerly toward the old warrior's grey one, as they went on down; Ari Knudson with the great

33

sword Wave-flame gathered into the crook of his arm. 'So the Red King has turned aside from Carlisle after all,' they heard him say. 'It seems that you are to have your holm-ganging this summer, Gille.'

It was no more the time for birch twig galleys.

## IV

## THE KING'S ANSWER

GILLE BUTHARSON LAY still as a basking grass-snake atop the great rock hammer that jutted among the bracken and boulders of the fellside, watching Red William's army encamped below him. Men and tents and horses, and the blue haze of many cooking fires hanging over all: a huge army, darkening all the low ground at the head of the Winding Mere, and centred on the grey square of the ancient fort that the Legions of Romeburg had built there a thousand years ago. A great stone fort where their three great Lake Land roads branched, one to Rafnglas and the coast, and one following the High Street Ridge across the roof of the world to Penrith; and between them, one, the Midgate, running north through the heart of the fells. The roads had gone back to the wild now; they were little more than a hardness under the heather, even on high ground, lost all together where bog and totter-moss had swallowed the ancient corduroys. But the passes were still there, and the Midgate and the Rafnglas road in Norman hands would be an ill thing for the Lake Land.

35

The voice of the camp came up to him in a faint sea-murmur of sound on the little brushing wind, together with the tang of woodsmoke. And somewhere among the darkly wooded hills through which the Mere wound southward, a cuckoo was calling. There was the faintest rustle through the fern behind him, and the low breath of a whistle, echoing the notes of the cuckoo; and Gille looked back over his shoulder, as another boy a year or two older than himself slid out on to the warm rock beside him.

'Anything stirring?' asked the newcomer at half breath.

'Nothing above the ordinary.' Gille turned his gaze back to the distant camp. 'They look like a great swarm of ants,' he said disgustedly.

The other grunted, drawing himself further forward to look down. 'Ever felt like a besom broom, set to hold back the Sell Beck in spate?' he asked after a moment, very quietly, still looking down.

'Yes,' Gille said, just as quietly. And then in sudden exasperation, 'My stomach is sick of this waiting! Why doesn't my father give the word for attack?'

The boy beside him made no reply, and it was as though some uneasiness in him touched Gille, so that he asked quickly, 'What's amiss, Hundi Swainson?'

'Nothing, so far as I know, but—they were marking out the Thing Mote at Fellfoot when I left, and the Chieftains have come in from Ryedale and all the outlying bands, to join the Council.'

Gille looked at him, frowning. 'Why should my father call a Thing at a time like this? What can there be still to talk of?'

'Nay, how should I know? Maybe it is naught but a change of plans. We shall know soon enough; maybe too soon, at that.'

Gille was silent for a moment, the frown deepening on his usually pleasant face. 'Curse you for a bird of ill omen,' he said at last, and as the other made no reply, elbowed himself back a short way, half turned, and slipped into the young bracken and bilberry cover of the fellside.

A short while later, safely over the skyline, he stood up,
shook himself like a dog, and started back for the main camp
of the Northmen at Fellfoot in Little Longdale. He did not
hurry; he never hurried—at least, he never seemed to hurry—
but his long fellman's stride ate up the moorland miles rather
more swiftly than usual; and the frown was still between his
eyes as he came down the flank of Loughrigg and struck out
along what remained of the Roman road to Rafnglas.

The ancient Thing Mount, where the beck came down
from Red Pike into the deep waters of the tarn, was black with
men when he came in sight of it, and the Host spread far over
the surrounding Thing-Field. And forgetting the hunger that
was grumbling in his stomach, in the uneasiness that was
grumbling in his mind, he made his way through the weatherworn bothies on the outskirts of the Field and plunged into
the crowd.

They were a silent crowd; clearly the unease that had
touched Hundi lay heavy on them all. They stood motionless,
waiting, their faces set toward the sacred circle of hazel rods
that crowned the Mount. And with the shadow—whatever it
was—falling every moment more heavily on his own heart,
Gille pressed on and upward.

Edging and shouldering his way through the tense throng,
he emerged at last on the rim of the sacred circle, and stood,
breathing quickly, with the hazel cross-rods against his breast.
On the low turf seats that rimmed the clear space within, a
dozen or more men were gathered; the Chieftains of the War
Host, among them those from the War bands encamped in
Ryedale to cover the Midgate that led through the heart of
Lake land. Their faces were grim, and no man spoke to his
neighbour. Ari Knudson sat with his great sword Wave-
flame between his knees, and his chin sunk on his mailed
breast. Beside him, Aikin leaned forward on his folded arms,
gazing straight before him.

Just as Gille reached the hazel ring, the Jarl his father had
risen; and now standing in the midst of the open place, tree-
tall in his bull-horned helm, he looked round him slowly, at his

37

Chieftains gathered about him, at his War Host darkening the slopes of the Thing Mount. His eyes lingered an instant on Gille against the hazel rods, and then passed on, seeming to gather them all in, to the farthest fringes of the vast throng. He towered over them, dominating them and drawing them to him, so that for the first time Gille realized what manner of leader his father was, who had held Lake Land free of the Norman kind for twenty years.

Then the Jarl began to speak, his great voice reaching out clear to his farthest warrior on the distant outskirts of the Host.

'Neighbours, I have called you together, here in the Place of Assembly, that we may take counsel together on a heavy matter. Neighbours, ye have seen the host of the Norman King that camps yonder at the head of the Winding Mere. They are as a swarm of ants, as the grains of the Furness Sands. Their numbers are so much greater than ours that it is in my heart that not even our knowledge of the land—and the All Father knows there is scarce one among us but knows the fells as a man knows his own kale-garth—that not even our knowledge of the land shall avail to right the balance.'

A rising growl of voices broke in on his words, and he flung up a hand to quell it. 'Friends, hear me out before you give tongue. You know, all of you, how long and how strongly we have held the Normans out of Lake Land; you know that ere this, all England lies under the Norman yoke, listed for taxing farm by farm in a monkish book for Norman masters. Now it has come to this, that we must make our last choice whether we shall stand forth once more to meet our foes in arms, and die as our foregangers died at Clontarf, and our women and our bairns fall to Norman masters to be thralled or slain as best pleasures them; or whether we shall lay down the sword and strive to make terms—what terms we can—with this Red Norman King.'

Once more the growl of voices rose, swelling this time into a fierce clamour of denial, and an angry surge of movement swayed through the crowd; and it was a while before the Jarl could make himself heard again above the uproar. 'Friends,

friends, we shall serve no purpose by a shouting and a clashing of spears; this is a thing for clear heads and cool blood.'

One of the Chieftains rose from among the rest. 'Jarl Buthar, we have been free men, paying scat to no man over us; and it goes hard with us to lay down our freedom and stand like oxen for an alien yoke. We have had close dealings across the Solway before now; let us therefore seek aid from Scotland in this matter.'

'Scotland is torn with troubles at home, and has no aid to give, even to Dolfin of Carlisle. There is not any man left beyond our dales to stand shield to shield with us in this holm-ganging. We stand alone, my brothers.' The Jarl's great voice had gone harsh and flat like a cracked bell. 'I also have been free.'

There was a long silence. The War Host was quiet enough now. The boy leaning against the hazel-rods brought up his hands and clenched them on the slender barrier until the knuckles shone white.

A voice cried out into the silence at last. 'So then, your counsel is for peace, Jarl Buthar?'

The Jarl had seemed to droop a little, as though with the weight of an appalling weariness; but he drew himself again to his superb height, his gaze sweeping the dark throng around him. 'You who have been my sword kin, my hearth companions, you know how hard it goes with me to play the nything. . . . The All Father help me! My counsel is for peace, if peace is to be had.'

And Gille, suddenly sick, saw all too surely the unwilling and angry agreement in face after face of the assembled Chieftains; in the iron set of Ari Knudson's mouth and the bitter brightness in Aikin's eyes.

There was much talk after that, hot and urgent and heavy talk, for at the Thing gatherings all free men had a voice and most men used it. And there were many among the War Host, both Northmen and Saxons, who remembered burned homes and murdered kin, and would rather go down fighting than bow their necks to a Norman yoke; and many more, remembering also, who had women folk and bairns, and who bethought them that in the end, a Norman overlord might be a lesser evil than a whole land laid waste. Gille, standing with his hands gripped on the sacred hazel-rods, sick and stunned, heard the roar of voices, but little of what was said, until at last his father's great voice came through to him again, so hoarse and strained that he scarcely knew it.

'So be it then. Tomorrow we send one under the Truce Branch, to Red William, offering to set our hands between his in fealty and hold the Lake Land for him henceforth, under Ranulf Le Meschin or whatsoever lord he may set over us.'

And he knew that the bitter choice had been made.

And now it remained only to choose out one of their number to carry the word to the Norman King. Gille, staring at his own white knuckles, was aware of voices all round him, calling for Aikin the Beloved. He looked up again, and Aikin was on his feet. He seemed very dark and slight beside the huge golden Jarl, but his voice, for all that it was a light voice, at most times edged with laughter, carried as truly as his brother's to the outermost ends of the War Host. 'Neighbours, I am the youngest and least of all the leaders among you, but if you will have me to go forth for you under the Truce Branch, I will carry your words to the Norman King, and do all that I may to gain peace between his kind and ours.'

But almost before the words were out, Ari Knudson had risen beside his foster-son. 'Nay, friends, if ye need a messenger, here stand I, Ari Knudson, to do your bidding. This is a task for one that has a grey head on his shoulders and a long knowledge of men. Ye have called me the Grey Wolf, ofttimes—send me now to prove my wolf's cunning in this seeking of terms with the Norman King.'

Ari Knudson had his way, and next morning, when a small company passed out of the camp and away down dale toward Amilside, he walked a little in advance with his battle-sark laid aside and a green birch branch in his hand, for a sign that he came in peace. Four of his sword companions followed close behind him, but it was Aikin, who must turn back presently, who walked at his shoulder.

Down Little Longdale they went, following what yet remained of the Legion's road under the heather and the arching brambles, until the fells drew away on either side, and the road lost itself in the marshy levels, and far ahead in the water-pale morning light, they could see the wattle huts of the nearest Norman outpost rising above the faint ground mist.

There they halted; and Ari Knudson turned to Aikin, his foster-son. 'It is here that our ways part,' he said.

Aikin nodded. 'We shall be at Fellfoot until you return to us with the King's answer.'

Ari had flung back the dark folds of the cloak he wore, and slipped free the shoulder girdle of his great sword. 'Take her and hold her for me until I come again, Aikin fosterling; and if I come not again, then do you give your own blade to young Gille, and keep her as a gift from me. I would not that Wave-flame should go to any other master.'

'I will hold her for you until you come again,' Aikin said deliberately and took the sword and slipped the shoulder girdle over his head so that the great blade hung beside his own. 'No need that we speak of the other. You go under the Truce Branch.'

'Maybe, maybe. Yet even under the Truce Branch, who can say what the next hour holds, save Wyrd who spins the web of men's destinies?'

'What is that you mean, Fostri?'

'I smell treachery,' Ari said quietly.

There was an instant's complete stillness, and then Aikin said, 'Therefore you thought to go in my stead?'

'If it should come to pass that the War Host need its leaders again, and must lose one of them, better they lose an old leader near to the end of his war-powers than a young one with his great days before him.'

They looked at each other in silence a long moment, eye into eye. Then Ari Knudson said, 'It is time to be away.'

'The All-Father be with you, Fostri,' Aikin said hoarsely.

He put his arm round his foster-father's shoulder and hugged him fiercely, as though he did not know how to leave off; then released him, and stepped back.

With the rest of his band, he stood watching the five tall figures walking forward into the mists and the cool light of the morning, until they reached the Norman outpost; then turned back toward the Thing Mount in Little Longdale.

There was an odd silence in the camp, all that waiting time. The decision to sue for terms was a thing too bitter and too big to talk about, and the men of the North were not much given to a pointless clatter of tongues. But as the second day went by, the silence seemed to deepen, and behind their eyes when they looked at each other, every man saw his neighbour's growing uneasiness. And they began, almost furtively, to re-burnish weapons that were already in battle trim.

All that waiting time, Gille kept well clear of his father. He had never been able to come very near to the Jarl, who indeed was rather a remote man. But he had admired him enormously, at a distance; never more than in that moment at the Thing Mount when he had fully realized for the first time the strength of his father's leadership; and what had happened after seemed to have shaken everything in him. On the second evening of the waiting he had betaken himself to Aikin's boothe, and sat on the piled fern of the bed-place, burnishing and reburnishing his kinsman's helm. There had always been a strong bond between him and Aikin, so that it was somehow comforting to burnish his helm, and Gille was badly in need of comfort. It was almost dark inside the boothe, and the mizzle rain which had come up with the dusk whispered faintly on the wadmal awning which had been flung across the four walls for a roof; but the tawny gleam from a nearby watch-fire, shining through the doorway, showed him the outline of the winged helm on his knee and one did not need much light for burnishing. One just rubbed, and rubbed, and rubbed. It was better than thinking.

A shadow cut off the firelight, and Gille looked up as Aikin himself came in, followed by Garm the half-grown hound puppy, who had never been willingly apart from him since, at five weeks old, he had staggered from his dam without a backward glance when Aikin whistled him to heel.

'Gille!' said Aikin. 'What is that you do here?'

'I burnish your helm. Is there any news?'

'None as yet.' Aikin folded up on the bed-place beside him, with a hand on Garm's neck. 'Why do you burnish my helm?'

'It is in my heart that you may need it,' Gille said doggedly.

Aikin was silent a moment. Then he said: 'In mine also.'

'I'm glad!' Gille rubbed more fiercely at the shining metal. 'Better that, than that we have the Normans crowing over our fells!' Then, as the other did not answer, ' If you had been the Jarl, would you have sued for terms?'

'Maybe not. It would have been much easier to do the other thing.'

'Easier?'

Aikin shifted in the piled fern beside him. 'I have fought at your father's shoulder since I was old enough to carry my shield, and I know what manner of man he is; I've known him hold a mountain pass against a whole company, with five men (I was one of them), but it is in my mind that the hardest thing he ever did was to stand up yonder on the Thing Mount two days since, and speak to his sword-kin of a laying down of swords. I think that I could not have done it. If I could, I should be a braver man than I am.'

Gille said nothing for a while, turning the thing over in his mind. 'Yes, I—had not thought of it so,' he said at last.

Before either of them could speak again, another figure stood black in the entrance under the dripping edge of the wadmal awning; a huge figure, bulked against the tawny gleam of the fire, and the Jarl himself came ducking in. 'Aikin?'

'I am here, my brother.' Aikin rose as he spoke, and Gille also, sensing the urgency that flowed from his father. The hound puppy growled softly and uncertainly in the dark.

'Hugin Longneb has come in with word of movement in the

43

Norman camp as though they made ready for the march,' the Jarl said quickly.

'So-o.' Aikin's voice was gentle. 'What now?'

'I am going down to take a look for myself, as best I can in the dark. Do you bring the Host down to the dale mouth and hold them ready for whatever happens. Send Sigurd and his archers across to Ulfa in Ryedale, that they may hold the Reytha gorge if need be until we can be across Midgate in strength. We can do no more until we know which way the Norman thrust will come.'

For an instant the two brothers faced each other in the doorway. Then Aikin said: 'It would seem that we are to have no choice but Clontarf, after all.'

'It would seem so, yes.'

'There is still no word of Ari and his fellows?'

'None.' Jarl Buthar was already turning on his heel.

Aikin drew a harsh breath, and swung back to the inner darkness where Gille stood. 'My helm, Gille. You were right, you see.'

The boy gave the winged helm into his hands without a word, and plunged out after him into the dusk and the mizzle rain.

He was still at Aikin's shoulder when dawn found them with the light war bands across the Longdale Beck and far up toward the pass into Ryedale. Behind them came the Jarl with the main War Host, ahead of them there was only the dun fellside in the rain-mist. Word had come in at cock-light that the Norman advance guard was on the move, heading up the Midgate for the very heart of Lake Land. Now it remained for the Northmen to get across Ryedale in time to close the way.

They pressed on and upward, quickening the long swinging stride of the mountaineer at times almost to a run. Dawn broke about them, quietly, the rain dying out into white mist, and the wild fowl crying over the marsh and the curlews over the heather; and still the dun slopes rose before them, heather and bilberry, and bare rock where the bones of the fell cropped through its hide; and the pass still beyond and above them, lost in the mist. But surely they must be almost up to it now, Gille thought, loping and running at Aikin's shoulder. Once they reached the pass it would be but short work to get down to Ulfa on the far side; only—how far were the Normans on their way by now? Well, Sigurd and his archers would hold them in play awhile.

They were almost into the mouth of the pass, and the mist was thinning out before the sun, when a swift brindled shape came racing low through the heather to fling itself in joyous abandon upon Aikin. Garm, with tail lashing behind him, flanks heaving with the speed he had made, and dangling from his collar the gnawed end of the hide rope with which Aikin himself had tethered him to a tent-post when they left him in the almost deserted camp.

He circled round his master, tongue drooling and tail sweeping, triumph and laughter in every squirming line of him. And Aikin laughed also, and stooped in his stride and caught the trailing end of raw-hide. 'On your own head be it, brother. I can't take you back, so you must needs come on with us now.'

So they pressed on, with the number of the War Host swelled by one gangling half-grown hound puppy.

The last pale rags of the mist were rolling away among the high fell corries as they came through the pass and headed down through woods of birch and rowan into Ryedale. Grismere and Ryedale Water lay clear and faintly gleaming under a dappled sky; and teal and wild duck burst up from the rushes at their approach, but save for the indignant beat of wings, Gille's straining ears caught no sound in all the emptiness of the morning. They were in time!

Ulfa's silent grey ranks were massed on the high ground that formed a steep nab between Grismere and Ryedale Water, all across the line of the Midgate. Runners ahead had warned him of their coming, and now the old Chieftain himself stood out to meet them, making his great pole axe sing above his head in greeting, crying to them 'So ho! You come in good time, friends and neighbours!'

And even as he called to them, from far down the gorge below Ryedale the first sounds of fighting broke upon the quiet of the morning.

The hidden archers among the rocks were going into action, and the skirmishers falling back before the Norman advance as the Viking Host swung into position across the dale. A position that gave them all the width of the dale behind them for elbow room, while the Normans must attack uphill from the narrow strip of lowland between Ryedale Water and the steep fellside.

Strangely, as the sounds of the fighting grew, a new stillness seemed to come upon the fells, a stillness heavy with waiting; and it seemed to Gille, easing his buckler on his arm and shifting his hold on his spear-shaft, that the waiting was for something quite apart from the coming battle, something that the fells knew about as they would not know about battles. And then, chancing to look eastward across the tossing waste of moor and mountain, he saw above the dark mist-girt lift of the High Street Ridge, a strange cloud forming. A long roll of cloud that seemed to rest on the high top as a helm on the head of a giant.

But there was little time for looking at clouds, for now he could see the flying screen of archers falling back toward them, and the skirmishers backing and breaking and re-forming, clinging like a wolf-pack round the snout of the Norman advance guard. Between the birch woods he could see the daleside below him black with men, a dense mass of horse and foot, a reed-bed of lances. He could hear the triumphant yawping of the Norman trumpets, giving tongue like hounds at sight of the quarry.

And on the high ground, the quarry waited. Grey close-knit ranks, braced for what they were sure in their hearts would be their last fight, and grimly prepared to make it a good one. Garm whimpered with excitement, pressed against Aikin's knee, and Aikin slipped the bit of hide rope from his collar, and gave him a pat; then drew Wave-flame from its sheath.

Nearer and nearer rolled the Norman host, carrying in the van a dark knot of standards, half seen, half lost among the birch trees. Standards that the waiting Northmen on the nab could not properly make out, but that puzzled and oddly disturbed them. Images of some kind, no doubt.

Gille, straining to make sense of those strange and somehow horrible standards, did not notice that the light against which he narrowed his eyes was turning livid yellow as a week-old bruise, nor the growing and darkening of that cloud above the High Street Ridge.

The skirmishers were falling back more swiftly now; colour was beginning to spark out from the dark advancing host, in shield and cloak and lance-head gonfalon, all kindled to a strange muted brilliance by the lowering light. A puff of wind came down the fellside, and the birch trees shivered and were still. And then, almost in the same instant, two things happened. The yawping of the trumpets was drowned in a hideous, whistling roar that rose from the direction of that strange roll of cloud and swept toward them like some gigantic demon rushing wide-winged and shrieking down the empty tunnels of the sky; and the Northmen realized that those five grotesque standards were the broken bodies of Ari Knudson and his sword-brothers bound to spears.

The Red King had given his answer in a red language that all could read.

For the Northmen, there was one stark moment of unbelief and then, even as full understanding broke over them, with a shriek and a roar as of wild triumph, the rushing horror out of the sky was upon friend and foe alike. Birch and alder were lashed into a turmoil, bending and streaming out before the blast as though striving to fly from the terror behind them, while in an instant the still waters of the lake were boiling into a yeasty race. The wind beat like great wings among the close ranks of men, tossing them this way and that, like a field of barley in a squall; and all the air was full of torn-off leaves and twigs and blown lake-spray.

To the Normans it seemed the wrath of God. They had

been uneasy from the first, muttering as loudly as they dared against the King who had ordered them to march under such ghastly banners. This was the outcome, this appalling thing that leapt among them like an unseen angel of destruction, striking right and left, bringing down horse and man and hurling those upon the bank into the boiling surf of Ryedale Water. It plucked the standards from the hands of the standard-bearers and flung them down, and the King's banner with them; and in an instant all was a plunging chaos of terror-stricken men and horses.

But to the Northmen it was the Helm Wind; their own Helm Wind come to aid them in their direst need. Even Gille, who had never felt it before, knew that it was the Helm Wind. And they broke forward into the teeth of it, crouching and stumbling against the blast, and yelling as they ran, to avenge the Grey Wolf and his sword brothers.

Between the fell and the lake-side, the Norman host was in wild confusion, with here and there some knight or man-at-arms of tougher fibre than the rest struggling to steady them and stem the rout. Panic was loose among the tumbled ranks; they were no cowards, they were not afraid to fight men, but who could fight the just wrath of God? As the grey avenging wave of Northmen swept down upon them from the nab, they abandoned the accursed standards and cast away their weapons and ran, sweeping the King and his household knights with them. And the Host of the fells ran baying at their heels.

Aikin and Gille and Garm hunted together through all that long chase. Gille never remembered very much about it afterward, but when it was all over, and they had drawn off, triumphant yet baffled, within half a bowshot of the old fortress walls at Amilside, he noticed with satisfaction that his spear-blade was as red as anybody else's, and though Garm had a gash on his shoulder, the blood on his brindled muzzle was not all his own.

They returned the way they had come, leaning back into the Helm Wind that beat and roared against their humped shoulders, gathering their own wounded as they went, and stripping the Norman dead of weapons and gear before they left them to the ravens.

There were many Norman dead, so many that Jarl Buthar, looking down in the livid gloom into the gorge below Ryedale Water, where knight and squire and man-at-arms lay tumbled together like the debris of a spate, cried above the wind to the men around him, 'Neighbours, it is in my mind that there will be no more of the Norman kind in our dales, this summer season!'

They found the bodies of Ari Knudson and his sword kin where the Helm Wind had cast them down, and freed them from the framework of spears to which they had been lashed. All five had been brutally murdered. Ari had all too clearly been singled out for the honour of being tortured to his death.

Many hours later, a little company of Northmen stood together on the highest crest of the Longdale Fells, where they had carried Ari and his comrades for how-laying. The brief gloaming of the summer night was all about them, and the low torn clouds flew blackly overhead; but away in the north the skies were clear, and the faint light lingered between sunset and dawn, a low daffodil web of light like an echo behind Skiddaw and Helvellyn. The fringe of the Helm Wind rushed and shivered through the dark heather, teasing out the flames of the torches so that they plunged and flared and flickered, casting weird lights and shadows over the face of the living men who held them, and the dead men at their feet.

'Here is an end to all talk of laying down of swords,' Jarl Buthar said, his head tipped up toward the ragged sky, and his great voice bit like a north-east wind. 'The King's Peace! If this be the King's Peace, my brothers, better that we kill our women and bairns own-handed and stand forth to slay and be slain in the last pass. Nay, but it shall be the Northmen's peace; and the Normans shall grovel on their bellies, whimpering for it, ere this day's work be forgotten. By the Old Gods I swear it, by Thor's Ring and Hammer, by the High Seat of Odin Himself, I swear it!'

49

'I also,' Aikin said softly. He stood with one hand twisted in Garm's collar, Wave-flame naked in the other, looking down at the torn and broken body of his foster-father, that had even yet something of unbreakable defiance about it; and his face was a white mask in the torchlight. 'It may be that it will not be given to me to blood-eagle this Red King with my own hands, Ari Fostri, but nevertheless, I will repay the debt to Normandy; I will repay it full measure and running over.'

And Gille, standing close beside him, knew by the dreadful gentleness of his tone that it was no idle threat.

## V

## HIGH AND EMPTY PLACES

IN BUTHARSDALE THE sheep-shearing was in full swing, for though the shadow of the Red King lay dark across the future, the sheep must be shorn. So the pens had been set up at the foot of the Sell Beck, and the little dark mountain sheep with their owners' law-marks nicked into their ears brought down from the high fell pastures; and all across the open turf below the mill house the shearers were at work. They were women for the most part, old men and young boys. There were no thralls in the Dale, for in this life that the Jarl and his folk had been leading so long there was no room for them. One could depend on the loyalty of free men; men who were unfree might be a danger to the rest.

But the women were well used to such work, and with their hair knotted up and their skirts tucked into their girdles, they handled the sheep as well as their menfolk could have done, while the boys ran them down bleating and protesting from the pens.

Frytha worked with the other children, carrying jugs of buttermilk for the thirsty shearers, sitting on the heads of troublesome sheep, and toiling to and fro with the baled fleeces. The fleeces were harsh and greasy to handle, and the smell of the yoke came up from them thick and heavy; her nose was full of it; her hands and hair and the front of her short blue kirtle all smelled of it, and her ears were full of the baaing and bleating of the sheep; and she did not see the distant figures of the runners coming along the lake-shore toward them from the direction of the pass into Burgdale.

But suddenly word of the battle was running from group to group like a heath fire, and work slackened as men and women abandoned the shearing to gather about the runners, demanding details of the fight, asking for word of husband or father, brother or son, while the fleeces lay forgotten on the ground, and the shorn sheep got loose among the kale-garths, bleating after their lambs.

Without quite knowing how she got there, Frytha found herself caught up in the silent fringe of children and older boys from the sheep-pens hanging round one such group, in the midst of which Njal Scar-Arm, his breast still heaving with the speed he had made, was telling of the end of Ari Knudson and his sword kin, and sparing nothing in the telling.

Frytha listened, not really believing, because it could not be true that *that* had happened to someone who had been with her and Bjorn up the Sell Beck such a little while ago. And then she saw Bjorn's face in the crowd, and she knew that it was true. Bjorn's eyes stared straight and wide before him, as though he saw something so horrible that he could not look away. He had gone dirty white, and was making little movements with his mouth, as though something had hit him in the pit of his stomach and he wanted to be sick. And then the crowd shifted and she lost him again.

For a while she stood quite still, feeling sick too, and lost,

and coldly afraid, because if *that* could happen to someone
who had been with her and Bjorn up the Sell Beck, nothing
was safe or certain in the world any more, and the high, steadfast fells had lost their strength to shut out the dreadful things.
Then somebody stepped back on to her, knocking her over,
and that seemed to break something, so that by the time she
had picked herself up, the cold-fingered fear had gone away.
But the fighting had come into her world, and could never be
comfortably shut out behind the fells again.

People were already drifting back to their sheep that must
needs be shorn—tonight, when the work was over, would be
time enough to talk over the news that the runners had brought,
and Frytha went back to work with the rest. She did not go
to look for Bjorn, because in some way that she did not understand, the thing that she had seen in his face held her back.
But a little later, when somebody sent her up to the sheep-pens
with a message, she looked round for him among the other
boys working there. There was no sign of him.

'Where's Bjorn?' she demanded of Ottar Edrikson, as he
came by.

Ottar, who was a boy of few words, nodded over his
shoulder. 'Up the beck somewhere. Went a while back,' and
turned to get a grip on the fleece of a protesting sheep.

But Erland set down the crock from which he had been
drinking, and wiped the traces of buttermilk from his mouth
with the back of one hand. 'Bjorn's run away,' he said with
scorn. 'He's run away to hide because he was afraid when
Njal told what the Normans did to Ari Knudson!'

'He didn't! He wasn't!' Frytha cried furiously.

'He did! He was!' the boy chanted in growing triumph;
and raised his voice tauntingly as the others gathered closer
to listen. 'I saw him! He looked as if he was going to be sick.
*I* wouldn't run away and be sick because I was afraid!'

'I hate you, Erland Ormeson! It was the yoke smell—anybody can be sick with the yoke smell!'

'Yah! I've sniffed as much yoke as he has, and *I* haven't
been sick.'

'Perhaps you will yet. You look green enough to me!' Frytha told him viciously, and before he could retort, turned on her heel with a furious whisk of her kirtle, and stalked away toward the armourer's shop.

From the armourer's shop she crossed by the log bridge, and once out of sight of the sheep-pens, took to her heels up the beck. She must find Bjorn. She must find him and bring him back because of what Erland was saying, and because—because she knew in her heart of hearts that it had not been the yoke smell. Maybe he would be terribly angry with her for following him, maybe he would never forgive her, but that could not be helped; the thing that mattered now was that he should come back.

She went on, past the three great birches above the mill, slowing to a trot as the glen grew steeper, and in a little while she met Grim coming down through the birch-woods, with a bobbing black flock of sheep that had escaped the round-up. Vigi, looking very like one of the sheep himself, circled at his heels, with lolling tongue. Vigi was growing old, but he was a fine sheepdog still. Frytha waded on through the bobbing, bleating flock as it flowed round and past her, until she reached the little hairy shepherd, and checked to ask breathlessly: 'Grim, have you seen Bjorn this way?'

Grim checked also, looking down at her thoughtfully through the black hair of his face, while Vigi thrust a cold muzzle into her hand in greeting. 'Aye, he were heading up yonder,' he said after a moment, jerking his head back toward the high sloping shoulder of Whiteless Pike. 'Happen he doesn't want company.' And then, raising his voice as she made to pass him: 'Nay, I'd not go after him—not if I was thee, I wouldn't.'

But Frytha was already off and away. 'Ah now! Come back, ye flaysome bairn!' She heard him call, and for a moment she was afraid that he might leave the sheep to Vigi and come after her, but when she glanced back from a little higher up, he was going on downhill after the bobbing black rumps of the flock, with Vigi's white-tipped plume of a tail waving beside him.

54

She left the birches and rowans of the beck after a short while, and passed out through the gap in the turf wall of the intake, on to the open fellside. The tawny shoulder of White-less Pike stretched up and away, vast and seemingly asleep in the sun, until it ran out into the high head of Grismoor, two miles away. The shadow of a cloud drifted across Grismoor; nothing else moved in all the emptiness, but somewhere up there was Bjorn. In times of stress he always made for the high and empty places, and she was quite sure of finding him.

She climbed on and on, up and up. The young bracken that had been thick against the intake wall grew thinner and thinner, and then there was no more bracken, and she was out on the high fell, where the grass was tawny as a hound's hide, and the few flowers that grew in it were little and bright and fragile. On and on, up and up, until she seemed caught in a vast dome of sky, and she felt as small as an ant on the sweep-ing fellside. She had never been so high as this before, and she was frightened of the emptiness, and her legs ached. But still she climbed on, doggedly, sometimes scrambling up the steep bits, sometimes finding easier going up a more gentle slope, but always making for the high head of Grismoor. She did not think that Bjorn could have gone so far as that, but if he had, then somehow she must get there too . . .

She came upon him suddenly, lying on his stomach below a rocky outcrop, with his chin propped between his fists. She was very near before she saw him at all, for the skin of his back and legs was burnt nut brown, and his woollen tunic, which he wore twisted round his middle like a kilt, was the dull deep colour of the unbleached fleece, while his rough dark head blended into the blackness of the slate outcrop, with the same glint of starling colours, where the light struck. That, and his utter stillness, had hidden him from sight until she was almost on top of him.

Her mouth was open to tell him what Erland was saying, and that he must come back—and then, suddenly, she could not. She didn't know why, but she knew she could not; it would be like breaking in on him in some private hidden place of his own. Instead, she sat down on her heels against the out-crop, and waited for him to come out.

Bjorn never moved, and Frytha sat as still as he. The fell-side dropped away from her with a rush and a falcon-swoop that almost took her breath away. Far, far below her lay the green ribbon of Rannardale with its thread of a beck winding between steep woods of birch and hazel, down to the Crumbeck Water. Down there at the head of the Dale she could make out the ancient steading of that Ragna who had given his name to the place in the early days of the Northmen's coming, part roofless now, and long since sunk to be a shepherd's boothe; and the little pattern of old fields, once deserted, that had come into their own again since the Jarl made his Shield Ring in Butharsdale.

Once she looked sideways at Bjorn. He was still staring before him, straight across to the hummocked crest of Rannardale Ridge; but she knew that he was not seeing it, and she looked away again. In a cleft of the outcrop close beside her, a clump of the tiny mountain campion raised its first white stars from a cushion of mossy leaves, fragile and perfect against the dark slate, and she turned her attention to it for refuge against the hugeness and emptiness of the high fells; against the thing that men had done to Ari Knudson, and the thing that Bjorn was looking at.

At last Bjorn looked round. He was still rather white under his tan, and Frytha thought that he had been sick sometime on the way up. 'I suppose they would have had him tell them about the Dale!' he said, as though they had been talking of Ari Knudson all the while.

Frytha nodded. 'Like the man who made the watermill.' And then, taking a deep breath, and gripping her hands together between her knees, she burst out with the thing that she had come to say. 'Bjorn, you must come back. Erland is saying that you ran away because you were afraid when they said about Ari, and you must come back and stop him. That was why I came after you.'

Bjorn never moved, only something flickered in the pale

brightness of his eyes; and she said again, with desperate determination, 'You *must* come back! Now!'

Bjorn did not seem to have heard her. 'Lonely, he must have been,' he said at last.

'There were five of them in it, Njal said, though they didn't torture the rest. Oh, *please*, Bjorn——'

Her voice trailed away, and there was an even longer silence, and then Bjorn said in a small dead-level voice: 'If that ever happens to me, I wonder if I shall tell them what they want to know.'

Frytha stared at him. 'But no one has *ever* told!' she protested. 'You heard what Ari said. He said they couldn't all have been brave men, but none of them had *ever* told!'

'I wonder what it would feel like to be the one who did,' Bjorn said, and began to pluck up grass stems with little sharp snapping sounds.

And then, even as Frytha sat watching him in bewildered dismay, he threw the bits of grass downwind, rolled over and sprang to his feet. 'We will go back now,' he said, and without another word, set off purposefully down the slope. Frytha sat for an instant staring after him, then scrambled to her feet also and ran to catch him up.

They made their way back down the long slope of Whiteless Pike, and in through the gap of the intake wall, and turned down beside the beck. And all the way, Bjorn stalked a little in advance, and said never a word.

It was drawing in toward evening when at last they came down past the mill house, where the swallows were busy under the eaves, and sheepshearing was almost over for the day. But there was a new activity in the Dale, for the first of the returning War-bands had come in, bringing the wounded, and while the smoke of many cooking-fires rose into the air, Storri Sitricson, who, being the priest of the Dale, was also its surgeon, had swept his host of helpers into action. Bjorn and Frytha passed him, trotting between the boothies of his little hospice, as they came down to the Jarlstead, his sleeves rolled high and his round face scarlet under the fiery curls of his tonsure, scolding softly to himself as always in times of stress, 'Tch tch tch!' like a startled blackbird.

The boys who had been busy all day at the sheep-pens were hanging about the returned warriors before the Hearth Hall; and Bjorn, his mouth shut and his eyes wide open, walked straight into them, with Frytha, whose legs were so tired that she could scarcely drag one after the other, still following loyally at his heels. Boys glanced round as Bjorn pushed past them, one or two pushed back in friendly fashion. Jon from the mill house demanded to know who he thought he was walking through, and Ottar Edrikson said something about people who went off in the middle of sheep-shearing and left other people to do all the work. But it was all perfectly good-natured; only one or two looked at him curiously, with the thing that Erland Ormeson had said behind their eyes. Bjorn seemed not to notice them at all; he shouldered in and out among them as though they had been so much under-growth, until he found Erland in their midst.

He went straight up to Erland, without fuss or stir of any sort, and hit him between the eyes as hard as ever he could.

Erland staggered back with an expression of almost ludicrous astonishment, and crashed into another boy, whom he sent sprawling, then recovered himself, and with a yell of fury came boring in. Bjorn ducked under his flailing fists, and winding his arms round Erland, hooked his legs from under him. It was all so quick that before the onlookers well knew what was happening, the two boys were a twisting mass of arms and legs on the ground at their feet. There was no outcry, only a gasp of excitement as the others crowded in on them. Frytha got ready for battle in case of need; but some-how it was clear to all the onlookers that this was a private holm-ganging, and no one attempted to join in.

Frytha stood with her hands clenched into small fierce fists, staring down at the two squirming, smiting figures on the grass. Erland had the advantage of almost two years and a lot of weight, but Bjorn had something else: a bleak white

flame of rage such as the berserkers of old had known how to
call up at will.

It was a bitter fight while it lasted.

But suddenly there was a movement among the crowd, as
though to let someone through; and then, just beyond the
flailing arms and legs of the battle, Frytha saw two feet in
rawhide shoon, a man's feet, not a boy's, and the bronze
chape of a wolfskin sword-sheath bound with faded crimson
hide. And something seemed to stroke her spine with an icy
feather.

Then the puppy Garm thrust forward into the circle and
sat down against the feet to lick a gash in his shoulder, and she
knew that it was not Ari Knudson with the torturer's mark
upon him, after all. With a gasp of relief, she looked up.
Aikin stood there, resting his hands on the pummel of the
great sword that had been Ari's, and gazing down on the
combat with a gleam of laughter caught somewhere in the set
grey weariness of his face.

'This is a most fine and bloody holm-ganging,' said Aikin.
'What is the quarrel, my heroes?'

Nobody answered. It seemed as though his voice could not
reach the two hating, struggling creatures at his feet, and as
they rolled toward him, he stooped and, catching Bjorn, who
was uppermost, lifted him off his enemy. 'Peace, puppies!'
Bjorn hung on like a small dog with a rat, and Aikin shook
him to break his hold, then set him down with a tooth-
rattling thump beside the other boy, and stood to watch them
come to themselves. Erland got up slowly, shaking his head;
then Bjorn, wiping the blood from a cut eyebrow with the
back of his hand. Aikin looked from one battered face to the
other, and asked again, in the same tone as before: 'What is
the quarrel?'

They looked at him, and then at each other, still panting.
They were not at all sure, now; or rather, they were sure, but
not in words. Bjorn could have said: 'Erland said that I ran
away because I was afraid when Njal Scar-Arm said what they
did to Ari Knudson, so I came back and hit him.' But that

was only the thing that showed on the surface, not the real thing. So they remained silent.

'So, a serious matter, after all,' Aikin said, after another pause. He looked at them searchingly for a moment, then nodded. 'Finish the work, then. Such work is better finished than left hanging for another day,' and whistling to the hound at his feet, he turned away. Garm gave a final lick to his wounded shoulder, got up, sneezing violently so that all his four legs flew in different directions, and padded after him.

Behind them, the two boys looked at each other again, uncertainly under their brows, while the crowd waited. Bjorn wiped the trickle of blood from his eye again; Erland was poking with his tongue at a loosened tooth. But somehow the moment was gone and the fire was out and there was no particular point in starting it again. Almost in the same instant, shrugging, and with an elaborate air of unconcern, both boys turned and went their separate ways.

But from that day forward it was hackles-up between Bjorn and Erland.

# VI

## A GAME OF RIDDLES

THE NORMANS PATCHED UP the old fort at Amilside, and leaving a strong garrison there, followed the King back to Kentdale. And later that summer, when reinforcements had come up to strengthen them, they headed for Carlisle. By summer's end, the stronghold was in Norman hands again—or a ruin that had once been Carlisle—and Dolfin Gospatricson and his men were clear away over the Solway.

And standing among the fallen timbers, the Red King said to Ranulf Le Meschin, 'Build me this place again, and when 'tis built, see that you win me those Lake Land roads, for I have a mind to them. But first and foremost, build me a strong castle here, and hold it for me with the strong hand.' He spoke very softly, and smiled as he spoke, but his lip curled up over his dog teeth. 'Hold it with the strong hand this time, lest there be no other.'

Four times the Sell Beck ran yellow with fallen birch leaves, and three times the birch buds thickened again, and the swallows nested under the mill house eaves. And in all that time, though there were constant forays, though the Normans came raiding in the Jarl's territory and Northmen ambushed the Norman convoys struggling up the Eden Valley to Carlisle, there was no great flare-up of the fighting that had been going on so long; and life in the Dale swung between seed-time and harvest, slaughtering and lambing, while the War-bands came and went.

And so the fourth winter wore away to a night some while after Yule.

Outside in the darkness, sleet blew down the bitter wind, and the night was full of the moaning of the birch-woods up the Sell Glen; but in the Jarl's Hearth Hall was warmth and company and peat firelight that made the wild winter night to halt on the threshold of the open fore-porch door. The doors of the Jarl's Hall stood always open, and at the evening meal not only the sword companions of his household sat down to eat with him, but all who had a mind to, Saxon and Northman alike, of Butharsdale and all the dales and glens of Lake Land. The women with the Countess on the cross benches at the upper end, the men with their weapons behind them, all down the length of the Hall.

The evening meal was over, such as it had been—for the end-of-winter shortage was upon them, the time that came every year when the salted meat was almost gone and the few cattle gave little milk and the meal-arks were low—and the long trestle tables, bright with long years of use and rubbing, had been taken down and stacked against the walls. The jars of ale and scanty buttermilk were going round, and men had emptied the Bragi cup that was the signal for song and story-telling, and the Hall harp was passing from hand to hand as man after man took his turn to entertain the company; and the womenfolk had come down from the cross-benches to mingle with their men now that the eating was done, as was the Viking custom.

Frytha had come down to the foot of the hall carrying an ale-jar, and being there, had settled herself in the rushes by the lower fire. She had been out all day helping Grim and his fellows at the lambing-pens and her hair was still wet. She shook it out, running it over her hands, pleased by the way the fire shining through it turned its usual russet to the colour of flame; and she looked at the scene through its bright wavering curtain. She saw the Jarl in his High Seat whose front posts were carved with the heads of Odin and Freya; and Haethcyn on his stool at the Jarl's feet, his beloved Sweet-singer cradled in his arms; and high above them, dim-seen through the hanging peat-reek that parted about it as once the sea-waves had done, the snarling figure-head of the Viking galley. She saw the Countess Tordis, who had brought her spinning to sit beside her Lord, and she looking, as she always looked, remote as a spear-maiden, with the bronze and silver arm-rings shining above her elbows. Gille sat on the rushes at her feet, playing Fox and Geese with narwhal ivory pieces on a chequered board with Gerd, the daughter of Hakon Wall-eye, who was his betrothed maiden. Gerd was as round-about at eleven as she had been at eight, though it was an appealing round-aboutness, like a tit's. She was cheating outrageously, as she always did when she played with Gille, and Gille was not noticing, as he always did when he played with Gerd. Sometimes Frytha wondered whether he really did not notice, and when Gerd annoyed her, she dwelt on the pleasure that it would be to tell him.

A little lower down the hall, Aikin leaned forward, drawing Garm's fluttering ears through and through his fingers, while the great wolfhound sat propped against his knee, head up and golden eyes half closed. Garm had more scars than one on his brindled hide by now, for he had gone into battle with his lord many times since that first time of all; until it would have seemed as unnatural to Aikin to go into battle without his grey, fanged shadow loping at his knee, as without Wave-flame in his hand.

Around Aikin the flower of the Jarl's young warriors

gathered in an uproarous group, and on the fringe of the group, among the boys who clung about it, Bjorn sat in the rushes, with glue-pot and strips of sinew beside him, putting the finishing touches to the bow he had been building.

Frytha, who by this time had a light bow of her own and could use it well at the butts, would have liked to go and sit beside him and help with this one; but he had not asked her, and she was a little shy of going unasked. It had been like that for a long while now, ever since the day of sheep-shearing, four years ago. 'If that ever happens to me, I wonder if I shall tell them what they want to know,' Bjorn had said that day up on the shoulder of Whiteless Pike. That was Bjorn's trouble. Other people did not wonder those sort of things; other people mostly couldn't picture very clearly (at any rate they mostly didn't) what it would be like to be alone in the Normans' hands, with the lives of their fellows and the thing they fought for hanging on their power to endure with a shut mouth. But Bjorn could picture it with a hideous clearness—and so he wondered; which was a bad thing to do. . . . And it was because Frytha knew about it, because she knew the thing about him that he could not bear anyone to know, that there had been the gulf between them ever since. No, not a gulf, only a gap; a narrow gap made of silence and an odd shyness that they could not cross, though at most times they almost forgot that it was there. And she could not go un-asked to help him with the bow.

Somebody near her set an ale-horn down empty, and shaking back her damp hair she picked up the jar beside her, and rose to fill it. Then there were other horns to fill, and in attending to them, Frytha forgot the vague sense of loss that had come to her only the moment before.

The harp was still passing from hand to hand, but it seemed that tonight, for no particular reason, no one was in the mood for serious harping, or the long sagas of the North. There was a breaking-up and a shifting in the Jarl's Hall; somebody flung more peat on one of the fires; indeed, it was a night for keeping the fires up, for the chill of the sleet was everywhere, and cat's-paws of icy wind stirred the rushes up and down the hall. A cluster of boys and young warriors had captured the harp now, and thronging round the fire, close to where Aikin sat, had begun to pass it among themselves, chanting to its accompaniment the long and complicated riddles that were dear to the Northmen, each boy making up his own as his turn came.

> 'I am the companion of a Warrior's arm,
> Not of gold as an arm-ring am I;
> Not of leather as the grip of his linden shield.
> Whiles, he sends me free,
> To kill and to return again . . .'

'A spear.' Somebody guessed, and was shouted down. 'Whoever heard of a spear returning from its kill? You have to go after it.'

'It's a falcon! A falcon, isn't it, Otter?'

And someone else took the harp and tried, striking the strings in time to the thoughts and images of his word-play.

Frytha heard them behind the deeper talk of their elders, as she bent to refill the ale-horn which Aikin held empty on his knee. He glanced up at her with a quick smile of thanks, not breaking the thread of his deep discussion with Hakon Walleye, who now sat beside him. 'The wind has blown light and fitful this long while past,' he was saying. 'All these four years past, since they butchered Ari, my foster-father. But now Le Meschin has finished his fine stone-built castle of Carlisle, and it is in my mind that soon the wind must rise again.'

'And whither will it blow this time, think you?'

'Down the road to Rafnglas.'

Hakon Wall-eye scratched delicately at the tip of his left ear, as he always did when thinking. 'What of the Midgate?'

'It is in my heart that they will leave that road to its dead,' Aikin said, smiling gently into the tawny depth of his ale horn. 'I think that the Midgate is closed for ever by certain white bones among the birchwoods—as by the cross of my sword that was once my foster-father's, every pass into Lake Land shall be also, by and by.'

There was a burst of laughter from the boys thronging the

65

fire. They were shouting down Jon's choice of a riddle, protesting that Hugin Longnab's nose was no fit subject for a riddle anyway, since it would take the whole evening to give a proper idea of its length; while Jon himself, more freckled than ever, sat smiling serenely down his own nose at his dirk, which he was trying to balance upright on the tip of one finger.

Then someone called 'Bjorn! Bjorn, don't go to sleep. It is your turn.'

Bjorn looked up, thrusting back his hair with a gesture that was typical of him, and his bright, faintly mocking gaze flickered over the laughing faces of his kind. 'Have we not had enough of rhyming riddles and riddling rhymes?' he asked.

'Don't hedge,' said Ottar Edrikson. 'Why should we scrape our wits for your good, and you do nothing for ours?'

Other voices joined in, laughing but quite determined; and Bjorn laid aside the bow-stave. 'Nay then, I am weary of your riddles and I'll not make a fool of myself like Jon with a limping rhyme for your pleasure,' he said lightly. 'If you must have a riddle to sharpen your wits on, you shall have it in a tune instead of words.'

He drew his legs under him and got up, his hand already out to take the Hall harp from the boy who held it. Then he checked, as though an idea had come to life in him, and glanced toward Haethcyn on his stool at the Jarl's feet. The old man met his eyes, nodded, and very slightly lifted the harp on his knee. Bjorn went across to him, and a long look passed between them as he took the treasure from his foster-father's hands into his own. It was five years now since Bjorn had taken the Sweet-singer without leave; five years since Haethcyn had begun to school him in those arts that belonged to a harper, the telling of stories, the chanting of song and saga, above all, the handling of his harp. A hard task-master, Haethcyn had been, as ruthless in his demands even as Trond Gyrdson, from whom Bjorn had learned the use of sword and spear and the great Viking axe. And suddenly they knew, sharing the knowledge as though it had been spoken between them, that tonight those five years had come to the testing.

Bjorn turned toward the rest, who were already drifting up
the hall in his wake, and setting one foot on the bench, settled
the harp on his knee and into the hollow of his shoulder as a
woman might settle a child; and so remained for a little while,
staring into the fire as though he were listening, utterly
oblivious of the impatient pack who crowded round him,
touching the strings without sounding them.

Frytha stood very still, forgetful of the ale-jar she carried
in her sudden intense awareness of something happening—
something that was to matter deeply, and that, for good or ill,
could not be undone. She watched Bjorn's absorbed face and
his right hand, seeing the firelight run and quiver on the
white-bronze strings of the ancient harp. He began to sound
the strings, hesitantly at first, then more surely. Just single
notes, in the beginning, that somehow made her think of Anlaf
forging a sword-blade; then gradually quickening and spinning them together into a kind of tune, a humming, thrumming, flashing tune. And it seemed to Frytha that she was no
longer listening to the forging, but to the blade itself, singing.

Old Haethcyn sat very still, looking up at his foster-son, his
lips parted smilingly, so that his long yellow teeth showed in
his beard. Gille abandoned his game of fox and geese, and
turned to listen. Aikin came strolling up from the lower fire.
Little by little the whole hall grew quiet to listen. Bjorn
played on, absorbed in the thing that he was making. And
now it was as though the sword raised its voice in triumph, in
the hot ecstasy of battle, singing as it drank blood; and now the
mood changed, and it was wailing—keening like a woman for
its slain. . . .

Suddenly Bjorn became aware that everyone was listening.
His hand stumbled: he swept a last fierce flight of notes from
the harp on his knee, and was still, his head tipped back, half
laughing. But it seemed to Frytha that there was something
of defiance in his gaze as it flicked over the faces that thronged
him round, and he looked rather white.

There was a moment of complete silence, and then Gille
said in a faintly puzzled tone, 'But it sounded like a sword.'

The Jarl looked down from his High Seat, smiling in the shadow of his golden beard. 'It seems that there are two harpers in Butharsdale, where we thought there was but one. Give you joy of your foster-cub, Haethcyn.'

And Aikin, with his hand stilled on Garm's twitching ear, said with a nod, 'I think that were I Wave-flame, and had the power of song, that is much the kind of fierce and flashing song that I should sing.'

The boys and young warriors were crowding round Bjorn, and a burst of voices filled the Hearth Hall; voices that tossed the answer to the riddle to and fro; voices that shouted their approval or disapproval. 'A sword! That's what it is—a sword-song, and a good one too. Well harped, Bear-cub! Well, how could *anyone* guess what a tune means?'

Bjorn grinned, and exchanged insults with his audience, then turned to give the precious harp back to his foster-father. The old harper took it from him, cradling it once more on his knee, and again the long look passed between them. Then he nodded. 'Aye, you have the music in you, from your fore-mother's folk, the true gift,' he said. 'Did I not tell you when you were a bairn, that it is the Saxon kind, and the British who were before the Saxons, who have the music?'

Erland Ormeson, sitting nearby, looked up from the spear that he was re-shafting, and raising his voice just enough to clear the voices all around him, demanded, out of the superi-ority of a whole season with the War-bands, 'Do the Saxon kind and the British who were before the Saxons always make their brave sword-songs before ever they have heard the clash of swords in battle?'

In the sudden hush that followed, Frytha heard very clearly the spatter of sleet against the stretched membrane of the high window-holes. That was like Erland, she thought; bitter-tongued, and always ready to pick a quarrel; above all, to pick a quarrel with Bjorn, any time these past four years. And any time these past four years, Bjorn had been more than ready to take it up. She could almost see the hackles rise on Bjorn's neck as he swung round, though nothing showed in his face

68

save the lazy mockery that could be so infuriating. 'I did not know Erland Ormeson was so great a champion on the Whale's Road,' he said; and there was a shout of laughter, for the subject of Erland's riddle had been the figure-head on the housebeam overhead, and it was well known that Erland himself could neither swim nor handle a boat so well as befitted his Northern stock.

Erland flushed as crimson as Bjorn was white. He sprang up, letting the newly shafted spear clatter on to the hearth stone; and for a few moments it seemed as though there might be real trouble, as the two stood facing each other, tensed like two hounds in the instant before they fly at each other's throats.

But before the thing could go any further, the great voice of the Jarl himself boomed across the silence. 'Peace, you young fools! I'll not have this snarling of whelps in the Hearth Hall! Gin you must fight like puppies, out you'll go into the night like puppies, and the sleet may cool your hot blood for you!'

The tension snapped like a harp-string. Erland stooped, muttering, to pick up his spear again, and Bjorn swung away to his unfinished bow-stave, and the thing was over as swiftly as it had begun.

Nevertheless, something had happened, for good or ill, that could not be undone. Frytha knew that, and the uneasy knowledge was still with her when, a little later, she followed the Countess from the hall with the rest of her maidens.

In the bower, old Unna, who seldom came into the Hall, sat crooning over the fire that she had built high with birch branches stacked among the peat, spinning her fine woollen thread. They gathered round the hearth, holding their hands to the warmth and shivering while the whistling draughts played up and down their backs. But it was time to make ready for the night. Frytha took the fillet of twisted silver from the Countess's head, and laid it away in her dower coffer, then brought her her comb of narwhal ivory.

They huddled over the fire, combing and braiding their hair, and talking softly. And presently they heard the gathering begin to break up in the hall, as men betook themselves to their quarters, and the benches were spread with rugs for the young warriors who slept in the Hall. The old woman Unna laid her spindle aside at last, and shivered. 'It is cold!' she grumbled. 'Aie aie, this wind has a sharp bite for old bones!'

'You are right, Unna,' said the Countess Tordis. 'See how the fire burns!' She finished plaiting her hair into two long braids, then rose and went to a great kist carved with writhing bird-beaked dragons, and opened it. 'Haethcyn will be frozen in that boothy of his. I have begged him to come in-by and sleep in the loft over Hall like a Christian, now that he grows old; but no, he will gang his own gate.' She brought out a fine wolfskin rug as she spoke. 'Frytha, do you take him this, to hold out some of the cold.'

So Frytha flung on her cloak, and gathering up the heavy rug, plunged out by the garth door into the bitter night. The ground was icy slush underfoot, and the sleet drove in her face as she sped between the byres and barns of the Jarlstead; and it seemed to her that she could catch in the wind's moaning the howling of the Skiddaw wolves who hunted close to the haunts of men in the lean time at the winter's end, and she thought of Grim and his fellows mounting the wolf-guard over their lambing pens.

She hardly expected that Haethcyn would have come from the Hearth Hall yet, but when she reached the boothy on the edge of the steading, that he had made his own, and beat upon the door, calling that it was Frytha, he answered her; and when she lifted the pin and went in, he had set his lantern on the crossbeam, and was hanging the Sweet-singer in its worn leather bag on the wall above his sleeping-bench, where it always hung at night. Frytha slammed the door behind her and dropped the pin, shivering and laughing as he looked round inquiringly. 'Phew! it is cold tonight!—The Lady Tordis sends you another rug to sleep under, since you will not come in-by and sleep over Hall like a Christian!'

'Na na, I am an old dog and I keep to my own lair,'

70

Haethcyn said. 'But give my thanks to the Lady Tordis for her rug.'

He made to take it from her, but Frytha went past him to the sleeping-bench, and setting the heavy wolfskin rug on its foot, began to straighten the chaos of coverings already there, making his sleeping-place ready for him. As she did so, her shoulder brushed against the hanging harp and set it swinging, and it seemed to her that she caught the faintest thrumming from inside the bag, as though in its sleep the harp was remembering the sword-song that Bjorn had made on it that evening. 'It was a fine harping that Bjorn made in Hall tonight,' she said, straightening the plaited straw pillow.

'It was a fine harping,' Haethcyn agreed. 'Yet it is in my mind that it has started a thing that will not be stopped until it has run its course.'

Frytha looked at him quickly. So he felt that too. But he was wrong; it had started five years ago, with a curlew's mating flight up on the shoulder of Beacon Fell. 'Is it a good thing, or a bad?' she asked.

'Nay, I am not old Unna, to read you the future in a candle-flame.'

Even as he spoke, there came a rattling at the doorpin, and the door burst open, and as they both looked toward it, Bjorn himself stooped in out of the sleety darkness, and slammed the door behind him, and stood leaning against it, shaking back his wet and white-flecked hair. He never looked at Frytha in her corner, for his whole attention was turned to the old harper. 'Haethcyn Fostri, I have just been with Aikin. I asked him that I might go with the War-bands when the time comes for the Spring Hosting.'

Haethcyn showed no sign of surprise. 'And what did Aikin say to that?'

'He asked me how old I was,' Bjorn said, speaking very fast, 'and when I told him that I should be fifteen next Fall of the Leaf, he said that, by the laws of our people, I could not be called on to bear my shield for nearly a year yet.'

'And then?'

'I said that, by the laws of our people, I need not wait to be called. And then he said: "Go you to Haethcyn your foster-father, and ask his leave; and gin he give it to you, you shall come!"'

He stood waiting, those pale bright eyes of his levelled on the harper's face; and again Frytha heard very clearly the sound of the wind-driven sleet, hushing this time, across the broom-thatched roof.

Haethcyn got up from the sleeping-bench on which he had been sitting, slowly unfurling his full splendid height in the little hut; and setting his hands either side of Bjorn's shoulders, turned him full to the light. 'I had not thought for this to come for another year yet,' he said, looking down into the boy's face, 'but I am content to rest by Aikin's judgement in the matter.'

'You give me leave then, Fostri?'

'I give you leave, aye, as I think that Bjorn your father would have given it to you,' Haethcyn said, and dropped his hands. 'Wait you, there is a thing that I have for you, laid by against this day.' He turned aside as he spoke, to the small carved kist at the foot of his sleeping-bench, and while the two watched in expectant silence, he freed the ancient clasp and raised the lid. His few belongings were inside: his best sark of dark blue wool, a shoulder brooch set with amber, the round bag in which he kept the fine white-bronze wire for his spare harp-strings; and he delved under them like an old hound looking for a buried bone.

When he straightened up, Frytha saw that he was holding something long and narrow, wrapped in saffron-coloured cloth. He began to unroll it, saying, as the last fold fell away, 'There, take it; it has been waiting for you a long time,' and into Bjorn's hands he put a heavy dirk, whose iron hilt showed in the lantern light inlaid with gold and age-darkened narwhal ivory.

Bjorn looked at it in silence a moment, then, still in silence, drew it from the sheath. It came easily, with a smoothness that spoke of careful greasing. The brindled badger skin with which the sheath was covered was rubbed bare in places, the

ornamental bosses dulled and dinted, the girdle-thongs that
hung from it deeply worn; but the blade was bright and keen
as a flame. Bjorn smiled at it, making the light run to and fro
along the blade from tip to hilt and back again. He made it
whistle as he cut the air, 'wheett—wheett '. 'This was my
father's dirk,' he said at last, half questioningly, half stating a
fact.

'Aye,' Haethcyn said. 'When he knew that the wound was
mortal, he bade me keep his dirk for you until you were of an
age to bear it.'

Bjorn looked at the thing again, and then set about freeing
his boy's dirk from his girdle, and knotting the man's dirk that
had been his father's in its place. 'I must put on fresh thongs,'
he said. 'These will not hold it long.'

'There is yet something more,' said Haethcyn; and Frytha
saw in the palm of his hand a small thing that caught green
fire from the lantern, as he held it out.

Bjorn took it from him and turned to the light; then
glanced for the first time at Frytha, and moved a little, as
though to share the thing with her. And Frytha, who would
not have come unbidden, came close to look at what he held.
It was a ring: a massive gold ring of ancient workmanship,
much scored and battered, with a bezel of dark green trans-
lucent stone, on which was engraved a device of some sort.

'What is this thing like a fish?' Bjorn asked.

'A dolphin.'

Bjorn turned the ring in his fingers, examining it from all
sides. 'This is not such a ring as our people make,' he said in a
faintly puzzled tone.

'It was none of our people's making,' said Haethcyn. 'It
was made by the people of Romeburg, the people of the
Legions, who made the Rafnglas road and the great fort at
Amilside.'

'How did it come to my father's hand?'

'It was his father's before him, and his father's father's before
that,' Haethcyn said. 'It came out of Wales with that British
foremother of yours that once I told you of, and it was old

73

even then, and had come down to her—for she was the last of an ancient line—from the high far-off days, from the people of the Legions whence her line was sprung. So the story has passed down with the ring, from father to son; and so now I pass them both as from your father, on to you.'

Bjorn slid the ring on to his left hand, and turned it under the light, watching the green spark wake and slumber and wake again in the engraved jewel.

'From my father, on to me,' he said. 'It has come a long way.'

## VII

## DAWN ENCOUNTER

THE MOON, RIDING high in a dappled and glimmering
sky, shone down on the dark ruins of the old Roman
fort that clung like a falcon's eyrie to the rocks, keeping
watch over the Hardknott Pass as it had done when Cæsar's
legions came and went that way. For half a thousand years
the fox and the mountain cat had laired in the ancient strong
point, undisturbed unless by stray ghosts drilling on the lost
parade-ground or marching their beat along the crumbling
ramparts. But now the fox and wild cat and the ghosts had
been driven out, and for a while there were men again, where
men had been before.

In the western angle of the ramparts, among the rubble of
the fallen corner tower, a tall stripling stood on guard,
motionless as the stones about him in the sliding silver light

that splintered on the iron comb of his war-cap and hung star-wise at the tip of the spear on which he leaned.

Bjorn was aware of the camp behind him, choked with men: men snatching a brief rest, wounded men in pain, men standing watchful like himself all round the fallen ramparts; but for all that he could hear of them, he might have been alone between the lop-sided moon and the Norman watch-fires. Far below him all Eskdale lay still in the moonlight: marsh and meadow, wild-wood and looping river, webbed and washed with the silver of the moon, between him and the desolate billows of the high moors that rose to Scafell beyond. Somewhere among those high moors, where the little glens came down to dale, lay Bjornsthwaite, he knew: the lost land-take and the ruins of the steading that had been home to his father and his father's father before him. Haethcyn, who had so often told him about it, said that it lay hard beside the way down into Eskdale from the north, but all the glens looked alike in the moonlight. . . . Close in here, under the shoulder of the fortress fell, the road dropped from the Pass, plunging down in wide swerves and loops to join the Esk, and so away down dale to the sea. The Legions' road to the coast. He could catch the gleam of it clear in places, where some stretch of ancient paving caught the moon before it was lost again in the encroaching wild. It was along the line of the road that the Norman watch-fires gathered thickest, but there seemed to be watch-fires everywhere, as he looked down; watch-fires circling the base of the fell shoulder, watch-fires right up into the dark throat of the Pass.

Bjorn, his gaze following that trail of fires, was remembering the months since he had carried his shield into battle for the first time. In the first days of spring, that had been, and the snow still lying thick on the high fells, when the Normans began their thrust along the Rafnglas road. Aikin had said that Le Meschin would not dare to take his men up Ryedale again, and he had spoken truly; for it could not put much heart into an army to bark their shins on the bare rib-staves of the men who had tried that way before them. Besides,

William Le Meschin with his strong stone castle at Mulecaster already held the western end of the road, all down Eskdale to the sea. That must have made the Rafnglas road seem an easier nut to crack. It had not been as easy as all that—a day's march from Amilside to Hardknott, and it had taken the Normans all spring and summer to make it. But now they were up to the Hardknott Pass, to the last truly defensible point of the way; and beyond that the road ran open down into Eskdale, down to the sea, and William Le Meschin, with his troops at Mulecaster, only held from joining forces with his brother by a desperately thin barrier of Northmen. He was remembering the stand that they had made, high in the throat of the Pass; shield to shield, with all Eskdale opening at their backs. A great stand it had been, but a hopeless one, from which at last they had made a fighting retreat in the dusk, carrying their many wounded with them, up here to the ruin on the fell shoulder that had been their burg these many weeks past.

So long as they held the old fort, the Normans would not have control of the Rafnglas road and they had held it like heroes for three days now. But they could not hold it much longer without reserves, and Jarl Buthar could send them none without leaving the rest of the Lake Land wide open to the Normans' trampling. The ranks of the War Host were growing thin of late years, Bjorn knew; too many young warriors going down in battle with no sons to take their weapons after them. And now it had come to this, that they could not hold the Hardknott Burg.

Only an hour since, with the last Norman attack not long beaten off, Aikin had called his captains and the young warriors of his Sword-band about him, and looked round on them in the mingled light of low watch-fire and rising moon, and said, 'It is time to be going, my brothers.'

Someone had said half sullenly: 'We are ready to stay, Aikin Jarlson.'

'And after we have stayed, what shall the Jarl my brother do for men?' Aikin asked very quietly. He tightened with his

teeth the piece of rag that he had been knotting round a
gashed forearm. 'Nay, we have no choice but to pull out tonight. And thanks to the clear skies and this accursed moon
that will not set until the sun is up, we are like to find it none
so easy. Therefore I have been making a plan. It may be that
one of you can better it, but'—he shrugged thin, mailed
shoulders—'I cannot.'

A low mutter of voices rose from the throng around him.
'Let us hear it then, Aikin. We are with you whatever
it is.'

'See then,' Aikin said. 'It is in my mind that we will wait
as long as maybe, for a low moon and long shadows; but we
cannot wait too long, for the wounded will be slow travellers.
When the time comes, we will send the main host out by the
Northern gate, and up dale to the ford above Heron Crags:
the wounded must cross there, where they will be sheltered
from the Norman outposts, and once into the fells beyond,
they will be safe on their road home. Then let the rest make
up through the yew woods to the glen-head under Stonesty
Pike and wait there for the rest of us.'

'For the rest of us?' somebody questioned.

'Aye—the whole fellside from the North gate up to the
Heron Ford lies full in view from the Norman outposts, and
there's little enough cover among the rocks—at least for
wounded men—since the Normans felled the scrub. Therefore
we must make cover of another kind, by keeping the Normans
so busy toward the Pass that they will not trouble with the
bare slope up-dale.'

'So ha! That is a plan indeed!' Njal Scar-arm, who had
stood at Aikin's shoulder in many fights, drew in his breath
approvingly through his teeth, and a little movement ran
through the crowd, and was stilled again. Garm, standing
against his master's leg, whined softly, as though sensing the
strain and the excitement, his eyes glowing in the low firelight.

Aikin looked about him as though to gather them all in.
'Four score of us should be enough. Three score or so to come

78

down on them this side, and a small band to get across the river behind them and into the skirts of Harter Fell.'

'An attack from two sides at once!' someone said softly; and there was a deep-voiced growl of approval from the men about him.

'Who leads the band from this side?' That was Hakon Wall-eye scratching delicately at the tip of his left ear as usual.

'I do,' Aikin said. 'And for the other'—he turned his head, searching the dark throng, and picked out young Gille, standing tall almost as his father among the rest, and leaning on the haft of the great pole-axe with which he was already earning a name for himself—'Gille?'

'Aikin?'

'Will you take the Harter Fell band?'

'Give me the little war horn, and I'll make Le Meschin think there's a whole War Host up that side,' Gille said simply.

And then they were thrusting in from all sides, low eager voices clashing together. 'I'm with you—and I—and I. I am your man, Gille. Aikin, I am for you.' There was no need for the Sword-band to give tongue, they were Aikin's to lead through Hell if need be, both by custom and their own choice, and he knew it as they did, but they thronged about him none the less. Bjorn remembered it vividly, the crowding faces, eager in the mingled light of fire and moon, the brindled head of the hound upraised and pressed against his lord's thigh; the ring and rattle of weapons and the low urgent grumble of voices, as plans were shaped and made perfect. Aikin's voice last of all, with its familiar edge of laughter. 'So. It will serve. Go you back to your own places now, and twiddle your thumbs awhile. We shall have something of a wait, since we cannot hurry the moon!'

No, Bjorn thought, they could not hurry the moon. Far up the dale, Heron Crags were beginning to darken as the light slid behind them, but the dale itself was still full of white radiance. Odd, how the moon drained the world of colour; the red sandstone of the ancient rampart was ash-grey where the moonlight fell, black in the shadow. He wished the moon would hurry; he wished that he could hear the others. The cold taste of defeat was in his mouth, and he felt most horribly alone; suddenly half aware in his aloneness of some difference between himself and his kind—between himself and Gille, for instance. Some difference that had come down to him perhaps with his ring from that far-back foremother out of Wales.

He moved his hand on the spear-shaft, and felt the pressure of the battered ring on his finger. It had been rather loose for him when he first put it on but it was not so loose now. It must have been made in the first place for a hand that was narrower than his; but it had been made bigger; you could see the place where more gold had been let into the shaft. He wondered if that meant that it had been made for a woman, but somehow he did not think so; it had not the look of a woman's ring. Perhaps the people of Romeburg had narrower hands than the Northmen; that would explain it. Suddenly he wondered if someone wearing his ring when it was bright and new, someone with narrower hands than his, yet who was part of him in some way, had come this way before; had helped, maybe, to build the road that had gone back to the wild so long ago, and looked down over Eskdale from the red sandstone fort, when it too was new.

Just for a moment, the thought made him catch his breath as though he were looking down an unbearable length and loneliness of time, and the wind blew cold out of its emptiness; and then it was oddly comforting, and made him feel less alone.

The shadows were beginning to lengthen across Eskdale, brightening the tawny gold of the Norman watch-fires as the moon westered. He heard the wild-fowl calling above the dark marshes of Dunnerdale; and then, within the camp itself, a long-drawn mournful cry that could pass, with those who did not know it, for the howl of a wolf.

There was a sense, rather than a sound, of movement in the camp behind him, and he knew that for Gille and his handful the waiting was over. He had wanted to go with Gille, but only seasoned warriors had been deemed worthy of that venture; so Bjorn must wait for the wolf to cry again.

The silence settled once more, a silence drawn out thin and long—long to snapping point, like overdrawn wire. Heron Crags grew darker yet, and the darkness crept out toward the river ford. And at last, the wolf cried again from the camp behind him.

Bjorn's heart gave a wild lurch, and steadied, as he turned from his watch-post and went to answer the summons.

The eastern corner tower still stood half its height, sheltering with its black cloak of shadow the tumbled breech in the rampart at its foot, and the men who were gathering there like deeper shadows themselves. Bjorn slipped into the growing throng, hearing the tense human silence, the quiet quick breathing of men all round him, feeling the wild-fire of the waiting moment leaping from man to man. Then, for the third time that night, the wolf called, this time from their very midst, and even as the call died away, the throng began to melt. There was a breath of soundless movement a slipping forward of shadows, and with the rest, Bjorn was out over the fallen rubble of the rampart, Ottar Edrikson before him, Erland behind, running low and soundless for the shelter of the ruined bath house, maybe seventy paces away.

In the shadow of the bath-house wall he checked an instant, seeing ahead of him the whole drop of the fellside empty of life, save for a dark thing near his feet and already disappearing into the bilberry cover, that was Ottar's right heel. Then he dropped on to his belly, and slid forward after it, into the thick mass of bilberry and fern.

For a little, he heard Ottar in front of him, and Erland behind, and then, as the band spread out, curving down toward the Pass, he lost the sound of them. He was aware of the others all around him, slipping forward and down, but he saw no more than the stealthy swaying of a bilberry spray, heard nothing but a breath of night wind. They were closing in, slipping from cover to cover, from bramble-break to rock hammer, from rock hammer to dry runnel bed, down and down. How had it gone with Gille and his handful? Bjorn wondered. They must be well across the Norman line by now, and there had been no sound of fighting. Behind and above him in the silent fort, the War bands would be waiting for the first baying of the War horns that would be their signal to pull out. Well, they would not have long to wait now. The shadows of the Pass were flowing up about him, the nearest of the watch-fires were very near. The Normans had felled the birch-scrub on either side of the road, but the rocky fellside was streaked and dappled black and silver by the moon, giving good cover still. Bjorn, belly-snaking forward with his spear at the trail, began to catch the glint of firelight on hauberk and helm, drawn sword and grounded spear; and when at last the moment came for waiting again, and he lay still, with quiet breath but racing heart, he could have tossed a pebble into the nearest watch-fire.

He watched the slow pacing of a sentry, heard the voice of the river and the wild fowl calling, smelled the first promise of dawn in the night wind through the grass. And then it came: the hollow booming of a War horn among the rocks of Harter Fell. Gille had got through! And even as the hot triumph shot through him, a thin flight of arrows came thrumming overhead into the camp below. For one instant he saw the whole scene caught in utter stillness, as a fly in amber; hands that seemed frozen on sword-hilts, the blank and startled look stamped on firelit faces, all somehow unreal and grotesque. The sentry he had been watching seemed to stand swaying for a long time, with a shaft yet thrumming between his shoulders, before he fell slowly, as a tree falls. Then the whole world burst into uproar, and Bjorn was up and running with the rest, hard on the heels of Aikin and the brindled snarling fury that was Garm.

The Normans gathered themselves and sprang to meet the attack; watch-fires were scattered as men crashed through them, and darkness engulfed friend and foe alike, and somewhere in the darkness a Norman trumpet rang brazen-tongued above the tumult.

The time that followed was a chaos of random blows, in darkness that made it hard to tell friend from foe, until some of the scattered embers from the fires caught the dry grass of summer's end, and the long curling swathes of flame scattered the battle as seeds that burst from a puff-ball; and once more for a while there was light to see by.

The Northmen's only hope was to make Le Meschin's troops believe themselves beset by the whole War Host. So, and only so, they might be held in play, while the true War Host, with its burden of wounded, won clear. They hung about the flanks of the Norman army, driving in on them now from this side, now from that, rather as a pack of hounds holding a bull at bay; melting into the darkness when the goaded Normans lunged back.

Slowly the sky grew pale toward the east, and the moon was on the rim of the Eskdale Fells; and at last the War horn boomed again, not from Harter Fell this time, but from far up among the mists of Hardknott. 'Come home now,' said the hollow peel. 'Break away! All's over! Come home! Come home!' Bjorn heard it as clearly as though the words had been spoken; and seeing the spreading pallor of the dawn with an odd surprise, because somehow he had expected the fire and darkness to go on for ever, knew that by now, if all had gone according to plan, the wounded would be well across Eskdale and far into the safety of the fells on their way home.

They would not have to kill their wounded, this time. He thought of it quite matter-of-factly. They had had to more than once before now, he knew. Sometimes you could not get your wounded away. When that happened, it was better to die quickly at the hand of friend or kinsman than be left to the Norman's butchery. But this time there would be no need to kill even the sorest scathed, he thought triumphantly, as he slipped into a little gully left by the winter rains, and began to work his way up it. There were Normans scattered and questing all up and down the dale, and the light was growing every instant. Well, all that was left now was to get clear and head for the meeting-place under Stonesty Pike. Probably soon, as soon as they were well into the fells, he would come up with others of the band.

The gully swung too far left, and he took to the open hillside, traversing behind an outcrop of black rock. He was not clear of the enemy yet; better go carefully—carefully. . . . And then among a steep tumble of rock and heather he came suddenly face to face with one, who, like himself, had become separated from his own kind.

For an instant he saw the mailed hauberk, the waspish glitter of black and gold on the kite-shaped shield; the young fleshy face with the eyes suddenly widening under the helmet rim; and then, shortening his spear, he sprang in to the attack, diving under the swift guard of the other's sword that came whistling to meet him. Somehow—perhaps it was the steep fall of the ground, perhaps because he had been so long without sleep that nothing seemed quite real or clear—he missed his stroke; but so did his enemy. Bjorn crashed into him, and the man's blade flew wide; he stepped back, caught his heel in a heather tuft, and went down, dragging Bjorn with him. The Norman had lost his sword, but even as he fell, he had contrived to whip out his dagger; Bjorn, still clutching his own shortened spear, caught the flash of the wicked little blade, and wrenched sideways just in time to take in his left shoulder the blow that had been meant for his throat.

He let go his spear, which was unmanageable at such close quarters, and grabbed the wrist of the man's dagger-hand before he could strike again. He could not come at his own dirk, he could only cling grimly to his hold. Close-locked together they fought, strength against strength, and not so ill matched as they seemed; for though the Norman was three or four years the elder, he was somewhat soft, while Bjorn was lean and hard as a wolfhound, and like all his kind, a wrestler born and bred. But Bjorn was bleeding like a stuck pig. There seemed to be blood everywhere, and his own strength going out of him on the red tide.

The face close to his own glared up at him, the lips drawn back over grinning teeth as the man struggled to free his dagger

84

hand. The first sunlight was spilling over the shoulder of Hardknott; below them Dunnerdale lay still in deep shadow, but suddenly the whole fellside was gleaming. On Bjorn's left hand, as it gripped the other's wrist, the green stone in the ancient ring, that was normally dark and cool as the leaves of the mountain juniper, caught the first level ray, and lit for an instant into dazzling green fire. For the merest flash of time the Norman's attention flickered from Bjorn's face to the pin-point blaze, and in that instant, with a last effort that started the world swimming into darkness, Bjorn twisted the Norman's wrist so that he gave a sudden snarl of agony, and the dagger slipped from his fingers. Through the buzzing in his ears, Bjorn heard shouts that seemed to come from two different directions at once, and the rush of running feet through the heather. He was dimly aware of his enemy twisting from under him like an eel, and then there was nothing but blackness.

He thought—'I'm blind!—but it was only my shoulder——'

And then there was not even blackness; nothing at all.

And then, slowly growing out of the nothingness, there was the solid darkness of rock outlined against a misty sky. It wavered on his sight as though he were staring up at it through gently running water, but gradually, by dint of much frowning, he managed to get it steadied. He turned his head cautiously, and saw a heathery slope running up to a grey crest of crags that had grown familiar in the past months. So he was not blind; and he was where he ought to be, in the glen under Stonesty Pike; and he realized that he was lying under the overhang of a long outcrop, sheltered from the soft mizzle rain that drifted across the glen. Voices reached him, and a faint smell of wood-smoke. There was a fire burning under the outcrop, and as he moved, a man turned from the group about it and came to one knee beside him, and he saw that it was Aikin himself.

'So, this is greatly better,' Aikin said, thrusting back Garm's inquiring muzzle.

85

Bjorn squinted at him accusingly. 'I feel as wankle as a wet sark!'

'That is scarce a thing to wonder at,' the other said with a quick flash of laughter, and turning back the sheepskin cloak that had been spread over him, looked at the tight-lashed strips of linen about his shoulder. 'At all events the bleeding has stopped.'

'They can't say we didn't give them good cover,' Bjorn said.

'They can't. We gave them most noble cover.'

'Did—they get clear away?'

'The wounded were safe into the fells when Hundi Swainson doubled back to bring us word of them. As for the rest, if you look about you, you will see them making camp.'

Bjorn drew a deep breath of relief; and then his eyes caught the waspish glitter of a shield propped against the rock beside him—a black shield on which three golden flames shone out fiercely in the morning light—and flew back frowningly to Aikin's face. 'The Norman—did he get away?'

'Aye; his own men were too near to be healthy for us; it was all that Ottar Edrikson and I could do to get you away, without troubling about him. We brought his shield away, though; the guige had broken, and you were lying on it.' Aikin smiled gently. 'It seemed a pity to leave it lying for the Normans to pick up.'

Bjorn became aware of someone else standing just behind Aikin, with a bronze cup in his hand. 'Have a drink and you'll feel better,' Gille said, with his slow grin; and put the cup into the hand that Aikin held up for it. Bjorn struggled on to his elbow, the world tilting as he did so, and heard Aikin say: 'Softly now, take it softly,' and felt a steadying arm under his shoulders and the bronze rim against his mouth.

It was not the buttermilk or ale that he was used to, but the fiery mead kept for special need; it ran down his throat like liquid fire, making him choke and splutter; but almost at once he felt the new warm life creeping through him. 'So, that is better,' Aikin said for the second time. 'Erland has

86

killed a buck to savour the barley bannock and there will be broth presently. That will put new heart into you.'

'I am well enough,' Bjorn said.

'You will be, by and by, when Storri Sitricson has his hands on you.'

'Na, I am well enough, I tell you,' Bjorn protested. 'There is no need that I go back to Storri Sitricson. I will stay here with the rest of my sword-kin, I——'

'You will go back to Storri Sitricson, and get that shoulder truly and fairly healed; and when Storri says that you may come out again, then come. We shall be here or hereabouts, so long as Ranulf Le Meschin holds the Rafnglas road.'

Something in the other's voice made Bjorn forget his protests and turn a little to get a clearer view of his face. 'A fine stronghold this would make, for harrying the Rafnglas road,' he suggested after a moment.

'A fine stronghold for harrying the Rafnglas road,' Aikin agreed.

Watching him, Bjorn said slowly, 'It is in my heart that I could be sorry—almost—for the Norman kind.'

Aikin was looking away down the glen. His face was as gentle as ever, but suddenly its gentleness was not good to see. 'If it were not for the thing that they did to Ari, my foster-father, it is in my heart that I also could be sorry—almost—for the Norman kind,' he said, very softly; so softly that his lips scarcely moved over his shut teeth.

# VIII

## THE ROAD TO NOWHERE

BY SPRING THE Normans were cleared from the
Rafnglas road again, leaving many of their number
dead behind them. It had been an ill day's work for
his own followers when Red William broke faith with the
Truce Branch and bound Ari Knudson's broken body to a
frame of spears; for if the Northmen had been hardy and
cunning fighters before, they were devils after. And by this
time Aikin himself had become a legend, and a frightful
legend, to the Norman troops; for there was more than one
among them to swear to having seen him change into a grey
wolf beneath their eyes, and come flying out of the mist at a
comrade's throat.

More than a year went by, more than a year of fierce though
fitful warfare; of Norman thrusts into the mountains, and wild
Viking forays in return. Bjorn, his shoulder long since healed,
was become a seasoned warrior; and the gold flames on the
black shield that he had hung among the other trophies in the
Hearth Hall were growing dim with peat-smoke.

It was a year that yielded a good harvest of Norman
weapons and armour, and stores that were worth all the more
because the summer had been bad among the fells, and the
grain harvest even leaner than usual. Of the weapons and

armour, the Northmen took what they wanted, which was little enough, for the heavy Norman harness was not suited to their kind of warfare, and sent the rest, as they had sent it for more than twenty years, to Ireland and Galloway, where such gear would always fetch a good price in grain. That autumn, more than one train of pack-ponies laden with fine war-gear wound its way out from the strong place at the foot of Crum-beck Water, by secret marsh tracks to friendly villages on the edge of the lowlands; and on through the darkness, lying up by day, to hidden places on the coast. More than one ship crept in under cover of the dark, with the desperately needed grain in exchange for fine hauberks and worked leather harness.

The communication lines of this night-bird trade ran through a certain low-browed ale-house on the riverside fringe of Workington. The large slow-moving Saxon who kept the place sold good ale, and much of it, to the men-at-arms of the small garrison, as well as to the country folk and the seafarers who came and went through the town. But many and many a message passed in and out under the ale-bush: messages breathed into the depth of a shared ale-stoup, or muttered with the lips scarcely moving, as one man brushed against another in the doorway; messages of which the men-at-arms dicing over their drink an arm's length away knew never a thing.

But it was no business of corn or harness that brought Bjorn that way, on a night late into the autumn. It was the matter of new harp-strings for his foster-father. Several broken strings that summer had brought perilously low Haethcyn's store of the fine white-bronze wire which only the Irish bronze-smiths made; and the old harper would not string his beloved Sweet-singer with any other. So at summer's end the word had gone forth to a certain smith in Leinster, known of old to Haethcyn; and with the word, a fine Norman dagger in payment. And in due course the wire would come, as other small packets had come before, by some passing shipmaster probably bound on the Normans' business, into the hands of mine host of the Workington ale-house. So now Bjorn, who had come up with the last pack-train of the year, was bound in the same direction, on the chance that it might have arrived.

It was a black-dark night, with a bitter wind sweeping down-coast from the Solway, as he made his way along the narrow riverside wynds; but he did not pull forward the hood of his heavy wadmal cloak, lest it muffle his hearing. He had been this way before—two or three times now—but still, he did not like towns. He had an unpleasant feeling of being caged and hemmed in as he threaded the narrow evil-smelling ways. A bunch of revellers shouldered past him, singing, as he turned down to the water-side, and after their passing, the dark wynd seemed quieter than before; a quiet that seemed to Bjorn, who had often slept alone in perfect ease in the utter silence of the high fells, to have an unpleasant suggestion of stealth about it, a hint of a knife-blade between the shoulders. He was glad when he emerged on to the water-side, with its familiar smells of rope and pitch, which only the cold tang of salt water made different from the smell of the boat strand at home, and picking his way in the dark among the litter of timber and cordage, small boats and lobster-pots, came at last to the open door of the ale-house.

Smoky light and the mingled reek of burning driftwood and warm company met him on the threshold; and a crowding life that at once made the silence of the wynd seem very far away. A couple of seamen, sharing an ale-jack by the fire, glanced up as he entered; a wall-eyed herd dog raised his head and growled, then subsided at an absent-minded kick from his long and lounging master. The ale-house keeper turned a face as flat and broad and formidable as a boar's from the man he was serving, and across the smoky chamber his gaze met Bjorn's for an instant; then he turned his back on him. But as Bjorn strolled across to the hearth at the far end of the room, somehow, the other was beside him.

'And what's for you, lad? A stoup of ale to drive out the cold?'

Bjorn grinned, sniffing a savoury smell from the one inner room. 'I am hungry. I'd sooner have kale broth.'

The taverner thumped him on the shoulder. 'Ah! You know a good thing when you smell it, you do! There's swine-fat in that broth, and beans and oatmeal, let alone the kale. Kale broth it is, Lordling, and a fine crusty wedge of wheaten bread to go with it.' His back to the room, he added in a quick mutter, 'Naught amiss, is there?'

Bjorn shook his head very slightly, and answered in his normal tone: 'I am from my master. Has the wire come yet?'

'The harp-wire from Ireland, is it? Aye, a man came by two-three days since, and left it. Bide you, and I'll bring it with the broth.'

And a while later, with the packet from Ireland stowed safely in his pouch, a steaming bowl of kale broth in one hand and a hunch of crusty bread in the other, Bjorn was settled very comfortably to his supper, in a smoke-blackened corner between the fire and the stacked ale-casks.

The driftwood burned with little snapping, crackling salty flames of blue and green and saffron: a good fire for staring into. The kale broth was too hot to drink as yet, but the steam of it, thick with oatmeal and swine-fat, curled into his nose, bringing a rush of soft warm water to his mouth, for he was very hungry. Also, he was tired, with the tiredness of a dog after a long day's hunting; and the little space of rest and shelter seemed all the richer because he knew that as soon as the broth was gone, he would be out again in the wind and the darkness, heading back to join the rest on the road home. The wind beat across the thatch, sending knife-edged draughts along the floor; the wall-eyed herd dog scratched ceaselessly for fleas, while his master sat staring into space and whistling, between pulls at his ale-stoup; the two seamen were hotly debating some question of a great herring catch that had, or had not, happened in the year that the grandfather of one of them had seen a seal-woman with his own eyes. It all made a background against which Bjorn's thoughts went wandering back

over the past few days, remembering, as he fished for lumps of
swine-fat with his crust, the pack-ponies trotting through the
dark, the tingling moments among the last trees of a little
wood while a band of men-at-arms went by on the road below
them; remembering the hidden cove a couple of miles south
of Workington, and the low-set vessel slipping in on the night
tide, the gleam of a shielded lantern, the slip and crunch of
sea-washed pebbles underfoot.

He was almost asleep, with the empty bowl still in his hands,
when a gust of the rising wind swooped against the house,
driving the smoke back in a stinging cloud from the smoke-
hole above the hearth. The door burst open with a crash, and
as though borne on the dark wings of the wind, a knot of new-
comers surged into the ale-shop and across to the fire, roaring
for the taverner as they came. 'House! House! House! Bring
us ale, and plenty of it! Saints! It's cold enough to freeze off
a cat's tail. Ale, man, before we pull the roof down!'

Bjorn, in his dark corner, watched them under his brows, as
the taverner came lumbering to answer their summons, and
they subsided on to the benches, stretching their legs to the
fire, and thereby keeping it from everybody else. He who
seemed to be chief among them was a red-haired man-at-
arms who could have compared for size with Haethcyn or the
Jarl himself; and of the other two, one was small and a thick-
set individual with a broken nose and a fierce and merry eye,
and the other an oldish, greyish man in the stuff tunic and soft
felt cap of an archer, with his bowstave across his shoulders.

This was not, Bjorn judged, the first ale-house they had
visited tonight. They were not really drunk, but they were in
a mood he knew well enough, with just enough ale in them to
make them quick to laughter or suspicion, quick-fingered on
their weapons. Best sit quiet for a time; if he left the instant
they came in, that might rouse their suspicions, or in their
present mood they might quite likely take it as an insult, and
then there would be trouble.

So he remained where he was, and in a little he set down
the empty bowl on the hearth stone, and delving into his

pouch, brought out the packet wrapped in a scrap of cloth, and from it, the small coils of harp-wire. Might as well make sure that they were all as they should be. Better to have something to do with one's hands, too. The white-bronze wire shone bright and new in the firelight, as he separated the slender coils; yes, the different thicknesses were all there. He turned them between his fingers, and the sheen of the flames ran silverly along the curve of the coils, like the music that lay in them made visible. Wonderful, that was, music lying in the heart of the slim white-bronze wire; but no more wonderful, now he came to think of it, than flame in the heart of one of those pieces of driftwood on the hearth, or a flower coming from its seed: a white briar rose—a whole summer, a hundred summers of white briar roses lying hid in one seed of a rose-hip.

Somehow that made the walls of the little smoky ale-shop that had begun to close in on him unpleasantly like a trap, with the arrival of the three Normans, draw back a little, so that it was not so hard to breathe.

The men-at-arms had been talking loudly together in the Norman tongue, as they passed the ale-jack among them. Bjorn knew a few Norman words from Haethcyn, who had not forgotten all his schooling at Bec Abbey; but not enough to follow what they said. And then, as the archer grew explosive, the huge man-at-arms cut in, his voice lazy and a little slurred; and Bjorn's ears pricked to the sound of a familiar tongue. 'Keep to the good honest Saxon, can't you? You're no new recruit just crossed the Narrow Seas, that you should jabber at me like a maggot-pie!'

He of the broken nose snorted derisively. 'And you're no Saxon Thane! Come off the high horse, Hammund.'

'Me father was from Caen and me mother was from the White Horse Vale,' said Hammund. 'Sober, I'm as Norman French as Roland's horn; drunk, I'm as Saxon as me sainted mother, who was as Saxon as the White Horse itself. Just now I'm pleasantly drunk, so we'll speak the Saxon, my brothers.'

'And why will we?' Broken-Nose was inclined to be truculent.

'Because I'm bigger than both of you put together,' said Hammund with slow simplicity, and reached for the ale-jack. As he set it down again, wiping his lips, he added gravely. 'What was it that you were saying, friend Dickon?'

'I was saying,' said the grey man, 'who would go for an archer, that wasn't a fool born and bred? I was saying as I'm sick of bogs, and arrows in the back, and no pay this past year and more. That's what I was saying!'

Broken-Nose laughed sharply. 'Be cursed to you for a croaker!—Here, take another pull and you'll see things brighter. Ho! Hammund, pass the jack.'

Hammund obliged, with a lazy largeness of gesture that would have deluged the gloomy one in ale, if the great jack had not by this time have been two parts empty. Archer Dickon caught it with a curse and buried his face in it, drinking deep and loud, his head tipping further and further back.

'That's a fine swallow you have,' said Broken-Nose between admiration and regret, as the other came up for air; and taking the jack in his turn, gazed into it sadly before putting it to his mouth.

Archer Dickon shook his head, grinning, but still gloomy. 'Nay, 'tis well enough for you to cry "Croaker". You're Brother William's men; you have the lowlands for easy marching, and the sea behind you, and your victuals coming in regular—and little enough to do save eat and drink, so far as I can see.'

'We've our share of fighting, too, from time to time, old lad,' said Hammund.

'Fighting? 'Tis easy enough to fight on a full belly! And you sitting in your fine stone-built castles, as plump as pigeons, the lot of you. 'Tis a different story for us poor devils of Ranulf's;—ah, and 'tis a story that'll still be a-telling, so far as I can see, when our grandsons are grey and toothless, for all the sign there is of it ever coming to an end.'

'Saints! And I'd not be surprised at that, if Ranulf's grandson has as little sense as his grandsire,' snapped the man with the broken nose, who seemed embittered by the small amount of ale he had found in the jack. 'And as for pigeons——'

'Who's talking of pigeons?'

'You were. You said——'

'Never you mind what I said, nor what I didn't say, neither.' The archer raised his voice a trifle. 'What might you mean by that about Ranulf not having no sense?'

'Why, man, if half a lifetime of this merry little war has learned us naught else, it has learned us something of the lay of the land. Every fool knows by now that this secret valley or fortress, or whatever it is, is somewhere among the northern fall of the mountains; yet your precious Lord of Carlisle goes on hammering away from the south-east, when 'tis as plain as the nose on his face—and that's plain enough in all conscience—that his only chance of smoking out the hornets' nest is to come down on it from the north.'

Tempers were rising fast, and clearly they had lost all thought of there being other people within earshot.

'If you know so much, you'd best go tell Ranulf how to handle his war,' snorted Dickon, the light of battle beginning to gleam in his eye.

'I reckon William's been telling him that long enough as 'tis,' drawled Hammund.

'Oh ye do, do ye?' Dickon got deliberately to his feet, and stood swaying a little, his face thrust into that of the huge man-at-arms. 'Well, ye can reckon again, my bonnie lad, as there'll be another sort of reckoning for ye!'

The other laughed. 'Na na, Manikin, you showed not so fond of Ranulf yourself, a while since, that all men must smear honey on their tongues, to speak of him in your presence.'

'I carried my bow from Normandy at Ranulf's heels when we was both on us boys, and I'll say what I like of him—but nobody else does, when I'm around, see?' roared Dickon, his hand shooting out for the empty ale-jack. 'And here's to ye, for an overgrown, blear-eyed, tit-brained coxcomb!' and with a hollow and resounding clunk, he brought it down with all his force on Hammund's head. There was a roar of fury as the

big man-at-arms rose and flung himself upon his assailant, and
a snarl followed by a string of curses, as the wall-eyed sheepdog, roused from sleep and not sure what it was all about,
fixed his teeth in somebody's leg; and instantly the whole place
was in an uproar.

Bjorn laughed softly, returned the harp-strings to his pouch,
and got up. Catching the eye of the tavern-keeper, who was
wading grimly into the battle, he held up the price of his supper,
then tossed it on to the bench where he had been sitting; and
stepping over somebody's writhing legs, turned to the door.
The little man with the broken nose reeled backward into him;
Bjorn caught him from a fall and punted him back into the
heart of things. Then he was outside in the bitter darkness,
and the fierce silent laughter snatched at him in gusts like the
wind as he went his way.

Jarl Buthar had been somewhat grudging in allowing them
to trade that dagger for harp-strings; it was a fine dagger and
would fetch a fine price in corn. 'Men cannot eat music,' Jarl
Buthar had said. And behold the dagger had bought not only
harp-strings, but a warning that might be of more value to the
Dale than many measures of corn.

.     .     .     .     .     .

Frytha had been down to the huddle of huts behind the
Jarlstead, where Storri Sitricson gathered his sick and
wounded; and now she was on her way back. The first snow
of the winter had fallen, and with the onset of the darkness, it
had begun to freeze. The air cut her face, and the yellow pool
of light from her lantern swung before her over the trampled
snow, and overhead the sky was a vault of stillness that seemed
to echo to the thin harping of the wind under the stars.
Frytha was suddenly and piercingly aware of the stillness;
a waiting intensity of silence that had come upon the Dale
when the ringing of the axes in Rannardale stopped at dusk.

Axes in Rannardale. . . .

All this first day, the ring of them had come small and clear
to the settlement between its two waters, as men felled the
birches in the path of the Jarl's new road. All day there had

been no escaping from the sound, nor from the deadly purpose that lay behind it. Yet now that it was stilled, Frytha was more aware of the road in the new silence than she had been before; aware of it, not as a thing just begun, but as something already complete, and living its own secret life; lying out in the darkness, waiting with the patience of the fells themselves, for its hour to come.

It had all started with the return of the last pack-train of the autumn; with something that Bjorn had said when he came back with Haethcyn's new harp-strings from Workington. There had been long counsels among the chiefs of the War Host; and the Jarl had listened to all men before he spoke himself. But when he spoke, it was to the purpose. Frytha, who had been in Hall, remembered how he had sat forward in the High Seat, pulling at his great golden beard that was beginning to be streaked with ash colour, while he looked down broodingly at his chieftains and warriors gathered below. 'It may well be that the thing will never come to pass,' he had said. 'It is but tavern talk, yet in such there is often a grain of truth, and it is as well to remember that.' And then he had chuckled, deep in his chest. 'That which we lack in numbers we must make up in guile. . . . The Normans are a people who have always the need of a road for their horses and heavy armed knights. Therefore, lest they should indeed think to come upon us from the north at any time, it is in my mind that 'twould be but neighbourly to build them a road for their especial use. A fine road, easy to follow, but leading maybe—somewhat astray.'

The sheer dazzling ruthlessness of the plan, when complete, had appealed strongly to the whole of the Jarl's folk. The Northmen loved a grim jest, and this would be a grim jest indeed.

The only track from the north came down the east side of Crumbeck Water, and at Hawes Point, where a great nab of black rock thrust out into the lake, blocking the way as by a wall, the track was carried up and over it by ramps of stones and earth. Now, the northern ramp was to be destroyed, so

97

that once again there would be nothing on that side but sheer black rock, and a new road built, branching from the old one, up Rannardale Beck. With the old road blotted out, it must seem to an invading army who did not know the secret that the road had always run up Rannardale. And Rannardale, with its steep sides, was the perfect place for a great killing. Yes, a very grim jest indeed.

And so they had begun felling the birches in Rannardale.

A bunch of young warriors were gathering in the shadow of the peat-stack and the Hearth Hall porch as Frytha reached it, just returned from the day's tree-felling, and hungry for the meal that the women were making ready, stamping the caked snow from their rawhide shoon, and shaking themselves like the dogs that padded in and out among them.

Frytha, pausing among them to kick the snow from her own feet, caught sight of Bjorn as the light of her lantern swung across the group, and called to him. 'How runs the Jarl's new road?'

'Well enough for the first day,' Bjorn called back. 'It will be a fine road—for a road that leads nowhere.'

Somebody laughed in the dark beyond the range of the lantern. 'The Road to Nowhere! That's a good name for it! And "nowhere" is like to be an ill place for the Norman kind, I'm thinking, if they come pushing their snouts this way!' There was a general laugh, and other voices caught up the new name, pleased with the sound of it. 'The Road to Nowhere! The Road to Nowhere!'

They began to drift toward the light of the Hearth Hall doorway; then checked their drift, falling silent with heads cocked to listen, as a new sound stole into the waiting night. A sound so faint that at first, as they listened, it seemed to be spun from the stuff of the winter silence; then swelling and sweeping nearer: a whistling, half-musical throb that seemed to pulse under the stars.

'Here come the wild swans,' Hundi Swainson said; and Frytha moved clear of the porch, to look up past the dark branching spread of the antlers at the gable end. She could not see the flying shapes, but she could trace their path by the singing beat of wings, far up in the frosty sky; the eerie, heart-catching music of the wild swans overhead. Right overhead now; sweeping across the bright stars of the Little Bear, and on toward Rannardale. Over Rannardale it seemed to dip, to swing out and back in a wide loop, as though the birds were circling low; then it rose again and swept on, fainter and fainter into the distance.

'They will be making for Bassteinthwaite Lake,' said Erland Ormeson, while the faint wing-throb still hung upon the air. 'That's a strange thing, that they should fly that way, at this time of the year.'

'Strange? Aye, strange it would be, and passing strange, were they no more than swans that have just flown over,' said a thin voice behind them; and they swung round to see the old bent figure of Unna, with her spindle still in her hand and her laden distaff under her arm.

Gille stepped out from the shadow of the peat-stack, saying with his slow kindliness: 'Come your ways in out of the cold, old Mother.—Why, what else should they be?'

She seemed not to feel the big hand he laid on her arm, but moved forward to gaze after the last echo of distant wings as it died away. 'What else should they be? Aye, well may you ask, you that fell the birches in Rannardale for a road that runs where *that* road runs to!'

Standing there among the young warriors, she seemed to straighten and grow taller; tall as the Countess herself and straight as an up-drawn flame; spearing further and further toward the sky as the dark splendour gathered upon her. An uneasy hush had fallen on the whole group, as always on the people who were near Unna when the Second Sight came upon her; and her voice rose in the silence like the crying of a nightbird, on a note that was no longer cracked; a high cold ringing that was clear and brittle as ice. 'What else should they be? Did ye not hear how they dipped low over Rannardale, circling the place where the Spear-Tempest will break? Seeking out the Place of Killing against the day that they come again to choose their slain?'

Cold fear tightened for a moment on Frytha's heart, so that she found it hard to breathe; and she wanted to get close to Bjorn, but she could not move. It was as though she were caught in the meshes of a nightmare. And the old shining voice rose higher yet. 'Blood in Rannardale; and the wolves smell it and come down from Helvellyn, and the ravens gather for the slain. Aiee! I see it! I smell it! Rannardale Beck running red to Crumbeck Water, and the water ripples red against the shore—blood—blood——'

The strange high voice shuddered away in a long-drawn wail; and there was a long silence. And then, from the growing crowd around the Hearth Hall door, Haethcyn stepped out into the light of Frytha's lantern, and in his hands the Sweet-singer, whose new strings had set the axes ringing in Rannar-dale.

'If ye see truly, old woman, then is it sure proof that we do not build the road without need,' he said, and it was as though his words broke a spell.

Old Unna seemed to shrink and crumble in on herself as the flame died in her, and suddenly she was half weeping. 'Na na, I spoke foolishness. It was the swans, nothing but the swans —what else should it be? I am an old woman and I dream dreams.'

'You have left the dream half dreamed, old Mother,' Gille said harshly. 'Finish the dream and tell us how this Spear-Tempest of yours will go——'

'Gille, *no*.' Frytha found her voice, and started forward with her hand held out. 'Unna, it is too cold for you here. Come in-by to the fire.'

'Aye, I will come in. I am cold—cold. . . . Na na, my bird, it was the wild swans, nothing more. . . .'

But even as she spoke, and Frytha, with an arm round her drew her in toward the Hearth Hall door, she craned back over her shoulder towards Rannardale. And once again, Frytha was piercingly aware of the road, lying out there in the dark, waiting, waiting through years maybe, for its hour that would surely come.

## IX

## THE CROWN AND THE LONG-SHIP

UNNA DIED BEFORE the spring came again. She was
very old—so old that nobody remembered her young;
so old that she never seemed to grow any older. But
after the night that the swans flew over Rannardale she
seemed to shrivel in the bitter winds, as though suddenly all
the life in her had run dry. And Gille, returning to the Dale
from a raid, to find her no longer spinning by the fire, grieved
for her more sorely than he would have done for his own
mother, because she had been nearer to him.

All that summer, between the sowing and reaping, threshing,
spinning and cooking, work continued on the Jarl's road, the
Road to Nowhere. Women and children, men too old for the
War bands and boys too young, they all had a hand in it; and
by late autumn it was finished. They had used what they
needed of the earth and stones from the ramp to build hidden
defences across the dale, and tipped the rest into Crumbeck
Water. Now there was nothing but the bare black rock
jutting into the lake, and a rough track winding innocently up
through the birches of Rannardale, so that the Jarl's people
coming and going from the north must round the nab by boat
or make the thousand-foot climb over the dale-head and down

into the Sell Glen. And it remained only for the wind and rain and the encroaching bracken to do their part in blotting out the traces.

That was a queer summer, a queer year altogether, and queer things happened in it; storms and floods and fire in the heavens, and rumours that the world was coming to an end that reached even into the Dale. And then at summer's end, about the time that the road was finished, word came of the King's death by an arrow as he rode hunting.

'So, the day of reckoning comes for Red William,' said the Jarl when he heard it. 'But the payment was too easy; it should have been the Blood-Eagle, not an arrow from behind a tree.'

Aikin said only, 'There are more Normans than Red William,' and he went alone, save for Garm stalking like a proud grey shadow at his heels, and walked the full length of the Road to Nowhere. Walked it slowly and lingeringly, looking at the defences by the way, as though he loved every yard of it.

More news filtered in from the outside world. Henry Beauclerk, the Red King's brother, had taken the throne; Henry, who was an Atheling—the English-born son of the King—and known to have Saxon leanings. And as winter drew on, one question grew in the minds of the Lake Land people: what might it mean to them, to all that they had fought for for so long, this change of Kings in England?

But winter passed without any clear answer to the question —save that the outlying war bands brought in word of extra troops at Penrith that did not make good hearing; and the birch-buds thickened, and soon the wild geese would fly north again. And the day came for Gille Butharson to take Gerd from her father's house-stead.

The day came, and Gerd was decked out in the silken kirtle that had been her mother's, with the heavy silver-gilt bridal crown that had decked so many brides before, upon her head, and brought out to Gille and his groomsmen in the Hearth Hall. And the Jarl set her hand and Gille's together over the fire. And the rest of the day was spent in harping and feasting; and the young warriors wrestled and ran foot-races against each other, and returned hungry again for more of the sweet mountain mutton, the gold and silver char and great bowls of barley bannock and ewe-milk cheese.

Now the day was far spent, and the shadows lengthening. The Jarl and his chieftains sat in the Hearth Hall, but the young warriors had gathered round the great fires that burned on the open turf before the door. And between the fires within the hall and the fires without, Frytha and the other girls went to and fro, filling and re-filling the drinking-horns. Presently the young warriors would grow wild, and like as not the night would end in fighting but as yet they were content to listen to Haethcyn's harping, to drink ale and more ale, and stretch their stomachs that were often enough empty, and enter into bragging matches one against the other, each striving to cap the other's boast with one yet wilder, to pass the Hall harp from hand to hand in the wake of the Bride ale.

Presently someone called for Bjorn to give them a song; and the call was taken up and echoed from all sides. 'Up with you, Bear-cub! Come now, a song—a new song for a wedding!'

Bjorn set down the ale-horn he had been holding on his knee, and took in its place the Hall harp, which Ottar Edricson was thrusting on him. 'A song for a wedding, is it? A song for a wedding—and about a wedding—it shall be.' He sprang up on to a pile of peats beside the fire, and stood poised above the crowding heads of his sword-fellows, swaying slightly to the rhythm of his hand on the leaping harp-strings. Then he began to sing.

He sang of another wedding, of a bride who was not quite as other women of this world. Frytha, listening, knew the words well, for old Unna had often crooned them in a tuneless undertone to the thrumming of her spindle. But Bjorn had given them a tune: a tune that was cold as the north, and lonely as the north. Many of Bjorn's tunes had the loneliness in them, as though that odd difference between him and his

kind found a voice in the music that he made. In ordinary
life he was armoured with that faint fierce mockery of his;
but there was no mockery in his music, and so no armour.
The tune ached with regret over things that were no more;
and somehow it laid a spell of stillness and listening over the
young warriors, and they came drifting from other fires to
gather round him.

'He bore her home at the daylight's dying,' sang Bjorn,
drawing toward the end of his song.

> 'And set her down by the warm red hearth,
> Out of the rain and the wild wind's crying;
> And she combed her hair in the peat fire's light,
> She baked his bannock and tilled his garth;
> But he saw how she harked to the grey geese flying.
> (Brother, the wind blows cold tonight).'

The silence and the listening deepened over the crowd of
young warriors; the light of the brightening flames began to
flutter on their faces as they pressed closer, warming them to
golden tawny against the first faint deepening of twilight
beyond the fire.

> '"What is the thing that you have not told me?"
> "Lord, 'tis a thing that I cannot say.
> If I shiver, your cloak shall fold me.
> The Call is strong, but I will not hear;
> The Call grows stronger: Away! Away!
> Nay, but your arms are strong to hold me."
> (Brother, the wind blows cold and drear).

> But the nights grew dark in the winter weather,
> And he heard the geese fly overhead,
> And felt her stir in the warm piled heather,
> And turned half sleeping, and slept again.
> But in the dawning beside his bed
> Nothing there lay but a grey goose feather.
> (Brother, I'm tired of the wind and the rain).'

There was a moment of complete silence round the fire as
the last notes died away. Even the voices in the great Hearth
Hall seemed to have stilled; and Frytha could hear the lake
waters lapping on the landing-beach with a loneliness to
match that of the harp-song that had gone before. Then a
burst of voices closed over the silence, applauding, protesting,

calling for another song. 'Give us "Cattle-raiding". Give us "Forkbeard's Wooing"!'

Bjorn shook his head and sprang down among them, thrusting the Hall harp into the hands of a sword brother. 'If you want "Forkbeard's Wooing", here's Jon can rant it for you as well as I. I have sung my song.' Then his eyes went out over the heads of the crowd. 'And here's a late comer—and one scarcely dressed for a wedding.'

Heads were turned in the direction of his gaze, and looking round with the rest, Frytha saw a man in war-gear coming between the outhouses towards them.

As he drew nearer they saw that he was weary and had the look of one who had travelled far and fast. 'It is one of Sigtrig's War-band, from over toward Blencathra,' somebody said, and somebody else cried out: 'Ha! Hogni, this is no way to come to a wedding!' Two or three of them had started forward to meet him, and the crowd opened to draw him in, pressing ale on him, demanding to know had he come to the wedding or did he bring news?—If so, what news?

He shook them off, refusing the ale. 'Na na, lads, my news is for the Jarl first; I will come back to drink wass heil to the bride later!' and made for the Hearth Hall.

'Ah, well,' Jon said, staring after him, 'we shall hear in time and in time. Meanwhile my horn's empty.'

So, it seemed, was everybody else's; and for a time Frytha and the other girls were kept busy filling them. And then suddenly the word was running from mouth to mouth; the Norman advance guard were out from Penrith, and among them were men who wore the King's badge.

And so the winter-long question was answered at last.

Frytha, standing ale-jar on hip, felt the swift up-keying of mood all about her; the change from merry-making to a fierce gaiety that swept through the young warriors like a dry wind, as man after man slipped away to fetch his weapons.

And when she looked for Bjorn, he was not there.

Beyond the range of the firelight the world was sinking into the clear northern dusk, and the shifting fringes of the crowd were already losing form and substance. Once, as the throng shifted, she glimpsed Gerd standing beside the tall figure of the Countess, her little round face pinched and white under the bridal crown that Gille should have taken off tonight. Once she caught sight of the Jarl's tall grey-gold head, and the sudden ripple of light on the strings of Haethcyn's Sweet-singer.

And then Bjorn was there again, standing with Jon and Hundi and Ottar Edrikson beside the fire, his head bent to make some adjustment to the belt-thongs of his dirk, and the firelight burning on the comb of his war-cap and the bronze boss of his skin-covered buckler.

Frytha dodged toward him through the crowd, and reached his side just as he looked up. 'You are away, then,' she said, finding nothing else to say.

'We are away,' he agreed.

'You will need food; wait for me, and I will bring some.'

He shook his head, touching the rolled-up cloak that he carried strapped to his shoulder. 'I've a full gorge, and a bannock in here; and we shall be up with the nearest of Sigtrig's band by midnight.'

Aikin came out through the Hearth Hall door, and the light of the peat-flames jinked on the spread wings of his helm and the hilt of Wave-flame, and cast a ripple of fish-scale gold over the fine ring mail that clung to his slight body as closely as a wet sark. Garm stalked close against his knee as ever; and Gille strode behind him with his great pole axe over his shoulder, his bridal finery doffed for his old greasy battle-sark.

In a little they were gone, Aikin and Gille, Bjorn and Erland and the rest of the sword-band. And behind them others were going every moment, Northmen and Saxon, chieftain and carl, taking their weapons and turning from the firelight and the Bride ale and the small white-faced bride, whose crown seemed suddenly too heavy for her, to their War bands waiting in the dark fells. Soon, save for the little company of reserves and runners that remained always with the Jarl here at the heart of things, the Dale would be left again to the women, to the sick and the old, and the very young.

Frytha found Haethcyn standing beside her, looking down at her reflectively under his badger-striped mane of hair. 'What is it that you are thinking, with your eyes so dark and your lip between your teeth?'

'I am thinking that it is bad—sometimes—to have been born to the distaff side,' Frytha said.

He smiled, showing the yellow dog-fangs in his beard. 'It is also bad—sometimes—to have been a warrior, and to be old.'

Frytha had never thought of him as either old or young, only as being Haethcyn, who had saved her from the terror of the Jarl's Hearth Hall, that first night of all. But suddenly she saw that he was old: old and frail despite his great height, so that the flesh seemed to hang thin and light on his great bones. And her throat ached over all the woes of the world.

'Are you not going to Gerd?' he asked.

Frytha shook her head. 'There will be Margrit and Signy and the rest with Gerd,' she said: and added fiercely, 'If I were Gerd, I think that I could not bear to be comforted, just now.'

'Nay, I know. I remember the night that first you came among us. You were four—or was it five? You could not bear to be comforted then, and you have not changed. But you are not Gerd: you are Frytha. Frytha who should have been born to the sword side and carried a ˙shield among the War bands . . . Aye well, it may be that, sword side or distaff side, you will have your chance yet.'

She looked up at him with a swift, unspoken question: and he answered it as though she had put it into words. 'The ranks of the War Host grow thin and ever thinner, of late years. It is in my mind that a day may come when the women must stand forth beside their menfolk at the raven's gathering.'

. . . . . .

It was as Haethcyn had said; the War Host that had been growing thin when they made their stand against the Normans at Hardknott was far thinner now. And it was with a fine full army of his own and the King's that Ranulf Le Meschin marched out from Penrith that spring, over the moors to strike

107

the broad valley running westward under Blencathra. And before cuckoo month the Normans were into Burgdale. They made their base camp on a piece of rising ground just south of the old cattle-steading of Keswic, and fortified it with earthworks and stockades, despite all the desperate attacks that the Northmen hurled against them.

From there they were a danger to Butharsdale itself; and the Jarl, faced with this menace, could only gather every man able to hold a spear from the whole of Lake Land and pour them in to swell the War bands of Skiddaw and the Derwent Fells. And as the need grew more desperate, the women and boys came out to take over the tasks that lay, as it were, behind the shield-wall, that every man should be free for the actual fighting.

Frytha worked among the rest, helping with the pack-ponies that brought up barley bannock and sheaves of arrows for the War Host, tending the wounded far up on the very fringe of the fighting, message-running between the scattered bands among the fells. In wet weather she slept under shelter of a few woven branches, with Gerd and Signy; on fine nights, in some hollow of the heather, wrapped in her cloak, with the stars of early summer wheeling over her. She was often with Bjorn—the old, unhappy silence between them seemed not to matter now, though she knew that it would matter again presently; and in a queer way she was happy.

She was with Bjorn one breathless evening of full summer, lying flat among the heather of a long spur that thrust out from the towering heights of Grismoor toward Burgdale. She had come up, running, with word from Gille that the last man had been safely pulled back from Wild Cat Mountain, before the Norman advance; and the message safely delivered to Aikin among his captains, she had crept forward to join Bjorn, who was on watch.

Lying outstretched there among the heather, she looked like a long-legged boy. She wore loose breeks cross-gartered to the knee, and a short kirtle of rough dark wool, and in the broad strap of undressed deerhide about her waist was thrust

Bjorn's old dirk, that she had worn ever since he had had his father's. Her hair was cut short to her shoulders like a boy's, to be out of the way, and hung forward about her face, sticking to her forehead uncomfortably in the heat. She blew at it from time to time, but made no movement to brush it back with her hand, though the Norman camp must be upward of a mile away, because perfect stillness at such times had become second nature to her in the years since she and Bjorn had first watched the curlews on Beacon Fall.

A few days ago the Normans had begun again their steady, relentless advance. The main part of the army had rounded the foot of Derwent Water and pitched another camp. And then they had pushed on again. That had been this morning. Only this morning, Frytha thought; how odd! All day the fighting had gone on, the Northmen slowly falling back, the Normans pressing remorselessly forward up the broad marshy valley of Keskadale, until at last they reached the place down there, where it branched into four glens with steep spurs between.

'I think that I would not choose to camp for the night in those marshes,' Frytha said softly.

Bjorn's voice beside her was lazy as the droning of the small amber bees among the first bell heather. 'Who speaks of choosing, then? They cannot push forward until they have cleared us from the glens and found which one they want. And even to their way of thinking, that must be a day's work at the least.' He laughed softly, his head between his arms. 'Besides, they are not to know that when we fell back today, 'twasn't the strength of their arms that did it, but Aikin up here, whistling his hounds in, ready for tonight's hunting.'

'I wonder if they know just how near they are to the Dale,' Frytha said after a moment.

'They can scarce help but know that they could toss a pebble into the Jarlstead from here,' Bjorn said.

That was a figure of speech; but you could walk it in an hour, if you knew the passes. The fighting had never come so near to Butharsdale before. Frytha lay silent a while, gazing down. Up here on the ridge one seemed in some strange way to be riding out, far out, over the dale below; it was like being in the prow of a gigantic long-ship, she thought, though she had never seen a ship. On either side of her the deep glens, choked and tangled with woodland, cut deep into the fells, and between them the slender long-ship thrust of the ridge, tapering down into the marshes where the Normans were hurriedly throwing up bank and stockade about their camp. Marshes that glowed tawny green below the grey and blue, russet and purple of the fells. Save for the distant swarm of figures about the Norman camp, there seemed not a living soul in all the sweep of country; nothing to tell of the fighting that had gone on all the sweating, blistering day.

The sun was westering now, but it was no cooler. Even up here on the ridge there was not a breath of air moving. The heather swam in the heat, and Frytha's kirtle stuck to her between the shoulders. But far away to the north, Skiddaw and Blencathra were shaking clear of the thunder-haze that had hidden them all day, lifting their heads as though from sleep, into the tumble of bright-topped clouds that were massing along the skyline; and even as Frytha watched, a small puff of wind came up the ridge, shivering through the heather and scattering the mingled scents of heath and hot turf and bog myrtle. It stirred the hair on her forehead with a dank coolness, and passed on, and the hot summer scents settled again; but she heard it behind her, soughing away, fainter and fainter, until it died into the lonely silences of the high fells. She realized suddenly the stillness of everything: no larks singing over the fells, no call of curlew or green plover. Everything silent as the birds fall silent under the shadow of a wheeling hawk.

'There is a storm coming,' she said, and felt it somehow fitting that it should be so, as though the long dry spell beating up to thunder were linked in some way with the long-drawn struggle that would come to its own storm-burst tonight.

A brindled muzzle slid over her shoulder, and as she turned a little, Aikin himself slipped low through the heather between her and Bjorn. 'A sharp storm to bring the becks down in spate,' he said. 'Well, since we know the marshes and they do not, that should hamper them more than us, I'm thinking.'

He was silent awhile, one hand on Garm's neck, looking toward the distant camp. 'It is a good place for a look-out, this; you can see a fly move, anywhere among the marshes.'

'It is like a ship,' Frytha said on an impulse. 'Like being in the prow of a great ship—looking down.'

He turned his head quickly, to look at her. 'It seems like that to you?'

'Yes. Oh, I know that is foolishness, and I have never seen a ship.'

'Neither had I, when first it seemed like that to me,' Aikin said quietly. 'When I was a bairn, before the Normans came, I summered in the Dale more than once, with my father's shepherds when they brought the sheep up to the high pastures; and this was ever the place that I loved best of all the fells. It was my own place, my true place, more than my father's hall or my foster-father's hall, or the hunting-runs of Eskdale. And always it seemed to me a great ship.' The laughter flashed up in his thin face. 'Many is the sea-fight that I have fought up here with the wind for enemy. Many's the time that I have sailed with Leif Erikson. I was a Sea King in those days. . . .'

He was silent for a while, his gaze going out, out beyond Skiddaw into the sunset; and neither of his human companions cared to break in on his silence. Only Garm thrust up his great savage head against his master's ring-mailed shoulder and whined softly, as though in protest at something; and Fyrtha, glancing aside at his face, saw it change: saw the gentleness grow terrible in it, though he was smiling—a smile that the men who fought with him knew. 'I little thought, then-a-days, that the time would come when I should fight me a battle in very truth—though a land one—from this ridge. Now I see another likeness—down yonder.'

Bjorn asked after a moment: 'What likeness is that, Aikin Jarlson?'

'A hand, with the marsh for palm and four glens for fingers; a great, quiet hand, waiting to close on the alien host within it, as my hand might close on a blackberry, and crush it to a bloody pulp,' Aikin said. And there was something in his level tone that made Frytha shiver, despite the heat. The Northmen were not much given to love their enemies, but this, she felt instinctively, was something more personal and more deadly than the hatred of Northman for Norman; and its strength was the strength of the bond that had been between Aikin and his foster-father.

The sun was gone now, and the clouds were creeping up the sky: dark clouds silver rimmed against the angry pallor of the sunset, their upper edges growing ragged, as though teased out by a high wind, while against the blue-black masses lower down wisps and feathers of pale vapour seemed to float becalmed.

Another breath of dank air stirred the heather, and a low mutter of thunder stole along the fell. 'Listen to Thor's hammer,' Aikin said. 'Thor stands with his own people yet.'

# X

## THE MAZELIN

THE STORM BROKE soon after dark, in a crashing, rend-
ing tumult that flung to and fro among the fells until
the whole sky seemed to ring with the tumbling boom
of the thunder, and the lightning leapt fork-tongued and
crackling across the livid sky. But by midnight the storm had
grumbled away into the distance, and in the black darkness
the only sound was the hiss of the rain. And in the Norman
camp, with strong guards posted, Le Meschin's men had lain
down sword in hand, to sleep; while out among the marshes,
the Northmen gathered, deadly silent, and very wide awake.

And then, somewhere in the darkness, an early curlew cried
as surely no curlew would cry in such rain, and instantly the
whole countryside sprang to life. There was no escape for the
Normans; and the night covered the grim butchery—for it was
butchery and no battle—that set the swollen marsh becks
running reddened down to Bassteinthwaite.

A few men escaped to stumble back to the base camp at
Keswic, with word of the disaster for Ranulf Le Meschin, who
waited there with the reserves he was to bring up that day

for the final assault. The rest lay in the reddened mud of Keskadale foot in the steady dawn rain.

But to Frytha and the others among the birch-woods of Keskadale, the night was a thunderstorm that terrified the picketed ponies; it was rain that drove through the thin wild-wood tangle and drenched them to the skin and made it hard to keep the fires going; it was the long, long waiting darkness, with every nerve on the stretch, with any sound from the dale-foot that might have come to them drowned in the roar of storm-water coming down the becks.

And then at last, in the sodden and drenching dawn, the first wounded and the first news came in together, and after that, both came in quickly for a while. 'Aikin is away to cut Le Meschin from Penrith,' ran the news. 'Nay, but Le Meschin is a soldier, after all; he is out of Keswic and making down Bassteinthwaite for William's hunting-runs.' 'A running fight, a fine fight—send up more arrows.'

In the darkest hour of the next night, Frytha, who had lain down to snatch a little sleep beside one of the fires, woke suddenly, shivering and with the sound of wild lamentation in her ears. She had been dreaming of the dreadful search that had gone on all day: the women gleaning for their own dead and wounded, across the marshes in the rain, and among the little ruined steadings of Bassteinthwaite that the Normans had sacked in the spring. Dreaming of finding Bjorn face down in the mud. But it was only a dream. It was Hundi Swainson that she had found like that, not Bjorn. Only a dream, after all.

Gerd, who lay curled against her, stirred in her sleep, and because it *had* been Hundi (though she had always liked Hundi), and not Bjorn, Frytha felt a warm rush of fondness toward her. Little soft spoiled Gerd, who had laid aside her softness and her spoiling to sleep hard and toil behind the War bands and tend wounded men among the heather. But in the same instant there rose eerily in the darkness a long-drawn howl; and she knew it for the sound of lamentation that had awakened her—the cry of a wolf.

There was an uneasy stirring round the fire. 'We don't often hear that cry in the summer.' A boy's voice spoke out of the dark, and a woman answered him sharply. 'We all know well enough what brings the wolves down. Go you to sleep again and let others sleep, Gunda Trondson.' Somebody moved to set fresh birch branches on the fire; and as the flames leapt up, far off through the wet woods a ragged burst of shouting came to their straining ears.

Instantly Frytha drew away from the other girl, who was wide awake also by this time. 'Something is wrong down at the picket lines,' she said, and got to her feet.

Torches were moving to and fro among the clearing where the pack-ponies were tethered, when she reached it, but the tumult was dying down, though the picketed ponies still fretted and fidgeted, snorting and showing the whites of their eyes in the torchlight, as the men and boys moved among them, soothing them and testing picket-ropes.

'What's amiss?' Frytha demanded of an old man as he passed. 'I heard a wolf. Are any of the ponies scathed?'

He checked, shaking his head. 'No, but the brute must have passed close up wind, and the whole lot of them are scared half crazy.'

Scared half crazy they were indeed; and when at last they were quieted down, Frytha found that Teitri, the red pony she had worked with all that summer, had dragged out his tether and was away.

'It may be that he is still close to the camp,' suggested Gerd, who, valiant, though shaking with fright, had followed down hard on her heels.

But Frytha shook her head. She knew Teitri. He was as wild as a curlew, and once free, there would be no hanging about the camp for him, even without the smell of wolf in the wind. She stood a moment trying to think. 'The wind is from the south-west,' she said at last, 'so the wolf-smell will move him over toward Skiddaw.'

'Unless the river turns him,' someone suggested; and somebody else agreed. 'The first thing would seem to be to draw the marshes this side the river, at all events. Who's coming? Gunda? Thorkil?'

But Frytha, remembering other times that she had scoured the fells for Teitri, had a feeling that the river would not turn him. She tightened her deerskin belt that she had slackened when she lay down to sleep; told Gerd with more certainty than she really felt: 'There's no danger in a wolf at this time of year—not for men and women, anyway,' and leaving the others to the marshes, set out into the darkness on her own line of search.

By dawn she was already well across the river and climbing steadily through midge-infested hazel-woods. She had half thought to stick to the low ground and work down the shore of Bassteinthwaite, but it was that way that yesterday's fight had gone, and it seemed unlikely that the pony would drift that way of his own accord. Mountain bred as he was, he was far more likely to have taken to the high moors and the glens running up to the mountain wall.

Looking up at the sheer dizzying skyward rush of Skiddaw, dark and sombre with the rain-squalls trailing across its high corries, her heart did fail her a little. She was very tired, having lain down far spent last night, and been up again before she had well lain down, and to search even the fringes of this vast and frowning mountain for a strayed pony seemed all at once a hopeless task and an oddly frightening one.

But she took a firm hold on herself, and went on; following always the easiest way, because Teitri would probably have done the same, pausing on every ridge to scan the world for a gleam of red, before plunging down into the next glen. The voice of running water was all about her, a thousand mountain freshets brawling down from the great silence of Skiddaw; and the rooty smell of bog, and the pipits calling. But she was scarcely aware of these things, for she was so tired that she could keep only one thing in her mind at a time, and the one thing was finding Teitri.

And a while before noon, far over on the western skirts of Skiddaw, she did find him, grazing peacefully beside a beck,

where the fleece of bog-myrtle had left a little clear patch of
turf. He raised his head and looked at her as she drew near,
his eyes bright and watchful behind the russet tangle of his
forelock, his ears pricked. But he made no objection when she
reached him and put up her hand to his head-gear, from which
the hide-rope still dangled; indeed, he seemed rather pleased
to see her, as though he had been growing bored with his own
company.

'Oh cowardly and wicked one!' Frytha said, rubbing his
rough nose with a hand more gentle than her tone. 'Are you
not ashamed to run all this way from the smell of a wolf?—
No, I've nothing for you. I did not come so far to bring you
honey-crusts.' Now that he was found, she wanted to do
nothing in the world but lie down in the heather and sleep for
a week. But the thing was only half done; somehow, she must
get both him and herself back to camp.

'Come then; we must be going, you and I,' she said, chiefly
because talking helped her to fight off the waves of weariness
that were like a drifting grey fog in her head. And a few
moments later they were on their way. Make for lower
ground, she thought dimly; and once clear of these glens and
torrent beds, Teitri could carry her back. He was not as tired
as she was.

It seemed a long while later that they came to a place where
the beck—or maybe it was another beck—gathered speed and
came leaping down over a steep rock scar. Dwarf rowan and
alder leaned together over the dark fall pool, and there was
something among the rocks, at which the pony started, snorting and pricking his ears. Frytha's heart jumped sickeningly to
the thought of Skiddaw wolves. Then she saw that it was no
wolf, but a man—a man huddled under the elder scrub, yet
somehow not as though he were hiding; indeed he seemed
more dazed than anything else, as Frytha, with a reassuring
hand on the neck of the startled and unwilling pony, moved
in closer. He was a smallish man, crouching perfectly still,
and staring at her with eyes that were as bright as though he
were in a raging fever. His face looked as though it had once

been round, but now there was no flesh between the skin and the broad bones, and great hollows showed bruise-coloured at cheek and temple and round those brilliant eyes. His rough dark head was bare, and he wore a tattered and rain-sodden leather hauberk strengthened on breast and shoulders with a criss-cross of leather strips secured by studs of metal. But Frytha was not yet aware of seeing any of these things, only of those terrible eyes fixed on hers, lost, and blank, and somehow piteous; and suddenly it was as though a great horror of blackness that was within him reached out to touch her, and she was more afraid of him than she could have been of a Skiddaw wolf. And then desperate pity drove out the fear; and she moved closer yet. 'Who are you?'

The man only shrank away a little, running his tongue over grey cracked lips.

'Who are you?' Frytha repeated, 'And what is it that you do here?' But she knew all too surely.

He cried something, weakly, in the Norman tongue; and reached out his hands as though in entreaty. And she saw that they shook like quaking-grass.

'This can't be happening!' she thought. 'It *mustn't* be happening!—But it is, it is; and oh, what am I to do?'

But before she could do anything, a flicker of movement caught at the tail of her eye, and casting a swift glance upward, she saw a knot of figures cresting the skyline. In the same instant a cheerful shout told her that they had seen her, and Jon and Erland altered course and came leaping and scrambling down the steep sides of the glen toward her, with several more of the sword-band at their heels.

Instinctively, without realizing that she did so, she moved a little to come between them and the wretched creature among the rocks.

'Frytha!' Jon called, laughing, as they drew near. 'What in the world brings you over this way?'

'It was the pony,' Frytha called back, her voice shaking a little in her own ears. 'There came a wolf round the camp last night, and it frightened him, and he broke out. . . . What news is there?'

They were down to the little beck now, and the two of them came across with a flying leap and a scramble on the near bank, before Erland answered grudgingly, 'Le Meschin is clear away into Alverdale.'

'Oh,' Frytha said. 'What is it that happens now?'

Erland shrugged. 'Nothing, seemingly. Even with his brother's men added to his own rabble, he has not the strength to come at us again; and we haven't the strength to follow him up. The hunt is over for this time.' And then she saw his eyes go past her and widen suddenly. He side-stepped, quick as a cat, and was staring down at the man crouching among the rocks. 'What—by the Ring! Here's somewhat else beside a straying pony!'

'He——' began Frytha. 'He——' but her mouth was dry.

'He is one of Le Meschin's crew. Maybe he's a spy. See Jon—Ottar—look, all of you. Here's a Norman spy.'

'He is not a spy,' Frytha said. 'You can see he's not. He's been left behind—and he's sick.'

Several more of the sword-band had leapt the beck by this time, and came crowding in, eager as young hounds at the kill. Erland's hand was already on his dirk.

She protested swiftly. 'Erland, no. You cannot do that.'

'I can,' Erland said with a flash of angry laughter. 'Do you suppose he and his kind would not do the same for any of us in like case, unless they hoped for something to be learned from us?' The light glinted evilly on the rippled blade as he drew it.

The man still crouched unmoving, like an animal at bay, his eyes leaping from one to another of the faces that hemmed him in. He cried out again in his own tongue, shaking his head from side to side; then, as Erland took a menacing step forward, he flattened against the rocks behind him, making no attempt to touch the dagger in his own belt; and from his cracked mouth came two stammered Saxon words. 'No more! No more!'

I                                     119

'Erland, stop!' Frytha shrieked, desperate for some means to stay the dirk. 'How do we know that there is nothing to be learned from him? If you kill him here and no questions asked, like enough we shall all rue it later!'

'Kill first, and question after, is a good word,' Erland said; but he seemed to waver an instant all the same, and Frytha followed up her advantage.

'Question when it is too late,' she flashed. 'He is sick now—you can see that he is sick—and he cannot speak; but how do we know that he has not turned from Le Meschin to us, and maybe brought with him tidings that we have bitter need to know!' And she watched the uncertainty grow in Erland's hot-tempered face.

Jon, unwontedly sober behind his freckles, said quickly: 'It is in my mind that there is truth in that.'

And Ottar Edrikson, thrusting up behind him, put in: 'Let us take him down to the camp. Better keep him all in one piece till Aikin or Gille have seen him, anyway.'

Erland hesitated an instant longer, then lowered his dirk, though he did not sheath it again. 'Well enough. There'll be little difference in the end,' he said, and stooping, caught the man's wrist as he flung up an arm to shield his face. 'Up, you.'

They dragged him to his feet, slipped the dagger from his sheath, and strapped his hands behind him with his own belt, while he stood swaying in their midst, dazed and unresisting, as though he were asleep on his feet. And Frytha, striving to soothe the scared and fidgeting pony, looked on, sickeningly aware that all she had gained was a very small breathing space.

The little band set off with the captive in their midst; and Frytha, following behind, her weariness for the moment quite forgotten, wondered in angry bewilderment why she was doing this. The man was an enemy, a Norman, and she still remembered the pale flame of burning thatch. Yet she knew that she could no more abandon him than she could have abandoned a stray hound that had crept for mercy to her feet;

and she was fiercely ready to fight for him, against the Jarl himself, against all the chieftains of the War Host if need be. But oh! if only Bjorn were here to fight with her!

They followed down the beck for some way, then crossed over again where it ran shallow at the tail of a pool, and curved away northward over the open moors. When Ottar spoke of taking the prisoner back to camp, she had thought of the camp in Keskadale; now she saw that they were heading the wrong way. But with the Le Meschins just across the border into Norman Alverdale, there would be many camps of the War bands among the north-west glens of Skiddaw.

The captive stumbled often, and once fell headlong, unable to save himself with his bound hands. The Northmen dragged him to his feet and thrust him on again, while Frytha, bright-eyed for battle, clung stubbornly to the rear of the party with Teitri butting and slobbering uneasily at her shoulder.

So at last they came into a wide upland valley, where knee-haltered ponies were grazing and men gathered round a cooking-fire, and brown awnings were spread over ridge-poles to make sleeping-shelters beside the stream. Heads were turned toward them as they came down the heather slope; someone called out, and someone answered, and Frytha found that they were the centre of a crowd. The men thronged in on them, silent for the most part, curious, hostile as they stared at the captive, who stood in the grip of Jon and Erland, gazing about him with bright dazed eyes. And then the crowd parted, and Aikin himself was in their midst, with Garm against his knee as usual, and behind him, Bjorn.

Bjorn grey-faced and older than he had been when she saw him last, in his stained and weatherworn battle-sark. At sight of him, relief and a sense of safety flooded over Frytha, and her widened eyes were fixed on his face, imploring, demanding that he should help her—now this instant, without asking questions.

Bjorn's quick glance had already taken in the scene, the dazed and drooping captive, Erland flushed with triumph, and the white fierceness of Frytha's face; and instantly, and asking no question, he signalled back with a quirked eyebrow that he was with her.

'What goes forward here?' Aikin was demanding.

Erland thrust the captive forward so sharply that he stumbled to his knees at Aikin's feet; and Garm pricked his ears at the sudden movement, and growled warningly, deep in his throat. 'Here is one of Le Meschin's crew. He was skulking among the rocks over yonder.' He jerked his head back the way that they had come.

Aikin stood resting both hands on the amber pummel of Wave-flame, and looked down at the wretched captive crouching where he had fallen. 'Was he so?' he said after a moment, then to the man himself: 'Is it that you thought to spy on us? Or have you but run from your own kind? If that be the way of it, you have run the wrong way, my friend.'

The man neither moved nor answered, but Frytha saw how his breast heaved as though he had indeed been running. A ragged murmur rose from the crowd. Then Bjorn stepped forward, and stooping, took the captive by the shoulder and turned him so as to look into his face. 'Here's no spy you've caught, Erland. The man's as daft as a broom!'

'Daft?—And who says so?' Erland began hotly in the midst of a startled hush; but Aikin, leaning forward a little on Wave-flame, was also searching the captive's face.

'I say so,' he said at last. 'You are in the right of it, Bjorn Bjornson.'

'Nay, he is but playing the mazelin for his skin's sake,' Erland urged.

Bjorn straightened up. 'He is playing nothing. Look in his eyes and see for yourself.'

'Le Meschin must indeed have been short of troops, that he has come to using witless men-at-arms!' Erland retorted with angry sarcasm. They had forgotten Aikin for the moment; they had forgotten their own kind gathered round them; and Frytha realized that though Bjorn had taken up the fight on her behalf, it had become a thing between him and Erland now.

'It may be that he had as many wits in his head even as you, a few days since,' Bjorn said. 'We can know naught of that. If they be broken now, by all the gods of Valhalla that once we prayed to, it seems to me small wonder!'

The two young warriors glared at each other for a long moment; and then, his hand tightening on his naked dirk, Erland turned toward Aikin, who stood silent and half smiling, looking on. 'If he be mazelin indeed, there's naught to gain by keeping him any longer. Say the word, Aikin.'

Frytha wanted to cry out, 'Leave him alone; he's mine! It was I who found him, not Erland Ormeson!' But before she could do more than take breath, Bjorn had countered: '*Since* he be mazelin indeed, there's luck to lose by killing him. Aikin, my hearth-lord and leader, if I wrought well yesterday, give the man to me for a battle gift!'

A gasp of astonishment rose from the onlookers. Aikin said quietly: 'You wrought well yesterday, and you know it. If these were the old days, with treasure in our halls, your battle gift should have been in wrought cups and red gold. Yet I have still one arm-ring here above my elbow, that came to me from my father. Will not that serve instead?'

Their eyes met steadily, while even Erland held his peace. 'No,' Bjorn said, 'it will not serve.'

'Why would you have this—creature?'

Bjorn's eyes flickered suddenly with the familiar mockery. 'Did I not say that there was luck to lose by killing him? A mazelin is lucky, so they say.'

Again there was a muttering among the close-packed throng; men glanced aside at each other, nodding in half-unwilling agreement. A mazelin was lucky; all men knew that; and to kill a thing that was lucky . . . 'That's true enough,' an old warrior said. 'If the All-Father's hand is on him, then there'll be ill-fortune to follow if our hand be on him too.'

There was a white flash of laughter in the face of Aikin the Beloved. 'So—you choose your reason well, at all events,' he said. His gaze dropped to the poor wretch crouching at his feet; and he was silent a few moments, with an odd still look in his face that was certainly not mercy. 'Since you have a fancy for the thing, take it, then,' he said at last, and ignoring Erland's hot protest, he turned away and whistling to Garm, walked serenely off in the direction of the tents beside the beck.

Behind him, Erland rounded furiously on Bjorn. 'And who are you that you should demand a battle gift from Aikin? I and Jon and the rest of us, have we not fought as well as you? Have not our blades bitten as deep, when we ran beside him against the Norman host? It was your shield that covered him when he stumbled—but would not our shields have served as truly, had it chanced to be one of us at his shoulder?'

'Quite as truly,' Bjorn said, standing over his property. 'Is it that you want a mazelin each, or would you share this one between you?' Suddenly he laughed. 'Nay then, I'll not take him as a gift, since ye feel it so. See now, I will pay head-ransom for him with a new song in Hall, as once Egil the Icelander paid head-ransom for himself to King Eric of Northumbria.'

Jon grinned. 'That's a fair offer, and I'm for taking it. How say you, Ottar?'

'Fair enough—but see that you make it a good one!' Ottar Edrikson said. And other voices joined in, 'Make it hot and strong! Put plenty of fighting into it, then! Make it about Keskadale!'

Bjorn drew his dirk, and stooped over the mazelin. The poor wretch saw the blade, and shrank from it, his wild dazed stare going up to Bjorn's face, and again he stammered out his two Saxon words, 'No more! No more!'

'No more,' Bjorn said, and slipped the blade between his bound wrists.

Somebody said, 'You are growing soft in your old age, Bear-cub.'

'He was always squeamish,' Erland said, with an angry snort of laughter. 'Lack-bellied! Why, when we heard of what the Normans had done to Ari Knudson, he ran away and was sick; don't you remember——'

'Foul blow!' Jon cut in quickly. 'That was eight years ago.'

Bjorn straightened up with the cut strap in his hand; and Frytha saw that he was white to the lips as he turned to Erland, and his eyes blazed. 'Concerning my lack of belly—shall we put it to the test? There are hazels by the beck; we can mark out the ground for a holm-ganging here and now.'

There was an uncomfortable silence. Erland knew, as they all did, that if he let the challenge go by he would never be able to bait Bjorn about his squeamishness again, nor about the mazelin. But one glance at Bjorn's face told them that when he spoke of a holm-ganging, he was not using the term loosely, as men used it nowadays, for any sort of fight, but in its true sense, for the old terrible duel-to-the-death of the Viking kind.

Frytha, standing by, with her hand gripping the pony's mane, had forgotten to breathe. But it was a challenge that, hot-blooded as he was, Erland did not care to take up.

Bjorn's gaze had grown mocking again. 'Well?' he demanded after a moment.

Erland, as red as the other was white, shrugged. 'Oh, don't be a fool,' he said; and turned away with hunched shoulders.

A while later, Frytha was looking down from the back of the little red pony, at Bjorn, who stood beside her. 'What will you do with him?' she asked.

'Hand him over to Grim, perhaps. He may be useful with the sheep; and Grim has a way with wild things.'

Frytha nodded wordlessly, looking back toward the camp below them, where she could see a small slumped figure beside the beck; the mazelin, fed and watered and tethered to a tent-pole.

'What really happened?' Bjorn asked.

'I was out after Teitri, and I found him crouching among some rocks up on the edge of the high fells. He was just as he is now.' Now that it was all over, she was tired again, so tired that the grey mist was rising thick inside her head, and she had to fumble for the words she wanted. 'There was—something dreadful in him. It seemed to—to reach out to me for help, and I felt it; and then Erland came, and Jon and some of the others, and Erland would have killed him at once, but I would not have it so—and Jon and Ottar stood with me; and so they took him down to the camp, but——' She turned her face to Bjorn again: 'If you had not come, they would have killed him, after all.'

'Maybe it would have been better if they had,' Bjorn said quietly.

'Better? Bjorn, what—do you mean?'

'Maybe the greatest mercy for him lay in Erland's dirk, after all. It is in my mind that Aikin thought so; and that was why he let him live; not because I claimed him as a battle gift.'

'Oh, no!' Frytha whispered, suddenly cold and sick, her eyes widening on Bjorn's face. 'Bjorn—is it like that? But I—I *couldn't* let Erland have his way! And you couldn't, either.'

He made no answer, and she urged him desperately, 'You couldn't, could you, Bjorn? It was not only because of me?'

Bjorn looked up at her. He was still very white, and there were dark smudges under his eyes. 'Maybe I could, if I was sure enough of my own breaking point,' he said; and dropped his hand from the pony's neck. 'You must be on your way. Half Keskadale will be out beating the marshes for you by now.'

## XI

## 'HE HAS COME TO HIS ADVENTURE'

I N ONE OF old Gospatric's manor houses, a few days later,
Ranulf Le Meschin and his brother spoke long together,
the elder brother pacing restlessly about the chamber as
he talked, the other sitting on a low bench beside the hearth
and watching him.

'I am tired, Will,' Ranulf was saying. 'It is in my mind that
I will lay me down and leave these accursed mountains to the
devils whose haunts they are.'

'You're a broken man if you do,' William said softly.

'I think I am that already. I shall lose the earldom of
Carlisle, and whatever favour I still have with the new King.
I shall be a landless knight this side the Narrow Seas, as I was
at the beginning. But my hopes are behind me now.' Ranulf
laughed sharply, angrily. 'Well, I can creep home in disgrace
to Bayeux.'

William chuckled. He was a little dark paunchy man with a
scar under one eye, and his chuckle was soft and infuriating.

127

'As to that—"charity begins at home," so they say, and far
be it from me to turn my own brother from my gate. There
will always be a corner for you at Mulecaster, and the fill of
your belly at my table.' He cocked an amused eye at his
brother, who had swung round on him with an oath. 'No?
Then we must try the King.'

'And much good that is like to do us!' Ranulf, who could
never keep his voice down in time of stress, cried out to him
shrilly like a woman. 'He was lack-willing enough with his
aid this last time, and who shall blame him. Thousands of men
spent through more than thirty years, and naught to show for
it but Amilside!'

William crossed one knee over the other and sat hugging it.
'Nay, brother, you take too dark a view. We have more than
thirty years' experience in mountain fighting to show for it.
We have learned the lay of the land, and within narrow limits
the whereabouts of this hidden stronghold. The trouble with
you is that you are too much a bird of habit. You drive in your
thrusts again and again from the south and east with all the
heights of Lakeland between you and your goal, and wonder
that each thrust goes the way of the last. Try once more, from
the north, and it may be another story. From Papcastle the
vale runs low and wide into the heart of the mountains;
there's little cover for ambush, and we can leave strong communication lines behind us as we go. The north is the weak
quarter of the Jarl's defences—I seem to remember telling you
that before.'

Ranulf, who had halted a few moments, flung away to his
pacing again; up and down, up and down, while the little
dark brother on the bench watched him. At last he checked
and turned back to him. His face was grey with strain and his
voice leapt joggedly when he spoke. 'So be it then, oh most
wise brother; I'll make trial of the matter once more; and may
God have mercy on me!'

Bjorn made his new song for the mazelin's head-ransom—
a dark song, of the massacre in Keskadale—and sang it in
Hall; and little by little the mazelin ceased to be an enemy,

ceased even to be a wonder like a chained bear, and blended into the life of the Dale.

As his first dazed state wore off, it became clear that he was not really witless at all; only what Bjorn had guessed him to be, a man tested beyond his endurance, who had broken in the testing. His memory was gone from him, and sometimes his wits seemed to wander; and when left to himself he would sit half a day together with his arms across his knees, staring straight before him with those bright tormented eyes that seemed always to be struggling to remember. . . . Yet after a while, Grim, who had been sullen-set against him at first, saying to Frytha 'I bade thee remember whose work it was, the night we watched thy home burning, but thee's forgotten, I'm thinking,' admitted that he was good with a lambing ewe, and the mossy-faced sheep-dog who had long since taken old Vigi's place would work to his whistle almost as well as to his, Grim's, own. Even the blackness that had swallowed his memory had stray glimmers of light in it. He did not know who or what he was, but he would talk sometimes about an orchard in Picardy—wherever that might be—and sometimes he would sing snatches of the songs of the Norman camp.

Frytha saw him often, and Bjorn, when he was in the Dale, spent a good deal of time with him. Sometimes it seemed to Frytha that Bjorn came near to hating the mazelin for having broken, and yet it was as though in some odd way he felt responsible for him because he *had* broken.

So from being with the mazelin, who had forgotten anything he ever knew of Saxon, Bjorn began to pick up more of the Norman tongue to add to the few words he had had from Haethcyn; began also to pick up the songs of the Norman camp, and add them to his own minstrelsy. And that was a thing that was to play its part in his life, and the life of all the Dale before long.

The autumn came, and the Sell Beck ran yellow with fallen birch-leaves. The snow melted, and the birch-buds thickened. Again the birch-leaves fell, and the wild geese came down from the north, and the wolves cried close in the bitter darkness

of the long winter nights. And while still the Road waited
—Frytha always thought of it as waiting like a living thing—
for its hour to come, Ranulf Le Meschin, having at last gained
a promise of help from the King, was overseas with the Royal
Warrant in his pouch, gathering a new army from Normandy.

And then, while the last of that winter's snow still lay
dappled on Grismoor and Beacon Fell, word came from the
scouting bands in the north of a great hosting among the
enemy, greater than any that had gone before. The Normans
were moving into the ancient Legion's fort that men called
Papcastle; they were making it strong again, and William Le
Meschin was bringing in every man he could scrape together
from the honours of Coupland and Alverdale. All over
Cumberland and Westmarieland, preparations were going forward for such an attack as had not been seen in the north
before; the armourers were working day and night, shoesmiths
and fletchers, and always on the skyline, the ships going up
and down to Workington with supplies. And in Butharsdale
too, in all the hidden dales of Lake Land, the armourers'
hammers rang early and late, and the men of the War Host
furbished their weapons for battle.

And now Ranulf was back from Normandy with his army
behind him, several thousand strong, to add to the muster at
Papcastle.

'It is in my mind that our fine new road will come into its
own before many moons are past,' said the Jarl, when news
of his return reached Butharsdale. 'Brothers, it is in my mind
that this will be the greatest of all our battles—and the last.'

At about that time, the Countess called Gerd and Frytha
after her one day, and going into the bower, opened the oldest
and most wonderfully carved of the dark kists that stood
against the wall, and brought out from it a flat bundle folded
in linen. As the two girls watched, she turned back the folds
and carefully shook out the thing that was inside. The cold
smell of age and the aromatic tang of herbs filled the bower,
and as the thing unfurled, it was as though a huge raven spread
its wings for flight.

Frytha found that she was looking at a square of fine age-yellow woollen cloth across which the black wings spread from side to side. She saw the cruel beak and savage talons outstretched to rend and tear, and realized with a feeling of awe that she was looking at a thing that she had heard of often, but never thought to see: one of the dreaded raven banners, the black banners of the Viking kind, that had carried terror inland from the seas of all the world, wherever the Northmen ran their keels ashore.

'More than two hundred years ago, men last carried this into battle,' the Countess said, spreading it carefully across the carved kist. 'That was when it came west-over-seas with the first of My Lord's line to follow the Whale's Road from Norway, in the days of Harald Fairhair. Since then it has lain like a sword in the sheath, but now the time is come for it to spread its wings once more.'

But the ancient stuff was ready to tear like tinder, and must be strengthened if it was to go into battle again. So the Countess brought out fine new linen that had been laid by for a shift for herself, and cut it to the size and shape of the ancient banner; and for many evenings after, she and Gerd and Frytha worked on it, stitching the age-rotten wool with infinite care on to its backing of strong new linen. And when at last the thing was done, the Jarl bade them make another Raven, a new Raven, 'For,' said he, 'as there are two ends to Rannardale, so there must be two Ravens to hold them fast, when the time comes.'

So the Countess Tordis laid the ancient banner carefully away until its hour came; and she found a piece of bleached woollen cloth—there was not much, in the Dale, for the wool was mostly spun and woven in its natural dark colour, which did not show up on a fell side—and another piece that she dyed glossy black with a brew of bog-black and oak twigs. And she cut them to shape for the new one.

But between the two banners, on a stormy spring night, the bairn that Gerd had been waiting for was born, and they wrapped him in soft deerskin and laid him in the old wooden

131

cradle carved with writhing dragon-knots, that had been stored away since Gille was a babe; and sent word to Gille, in the north, that his son was born. And after that, for a little while, there was only Frytha to work with the Countess on the new Raven banner.

But Gerd was back with them long before the task was done; and on an evening almost into summer, the three of them sat together at the women's end of the Hearth Hall, the Countess in her great chair, Frytha and Gerd on stools drawn close to her knee, setting the final stitches to talons and wing-tips. Gerd had not brought the babe out, thinking that the crowd and noise in the hall would not be good for him, but the bower door was open so that she would hear if he cried.

The green twilight had deepened into the dark beyond the narrow windows under the eaves, and the shadows crowded in from the corners; warm shadows with a bloom of peat-smoke on them like the bloom on a bilberry. The three embroiderers had a mutton-fat dip to work by, but for the rest of the hall there was only the firelight. One did not need much light for spinning, nor for burnishing one's weapons, nor for listening to old Haethcyn, who sat at the Jarl's feet, his hand moving now fiercely, now caressingly on the strings of his beloved harp while he half sang, half recited the familiar and well-loved story of Beowulf. Those who needed more light drew closer to the row of fires, and settled on the rushes among the sprawling hounds.

How peaceful it all looked, Frytha thought, casting a swift glance down the hall between stitch and stitch. Peaceful and sure and—*continuing*. And yet soon, very soon now, the last and greatest struggle of all would be upon them. And after it was over? Maybe they would bear home their shields in triumph, and sit here in the Hearth Hall polishing their weapons again; or maybe they would lie out on the slopes of Rannardale for the wolf and the raven; or maybe they would be the thralls of Norman masters. Her glance flickered over them, questioningly. Aikin—Bjorn—Erland; no, they had not the look of thralls.

Far down the hall, Haethcyn's deep old voice went on, passing from speech to song and back again; joined sometimes by the voices of his listeners, as the excitement of the story rose in them. The tale was drawing to its close, Beowulf making ready for his last fight.

> 'Then he greeted every well loved man
> For the last time, his comrades loyal found,
> Brave men in helmets: "I would not take a sword
> To the serpent or any weapon, if I knew
> How else to grapple down his pride
> As long ago to Grendel I did do,
> But I look for fire, embattled heat,
> Breath and poison, for which cause I wear
> Shield and corselet——" '

Frytha took another strand from the black tangle beside her, and re-threaded her needle. 'There must be runes for a task such as this,' she said suddenly. 'If only we knew the secret, we could weave power into it, that it might always lead our men to victory!'

Gerd looked up from her own work. 'I have been thinking that,' she said. 'If old Unna were still here, maybe she would have known the way.'

'The Raven has power enough of its own without the aid of spells stitched into it,' the Countess said. 'And such magic as you have in mind is apt to be double-edged. Did Unna never tell either of you the story of the banner that was worked for Jarl Sigurd of Orkney, by his sorceress mother?' Then, as they shook their heads, she went on: 'It was a fine banner; when the wind blew it out it was as though the Raven spread his wings for flight, and always it would lead men to victory, but always at the cost of its bearer's life. Many times it gave Jarl Sigurd the victory in Scotland and when he went summer Viking down the coasts, and many a fine young warrior paid its price. But at last and at last Anlaf the White, King of Dublin, sent to Sigurd for help against the Irish who were rising to overthrow the Norse rule; and Jarl Sigurd gathered men from all the Orkneys, and from the Sudreys— my great-grandfather was one of them—and sailed for Ireland. And at Clontarf there was a great battle. And in the battle man after man was killed carrying Jarl Sigurd's Raven that his mother had worked for him, until at last there came a time when no man would take it up. Then Sigurd said; " 'Tis fittest that the beggar should bear the bag," and he took the banner from its staff and bound it round him under his cloak. And a little after, there came a chance-flung spear and took him through the heart. And with Jarl Sigurd dead, the magic that his mother had prisoned in the Raven broke loose, so that the battle ended in most bloody defeat for the Viking kind. They used to say, when I was a bairn in Barra, that for years afterward there was not a threshing-floor in all Ireland but had its chained Viking threshing on it.'

A sudden stir at the foot of the hall made Frytha look round as the story ended. A man stood in the open fore-porch door-way, with the dark behind him. He seemed far spent, and stood a moment leaning one hand against the door-post as though to get his breath back, then pulled himself together and strode forward into the firelight. And Frytha saw that it was one of the scouts from the north.

Old Haethcyn broke off the song of Beowulf between word and word, and the Jarl turned in his High Seat as the new-comer strode up through the crowded hall, saying: 'God's Greeting to you, Aan Olafson. What news do you bring?'

'God's Greeting to you, Jarl Buthar,' said the man, halting before the High Seat. 'This is the news that I bring: that the Normans are across the Derwent, and make another camp on the land-tongue where the Cocur joins it.'

The Jarl nodded, pulling at his beard, and said something in reply, but what it was Frytha did not hear, for even as he spoke, the man swayed a little and put out a hand to the nearby roof-tree to steady himself: and at the same instant, the bairn in its cradle set up a bleating cry. Gerd had dropped her needle and was gone through the bower door, and the Jarl was calling for food and ale for the spent messenger; and the Countess, rising and laying aside the Raven banner, bade her 'Go you to the kitchen-house and bring food—the best that you can find quickly.'

Frytha flew to do her bidding, through the bower where Gerd was just taking her wailing son from his cradle, and across the garth to the kitchen house. A few moments later she was back, with porridge from the great pot in a bowl of flame-grained birch, with barley bannock and ewe-milk cheese and a hacked-off wedge of cold mutton. The man was sitting on the skin-covered bench below the High Seat, with his legs outstretched before him, and his head hanging between his shoulders like a foundered pony, while many of those in the hall had left their places to gather in a silent crowd around him. They opened to let Frytha through, and she saw Countess Tordis already there, with the great silver guest-cup in her hands.

'Eat,' the Jarl said. 'Eat first, and talk after.'

And the man looked up, nodded dumbly, and took the food between his knees. Then his gaze went past Frytha, to Gerd, who had slipped through the crowd after her. 'That was the bairn crying? Lusty, he sounds. I will tell Gille, when I go back, that I have heard his cub give tongue.'

'It is well with my Lord, then?' Gerd said eagerly.

'It is well with him. He sends greeting to his mother, and to his son's mother.' Aan took the ale-cup from the Countess, and raised it high, turning to the Jarl and the circle of warriors about him. 'Wass heil!' he said, and drank, and returned the cup. Colour was coming back into his face already. 'That is vastly better! Nay, I will talk and eat at the same time; there is little enough to tell. The Normans are across the Derwent, as I told you; this has been a dry spring and the ford was easy. There was little we could do against such an army in daylight and in open country. Already they make strong the new camp with earthworks and stockades. . . .' He began reeling off the details of the latest raids like one telling over a list learned by heart.

Buthar, his great head sunk on his breast, listened attentively, asking many questions, while Aikin, lounging sideways on one of the massive table-trestles nearby, played with Garm's ears, and put in a searching question of his own from time to time. Between mouthfuls of porridge and bannock, Aan Olafson did his best to answer all these questions, but at last he shook his head. 'Nay, I can tell you no more. I do not know their number, nor how they are divided between mounted and foot, nor how many knights there are among them. They are a great army, an army such as might serve to conquer all Scotland, and more troops were coming up from Workington this morning, even as I set out. These things that you ask—all these other things—only a man within the camp could answer them.'

'A man within the camp,' said the Jarl after a pause, and looked at him with a suddenly arrested eye. 'A man who could speak the tongue. . . . Aye well, drink up, man; you need it sorely.'

Something made Frytha glance across at Bjorn. She saw his head go up slowly, and the white stillness of his face; and suddenly, her heart began to race, though she did not yet know why.

Slowly and deliberately he sheathed his dirk, which he had been burnishing and still carried in his hand, tucked the scrap of burnishing leather into his belt, and stepped out into the clear space before the Jarl's High Seat. 'Lord Buthar, I have somewhat of the Norman tongue—enough to serve the purpose. I will go.'

There was a sudden hush, a wave of silence that seemed to flow up the great Hearth Hall. All eyes were on the young warrior standing like a spear before the High Seat. The Jarl leaned forward, his hand on the carved front-posts of the great chair, his ice-blue gaze on Bjorn's face. At last he said: 'Up into the Norman camp, Bjorn Bjornson? Alone?'

'Yes,' said Bjorn, steadily.

Frytha's heart went on racing. She alone of all those in the Hearth Hall—the Jarl himself, the women, Bjorn's sword-companions, even Aikin, gentling his hound's ears while his quiet gaze went out like a touch to his young warrior—she alone of them all knew quite what Bjorn was doing. And then in the crowd beyond him, she saw Erland lean forward a little, as though for a better view. And catching the look in Erland's eyes, she realized that there was one other beside herself, who knew.

'And how would you be making your way into the camp?' Jarl Buthar asked.

'A harper is free of any camp.'

Thorold Forkbeard, who had been a sword-brother of Ari Knudson's, spoke up from the edge of the fire glow. 'Na na, heed him not, Lord Buthar; he is little more than a boy. If you would send one up into the Norman camp—I learned something of the Norman tongue in my youth, and I have not lost it all. Send me.'

Bjorn rounded on him, his eyes light and bright and fiercely mocking. 'In what guise? Are you then also a harper, Thorold Forkbeard? Is there any man here, having enough of the Norman tongue, that has also the harp-music, the gift of song, to open to him the Normans' gate? Is there any man here, saving Haethcyn my foster-father, who can do *thus*?'

He turned to where Haethcyn sat at the Jarl's feet, and as though the thing had been arranged between them, the old harper held up the Sweet-singer to him. Bjorn took the harp, and next instant, with one foot on the bench beside his foster-father, just as he had stood to make his sword-song in that same place, more than six years ago, he had taken up the song of Beowulf, where the other had laid it down.

> 'Then valiant, by his shield he rose,
> Got to his feet, and went with shirt of mail,
> Hard under helm, beneath the stone-gap close,
> Trusting the strength of one man would not fail:
> This is not a coward's course!
>   Having warred through many days,
> And combats tried, when armies knit their force,
> Brave with the best, and full of praise,
> He has come to his adventure. . . .'

Then, with a bewildering change of mood, he set the harp-strings dancing, prancing, and swung into one of the guard-room songs that the mazelin sang in his lighter moments, at sound of which the mazelin himself, sitting on the beggars' bench beside the door, roused and raised his head as though to listen to something a long way off, then sank back into his usual brooding state.

There was a moment's silence when the song was done, and then Aikin said: 'No, there is no other here, save Haethcyn, who can do thus, Bjorn Bjornson.'

Jarl Buthar was tugging at his beard as always when deep in thought. 'It is an old trick,' he said at last. 'Alfred of Wessex played it in the camp of our people, two hundred years ago. Well, it served his turn then, it may serve ours now.' The cold blue gaze went on to Aikin. 'He runs with your pack, Aikin my brother; how say you then? Does he go?'

Aikin lifted the old hound's head from his thigh, and got up. 'Yes,' he said. 'He goes.'

Bjorn, who had stood unmoving since the last harp-note died away, brought his foot down from the bench, and turned to give the Sweet-singer back to Haethcyn.

The old man made no move to take it, but sat with his great hands locked round one knee, peering up at Bjorn under his striped mane of hair. 'And what will you use for a harp, in the Norman camp, Bjorn Fosterling?'

'The Jarl shall lend me the Hall harp, maybe,' Bjorn said.

'Nay, but he shall not, for you shall take my harp, my Sweet-singer.'

'What if harm come to her?'

'That is as the All-Father wills. You know what she is to me—therefore do I give her to go with you into this, in my stead, because I am too old to go myself. She will be yours after me, anyway.'

There was a moment's silence, and then Bjorn said, more gently, Frytha thought, than she had ever heard him speak to anybody before, 'If I come back myself, I will bring her back to you, Haethcyn Fostri.' Then, still holding the harp, he turned back to Jarl Buthar. 'When would you have me go?'

'As soon as maybe,' said the Jarl. 'Yet there are more matters than one to be dealt with first; matters on which we must take counsel; and a few hours' sleep are good before the start of wayfaring. Time enough for you to set out in the morning.'

Frytha found Gerd beside her suddenly. 'The Countess bids us come,' Gerd whispered, pulling at her sleeve. 'If we go back to our needles now, we can have the Raven finished before it is time to sleep.'

Frytha pulled her gaze from Bjorn, and turned after her, and went back to the women's place, where the Countess had already taken up her needle again. But all the while she was thinking, 'Ari Knudson did not go alone. At least Ari Knudson did not go alone.' And she pricked her finger so that a speck of crimson stained the white wool.

## XII

## THE LOST STEADING

THAT NIGHT FRYTHA lay wakeful in her little closet
opening from the bower, watching the pearly square of
the smoke-hole in the blackness of the bower roof, and
the bright silver sword of moonlight that slanted down from
it as the moon rose higher.  She could hear Gerd breathing
quietly in the other closet, where she lay with the bairn beside
her.  Gerd was asleep; everybody but herself was asleep, it
seemed, in all the world, save perhaps Bjorn.  Would Bjorn
be awake and making plans? she wondered.  Perhaps they
were all made.

He was to make for Rafnglas, she knew that, and find means
to join up with the constant stream of men and supplies going
north.  It seemed a long way round, but it would leave a well-
laid trail behind him that would bear looking into without
betraying him.

She tossed and turned, trying to sleep, but always her mind
went back and back over the evening that was past, and she
was seeing Bjorn standing like a spear before the Jarl in his

High Seat. Sometimes she skimmed along the surface of sleep like a mayfly on the surface of a stream, so that though she never lost consciousness of the dark bower and the sword of moonlight, Bjorn got confused with Ari Knudson, and both of them with Beowulf. Beowulf and the Firedrake; Bjorn and the Firedrake—but that was just what it was: Bjorn going out alone to face his own particular Firedrake. 'He has come to his adventure . . .' For a moment she saw him through the dark wing-spread of the Raven banner that they had finished that evening, going down into the valley of the Firedrake, alone. 'But Ari Knudson did not go alone,' she thought, 'and in the end Beowulf's shield bearer ran to be with him . . .'

And then she was broad awake again, the silver sword was slanting further up the wall as the moon westered; and suddenly she could bear to lie there no longer. Taking infinite care not to rouse Gerd or the others, she slipped from under the deerskin covering, and felt for her cloak hanging at the foot of the sleeping-bench, and her shoes beneath it. The door into the garth always stood open save in wild weather, and she slipped through into the white night beyond, and flinging the cloak over her shoulders, sat down on a chopping-block to put on her shoes. It was cold in the night air, with the fresh chill that comes a little before dawn.

She would go into the apple-garth, she thought. But when she came to the gate in the turf wall, and went through, she found someone already there, sitting on the grass under the trees, with his head bent and his arm across his knees in the white moonlight, and she knew by the position, even before he looked up, that it was the mazelin.

'Mazelin!' she whispered. 'What is it that you do here?'

He shook his head wearily, and looked about him as though to discover where 'here' was. 'Perhaps I was looking for a strayed sheep,' he said, 'but there would not be any sheep here?'

'No,' Frytha said. 'There would not be any sheep here.'

The mazelin rubbed the back of one hand across his forehead in the wild and weary way he had, and looked at her as though hoping that she might be able to help him. 'Why did Bjorn sing "The Duke and the Jester" in the hall tonight? Where did he learn it?'

'You taught it to him,' Frytha said, resting her hand on the rough bark of an apple-branch, and looking down at him. 'Do you not remember?'

The mazelin had both hands to his temples now, his fingers working and working into the roots of his wild dark hair. 'Remember? I do not know what I remember. Sometimes I think I almost remember everything; and then—it is all gone again.' He dropped his hands and sat looking up at her help-lessly. 'What is it that I ought to remember?'

Completely caught up in Bjorn's affairs as she was, some-thing in the piteous appeal touched home to Frytha, and she said swiftly: 'Never heed it—it does not matter. All that matters for you to remember is the orchard, and you remember that.'

The wildness left him at once, and the face he tipped up to the moonlight was quiet again. The last of the blossom was gone from the low-hanging apple-branches, but in the white radiance of the moon the leaves themselves seemed made of silver, so that the trees were like the trees in a legend. 'The orchard?' he said. 'Aye, I remember the orchard. A fine fair orchard. Pear-trees there were in it, as well as apples, and the pear-blossom came first, in the spring. . . . There was a hedge round it—not a turf wall—a leafy hedge that smelled of honey and wine when the sun warmed it. There was someone else there, too—another boy—and a dog. Or maybe that was in some other place. Nay, I—I cannot remember.'

Frytha touched his shoulder. 'You can remember the orchard. That is all that matters.'

She was on the verge of turning away to wander somewhere else, when he asked. 'Where has Bjorn gone?'

She caught her breath. 'Gone?'

'I saw him go—a while and a while since—up that way, toward the Water-head. Where has he gone?'

Frytha stood quite still a moment, feeling as though someone had dashed cold water in her face. So Bjorn had gone already. No leavetaking, just a setting out, by his lone. That was like Bjorn. 'He has gone on a wayfaring,' she said at last.

'But he will come back?'

'He—will come back,' Frytha said.

She turned away, leaving the mazelin sitting under the moon-silvered apple-trees, and made her way back toward the bower. It did not seem to her that she had just made up her mind; it was as though her mind had always been made up, from the moment when Bjorn had stepped out before the Jarl's High Seat, last night. She reached the bower door and slipped through into the darkness within. Moving with infinite caution so as not to wake the sleepers all around her, she made her way to her own sleeping-bench, and knelt down, feeling for the kist in which she kept her few belongings. It seemed to her that the faint squeak of the lid as she raised it must wake the whole bower and the Hall beyond it; and she waited in an agony, her breath held to listen. But no one roused, and after a few moments she began to feel inside for the things she wanted.

Having found all she needed, she eased shut the lid of the kist, rose to her feet with everything bundled under one arm, and stole out again, across the whitened garth to the weaving-house. She raised the pin and slipped inside, leaving the door ajar to the sinking moonlight, and hurriedly began to pull on the short kirtle and loose breeks that she wore on the fells. She bound the cross-gartering from knee to ankle, tightened the deerskin strap about her middle, and thrust into it Bjorn's old dirk. She could pass for a boy, she knew that; even her voice would pass, for it was husky, like a boy's that is near to breaking. Only her hair had grown again in the two years since the massacre in Keskadale. She found the weaver's shears and hacked it off short and ragged to the base of her neck; and leaving the honey-brown braids to lie with the shears beside the loom, flung on her cloak again and went out into the garth once more, heading this time for the kitchen house.

There were generally folk sleeping in the kitchen house, but she must have food, lest Bjorn, who would have taken only enough for himself, should feel that he must share his with her. Keeping well in the shadows she made her way to the door, lifted the pin and went in quietly, but not so quietly that it would seem like stealth to anyone wakeful within. It was wolf dark, save for the red glow of the embers under the porridge pot; and someone stirred and mumbled a sleepy question. 'It is only I,' Frytha said, making her voice deeper than usual. 'I am hungry,' and she turned to the bread closet, and took a bannock from the top of the pile, and went out again, quickly and quietly as she had come.

Out from the familiar Jarlstead, and across the log bridge that spanned the river, hearing the soft rush of water below her in the darkness, and away up the west side of Butharsmere toward the pass into Ennerdale. The moon was low, and the shadows growing transparent, as she came up over the pass, and the rock ramparts of High Crag were already catching a promise of the coming day, though the darkness still lay like stagnant water in Ennerdale. But as she dropped downward, the shadows seemed to sink away as though the water were running out, and full dawn came up with the speed of flying, and overtook her before she gained the next pass; a dappled dawn, that seemed full of the wings of birds.

She broke her bannock in two and ate half of it as she walked; and that made her thirsty, so that when she found a pool like a silver targe among the heather, she knelt down to drink from her cupped palms, her own face looking up at her strangely with the short hair falling forward about cheeks and temples, before the reflection shivered to pieces as she dipped in her hands.

When she had drunk her fill, she got up, and went on again, following the thread of a beck down into the head of Wasdale. Through the long hours she held on, skirting as well as she could the dark and stinking forest that choked the glens, where living oak and yew and alders propped up others that were dead, and any step might carry one through the rotten trunk of some long-fallen forest giant into an ant's nest: by the open birch-woods of the lower fells, across great billows of high moor, where the young bracken was shooting among the rocks and she seemed alone in a world that held no sound save the cur-lews calling and the faint siffling of the mountain wind. She did not know the way, but to anyone bred to the fells as she had been, it was not hard to find; she had a hunter's eye for country, that showed her where the passes were likely to be, and the acute sense of direction of a wild thing; and she held on, unhesitatingly, until at last, far over beyond Burnmoor Tarn, she checked, gazing down and away into the misty green flatness that she knew must be Eskdale. Softly rolling woods dimmed with a blue haze of early summer, and the winding silver loops of a river; all spread far and fair and remote as a dream below the grey and russet fells. Cuckoo country, she thought, just as up here it was curlew country. A strange land to her, used as she was to the wild plunging heights and depths, the steep glens and leaping torrents and bare black crags of the Northern fells.

From here, the way ran clear down Eskdale to the sea; from here also, it ran through enemy territory. Better to turn aside from the clear way, lest someone should see her coming down out of the Viking country, and perhaps think awkward thoughts.

Scouting for a more hidden way down, she found herself after a while dropping down over a steep tumble of rocks and bilberry into the head of a shallow glen; and looking down it, as it opened from her feet, saw below her the ragged hum-mocks and half-lost walls of a ruined steading beside the beck. She could trace the outlines of byres and barns whose timbers had long since fallen away into the tide of bracken that had flowed in over the intake wall, and the turf-bank still standing about the tattered remains of an apple-garth run wild. The house-stead seemed to have been dry-stone built, and the walls still rose steadfast and defiant amid the wilderness, though the roof had fallen in, as though guarding the place for its master until the day that he came back to it again.

145

And even as Frytha looked, she thought that she could make out the faintest wraith of smoke rising from its midst, like the ghost of the thick blue house-reek that must have risen there when the master was at home.

Then Bjorn came into view round the gable end, and stood looking away down the glen toward the distant lowlands of Eskdale, and she knew that the master was at home. Odd, that she had not realized until that moment that it was Bjornsthwaite down there.

Only a moment Bjorn stood there, and then he was gone again; and Frytha was moving forward. But suddenly, as she went down past the dry-stone wall of the sheepcote, following the beck, she was unsure. Until now, she had known only that it was the natural and inevitable thing that she should go with Bjorn. She had known it so strongly that there had been no room for any holding back. But now she wondered for the first time how it would seem to Bjorn himself. Would he be angry with her for following him? Would he be angry at her breaking in on him, in this one place of all the world? She did not know, she only knew that she must go with him; and she went on down toward the steading. But the uncertainty made her move very quietly, almost as though she were afraid of his hearing her, as she came through the run-wild apple-trees to the place where the house-stead door had been.

There were ferns growing in the chinks of the dry-stone walls, and inside, she saw fallen beams burrowed deep in docks and nettles and young foxgloves, and an elder sapling that had taken root on the turf of the fallen roof and was curded with milky blossom. But the nettles had been cleared back from the hearth-stone in the centre, and Bjorn squatted beside it, half turned from her, tending a small fire of birchbark.

She must not watch. Instinctively she knew that if she watched him now, in this place, while he thought he was alone, that was a thing that he would never quite forgive her for.

'Bjorn,' she said.

He was up and facing her in a flash, his hand already on his dagger. Then he checked, his hand falling away from the weapon, and stood regarding her with down-twitched brows.

'Frytha,' he said at last; and then, 'What do you here?'

'I—came after you.'

He studied her a moment longer, then glanced up at the sun, which was still high in the sky. 'Surely you must have borrowed the troll's rolling-breeks to have come so fast on my trail!' he said lightly.

'I was not far behind you from the first. I could not sleep, and I got up and went into the apple-garth, and the mazelin was there and he told me that he had seen you go.'

They stood looking at each other. Bjorn seemed different. It was partly the clothes, of course. They had ransacked the store kists last night to find him garments more suitable to a gleeman than his old dark wadmal; and now, under his own cloak, his kirtle was golden brown, long-sleeved as the Normans wore them, and banded with embroidery at the neck and round the upper arm, while his skin-fitting breeks were cross-gartered in violet blue. But it was not only the clothes, it was something in Bjorn himself; as though in setting out on his adventure, he had somehow grown up.

He was the first to break the silence. 'What if I say to you that this is my hunting, and bid you turn back from it?'

'I do not know,' Frytha said simply. 'But I also have the Norman tongue from the mazelin, and—we have always shared the hunting, you and I.'

Bjorn hesitated a moment, then turned back into the roof-less house-place, saying, 'Since you are here, come in-by to the hearth, at least. The rest can wait a while.'

It was not until they were squatting on opposite sides of the little birch-fire that either spoke again, and then Frytha said: 'Is it safe to kindle a fire so near to the Normans' hunting runs?'

'They do not come so far into the fells, and if they did, what harm in a stray harper kindling a fire where he pleases?' Bjorn said, leaning forward to feed the flames with a sprig of heather. 'And it is my own hearth.'

'I know. Have you ever been here before?'

He shook his head, reaching for the leather wallet that lay beside him. 'Never, but seeing that I must pass so near, I was minded to turn aside, to warm the hearth again and break bannock in my father's house.'

Frytha watched him as he opened the wallet and brought out one of the round flat loaves; then reached for her own bundle. 'I have brought bannock of my own,' she said quickly.

Bjorn brought out a long leathery strip of smoked deer-meat. 'You think of everything,' he said; 'but dry bannock makes dull eating. This will serve to sweeten it,' and drew his dagger to divide it in half. And she saw that it was not his dirk but a small Norman falchion with a cut silver hilt.

He looked up and caught her gaze upon it as he gave her share of the meat across to her. 'I left my dirk with Haethcyn, as hostage for the Sweet-singer. It was an unlikely weapon for a glee-man to carry.'

They ate together, almost in silence, both very aware of the ruined walls and fallen beams around them that had been a living homestead; of other fires that had burned on the hearth-stone, and other men and women who had sat beside them, way back to the first Bjorn, and the half-unwilling woman out of Wales, beside the first fire of all. Very aware, both of them, of the quiet backwater moment that they would remember afterward in small bright birch-flames and the scent from milky moons of elder blossom, before they set forward into the stress and the danger that lay ahead.

Somehow there had ceased to be any question of Frytha turning back. But when they had finished, Bjorn, cleansing his dagger by stabbing it into the turf, asked, 'Why did you come, Frytha?'

'Because I wanted to,' Frytha said quickly.

'And because?'

Through the faint wisp of smoke his gaze was mocking her, challenging her, and she knew that there was no escape. 'And because Ari Knudson did not go alone,' she said defiantly.

There was a long silence. A long, long silence, stretching between them, made up of the things that they had never been able to speak of, since that far-off day at the sheep-shearing. For a moment, Frytha thought that it was going to break, and she was half glad and half frightened.

Then Bjorn said, 'We have ten miles or more yet to do. If we push on now, we can have most of them behind us ere we find a sleeping-place; and come down into Rafnglas at early morning.'

Frytha got up instantly, leaving him to quench the little fire. In a short while he joined her, slipping the strap of the ancient harp-bag over his shoulder, and they stood together looking down the glen. 'A good place, it must have been,' Bjorn said, 'with the barley white in the beck fields, and sheep on the fell pasture, in the days when the Jarl sat in his high hall down yonder in Eskdale.'

'If the Normans had never come, it would have been like that still,' Frytha said. 'Maybe you would have been standing here now, with a hawk on your fist, setting out to join the Jarl in his hunting—or maybe you would have this moment come up from the beck fields, and turned here in the doorway to look back over the work.'

'And you?'

Frytha laughed. 'I should have been somewhere south of Lancaster, and doubtless safely wedded to some burly thane whose manor boundaries marched with my father's. . . . How strange it would be, to live that kind of life.'

Bjorn was silent; his pale bright gaze seemed to have gone out beyond the green flatness of Eskdale into some unknown future. 'One day, not far distant now, all this will be over, one way or the other,' he said at last. 'Frytha—have you ever thought that if this great battle that is brewing up is indeed the end of the fighting between us and the Norman kind; and if there is—an after-time for us, at all—it will be the end of the only life we know?'

'I have thought, yes, and been afraid,' Frytha said. 'But I suppose the new one will be an adventure, too, in its way.'

## XIII

## THE WEB OF WYRD

IT WAS STILL very early next morning when Bjorn and
Frytha came down the last slopes of Mulecaster Fell,
under the very walls of William Le Meschin's stone-built
castle, and headed for the town that they could see ahead of
them, on the banks of the estuary where three great Lake
Land rivers came to the sea. Shallows and mud banks gleamed
silverly in the morning light, sheep and cattle grazed on the
low coast-wise meadows, and between the two huddled the
thatched roofs of Rafnglas that had been first a Viking winter
camp, and then a settlement of Northmen grown more peace-
able, before ever the Normans came.

It was market day, and they joined the trickle of men and
beasts that was already passing in through the East gateway
in the turf wall. Frytha had never seen a town before, and the
smells and bustle and uproar within the gates seemed to break
over her in a wave. The narrow streets were full of frightened

sheep and cattle and barking dogs, as well as the men and women and children thronging up and down. They were engulfed in a shifting, many-headed, many-voiced crowd, shouting, bleating, bellowing, jostling and pushing, and when Bjorn drew her aside into a low doorway out of the main stream, she felt very much as if she had been rescued from drowning.

She laughed breathlessly. 'If this be a town, I like better the wild places.'

Bjorn nodded. 'Bide here a while, and we shall grow a little used to it.'

And so for a while they stood together in the low doorway, watching the people jostle by. A very brightly coloured crowd they seemed to Frytha, used to the dark greys and browns of the undyed wadmal the Jarl's folk mostly wore. She had thought Bjorn bright as a jay in his golden-brown kirtle and the violet gartering of his hose, but beside the blues and greens and crimsons that flickered through this crowd he seemed quite sombre; almost as drab as the poor folk she saw here and there in earth-stained clothes with wisps of straw round their ankles, who she supposed must be settlers brought in from the south to farm the land for their Norman masters. There were women with market baskets on their arms, friars with their beads swinging from their girdles, craftsmen with the tools of their trade; and everywhere, men-at-arms in greasy leather and cuir-bouilli and brown or burnished mail, so that one could not forget that this was a town on the fringe of fighting, caught up like all Cumberland in the preparations for battle. A vendor of little rich pies went by, crying his wares; a knight on a tall roan horse, his head almost on a level with the upper windows of the houses, forcing his way through the crowd heedless of who he thrust into the reeking kennel; a boy in hot pursuit of a squawking escaped hen; a leper with his bell and his desolate cry 'Unclean! unclean!' for whom the folk scrambled to make way even more readily than for the knight. A lady passed, with a servant and a little gaze-hound at her heels, her skirts gathered high out of the dirt, and her

thick braids round her head as the Norse women wore them
sometimes for coolness in summer weather, or to be out of the
way when they were churning. Not that *that* one was like to
do much churning, Frytha thought; and she watched her until
she was lost to sight in the crowd, and then turned back eagerly
to Bjorn.

'Bjorn, did you see?'

'Did I see what?' Bjorn was watching the gulls wheeling
above the roof-tops.

'She had amber drops in her ears—like long drops of
honey!'

'Why shouldn't she, then?'

Frytha, feeling snubbed, said, 'I only thought—it must be
fine to have amber drops to hang in one's ears.'

He looked down at her, his light eyes flickering with
laughter. 'They would go but ill with your present guise.'
Then, as she remained silent, he said in surprise: 'Truly? Is
it that you would truly care for such a fairing?'

Watching the coloured crowds of Rafnglas on market day
go by, Frytha had all at once a disgraceful aching in her
throat, a longing for the soft and pretty things of life that she
had never even thought about before. 'Yes,' she said wonderingly. 'I have never had a thing just because it was beautiful
in all my life; such things do not come our way in the Dale,
and I have never thought of it. And now suddenly, when
there are things so much more important to think about, I
want amber drops to hang in my ears.'

Bjorn looked at her for a moment, with the mockery all
gone from him. 'If ever I grow rich, Fryth, you shall have your
amber drops to hang in your ears,' he said at last quite gravely.
Then he put a hand to the strap of the harp-bag over his
shoulder. 'We must be striking out again, lest we lose our
chance by standing here.'

He plunged out into the stream once more, and Frytha,
squaring her shoulders, plunged out after him. 'Where are we
going?' she asked breathlessly, as the crowd took them again.

'Down to the waterside first.' He tossed the words over his

shoulder. 'Waterside taverns are always good hunting grounds for a harper—and for making the right friends.'

There was no need to ask the way; they simply chose a street that led westward and followed it, until the smell of the market-place fell faint behind them, and they caught in its stead the river smell and the whiff of tar that was like the smell of the boat-strand below the Jarlstead. And as they turned a corner, there between the crowding house walls was the silvery sweep of the estuary.

The wynd petered out into a huddle of boat-sheds and rope-walks above a shingly landing-beach. The tide was out, and the silvery sand-banks were alive with curlew and dunlin feeding on the ebb. And a long transport lay like a stranded sea-monster just above high-water mark, at sight of which Bjorn checked an instant, saying softly over his shoulder to Frytha, 'Maybe there lies our way into the Norman camp, if we can but win aboard her!'

The vessel had been beached on the high tide, and lay heeled slightly over, showing a gaping square of darkness below the water-line, through which horses were being urged on board. There were men-at-arms everywhere, seamen and onlookers from the town and the rag-tag that always moved with an army. The landing-beach was black with them, loud with curses and laughter, shouted orders and much advice, and over all, the wheeling, crying cloud of gulls.

Bjorn strolled down into the midst of the hubbub, with Frytha at his shoulder, and presently they were close beside the transport, watching the sweating men-at-arms as, goaded by much advice from the onlookers, they struggled to get the scared horses up the ramp and into the darkness of the horse-hold. Bjorn had seen ships before, on his trips to the coast, but they had been of another kind than this; light, fine-lined craft little changed from the Viking long-ships, and his eye ran over the transport, finding her impressive as a cow-whale, but clumsy. He turned to a small wiry seaman beside him, and speaking in the Norman tongue (they had decided to do that as much as might be, and explain their shortcomings by claiming to be in the first place from the Norse colony in Pembrokeshire), asked, 'Are the horses for Workington?'

'Where else should they be for?' said the little seaman.

'Nay, I do not know; but it seems to me an odd thing to send horses by sea up to Workington from this place. One was telling me only a day or so since, that Le Meschin holds all the tracks along the coast, and surely it would be a simpler matter to send them by land?'

'Aye, but 'tis quicker by sea, in the long run,' explained the seaman, with acid patience. 'And seeing that the transport was lying idle for the while, them as orders these things thought to send up a load of horses in her, if you've no objection.'

Bjorn nodded. 'Have patience with me. I am a harper and no seafaring man. It seems that these men-at-arms are in a great hurry.'

'And well they may be.' The little seaman spat. 'When the last of those brutes is safe aboard, we shall have to get the door closed and made water-tight, *and* give the sealing time to set afore the tide lifts her off.'

'Sailing on the next tide?'

'Aye.'

'I wonder now, if there might be a chance of sailing with her,' Bjorn said thoughtfully.

'What should you want with Workington?'

'With Workington nothing; but I've a mind to follow up this company. A war camp is ever a rich hunting ground for a harper.'

'Never a hope,' said the small seaman. 'She'll be sailing as full as she can carry, as 'tis.'

'I—wonder,' Bjorn said; and then in sudden concern, 'What in Hel's name does the fool think he's doing? He'll never get him aboard, jabbing at his head like that; can't he see the poor brute is terrified?'

The black stallion who three men-at-arms were at that moment struggling to get on board was certainly badly scared, his ears laid back and his eyes rolling. He did not like the ramp, and he did not like the dark hole at the head of it.

Maybe he had made a sea voyage before, and knew the horror of the horsehold, or maybe the opening in the ship's side looked like a trap; and the jabbing of the men at his head was doing nothing to quieten his fears. Almost as Bjorn spoke, he squealed shrilly, and went up in a rearing half turn, breaking from the men who held him, and came clattering and slithering down the ramp, shaking his head.

Bjorn slipped free the strap of Haethcyn's Sweet-singer, and thrusting it upon Frytha, stepped forward into the path of the scared and angry animal. There was a moment of trampling confusion, and then he had caught the stallion's head-gear and brought him to a standstill, while the men-at-arms, seeming only too thankful for somebody else to take charge of the black devil, stood back to give him room.

Bjorn was drawing his hand again and again down the black nose, soothing him with voice and touch. 'Softly, softly, brother; no need for such a squealing and trampling.' Then, slowly, began to turn him back toward the transport.

The stallion started and began to tremble again as he caught sight of the dark hole, but Bjorn's hand was on his neck and his voice quiet and encouraging. Frytha saw a laid-back ear flick responsively and swivel round to catch the reassuring voice. 'See, there is nothing to fear; easy now, easy, black brother.' Bjorn was edging him slowly up the ramp, letting him take his time, letting him stop to snuff at the edge of the hole when they reached it. The men-at-arms standing in the opening made as though to catch the halter and drag him in, but Bjorn said quickly, 'Leave him alone, man; would you have all to do again?'

He and the black stallion disappeared together into the interior of the transport, and Frytha felt all at once very much alone. Two more horses followed, with a loud clatter and scramble of hooves on the makeshift ramp, but without giving much trouble; and then Bjorn reappeared and sprang down to rejoin her, his hand already out to take back the precious harp.

'Got him roped safely?' said a voice at Frytha's shoulder,

and she swung round to see a man who, unnoticed by her, had checked in walking past to watch what was going on. A thick-set, oldish man, clad in fine lizard mail, with a great sword at his side; clearly a man in authority.

'Quite safely,' Bjorn said after a moment, settling the strap of the harp-bag.

'You have a way with horses,' said the knight. 'Have you as fine a way with a harp?'

'It would ill become me to say so,' said Bjorn, smiling. 'I've a mind to put the matter to the test in your great camp up north, Sir Knight. Therefore my interest in this ship that they tell me sails for Workington on the next tide.'

'The coast-tracks lead north at any tide,' said the knight, with a glint of humour.

'Aye, but I am weary of walking; I am but just come up across the Duddon Sands, and if I cannot travel north by another means than my own feet, I'll not go north at all,' said Bjorn, with cool effrontery.

The man studied his face reflectively. 'A gleeman in a war camp is a luxury that we can do without,' he said at last. 'But a man that has your knack with a frightened horse is surely worth his room in a horse transport.'

'Erik, my boy here, has a knack with horses, also,' Bjorn said.

The knight looked at Frytha. 'Not so fast. Can you juggle, or dance on your head, boy?'

'No,' said Frytha blithely. 'I am naught but my master's squire.'

The small dark eyes began to twinkle behind the nazal of the knight's helmet.

'I never knew that harpers also had squires to follow them.'

Bjorn laughed. 'Nay, Sir Knight; King David had an armour-bearer, and he was a harper, if I mistake not; and surely what is good enough for King David is good enough for me.'

The knight laughed outright. 'So be it; bring your armour-bearer, oh most modest of harpers. If the ship-master raise

difficulties, tell him Roger de Lacey gave you leave. And when
we reach camp, you shall give proof of your skill in the harper's
art.' He nodded brusquely, and tramped off, his mail ringing.

'Sa ha, that is safely accomplished, and we shall come to
our camp in fine company,' Bjorn murmured, his head close
to Frytha's, as he pretended to tighten the buckle at his
shoulder. 'But I care not for this Norman trick of using horses
in battle.'

The horses were all on board now, and soon the heavy
timber shutter was wedged in place over the hole, and the
seams caulked and pitched to make them water-tight. And
when the tide rose, the seamen and men-at-arms, with Bjorn
and Frytha in their midst, set their shoulders to the vessel's sides,
and shouting and cheering urged her down the last few feet,
splashing into the shallows, until the water took her and the
rollers under her keel could be drawn clear.

And when she went wallowing out on the evening tide, with
her poppy-striped sails curving to the light wind, and her
cargo of men-at-arms on deck and war-horses in the hold,
Bjorn and Frytha crouched side by side in the lee of the weather
bulwark.

.     .     .     .     .     .

The tongue of land between Derwent and Cocur had been
overgrown with scrub and coppice when first the army advanced from Papcastle. It had all been cleared now, and the
hazel and hawthorn and birch had provided the sharpened
stakes for the camp stockades and brushwood for the cooking-
fires. But one great tree still stood defiant, lifting bare arms to
the sky, a lightning-blasted ash, outrunner of the vast forest
that swept like a dark fleece over most of northern England,
left there because being dead it could give little cover to an
enemy, and being iron hard it was too much trouble to cut it
down.

The hummocky turf around its huge silver bole had become a
favourite meeting-place for men-at-arms in their leisure hours.
They built fires between its spreading roots, and gathered there
to amuse themselves as best pleased them, to dice or sleep or

quarrel, to pit their fighting cocks against each other, or listen to the gleeman who had come in along with a draft of horses from Workington three days since. There were several groups scattered round about this evening, sprawling round the small fires that they had built there. The evening meal was over and done with, the horses in the picket lines had been watered and fed, the guard had been changed—they mounted strong guards, here on the fringe of the Viking country—and it was time to take one's ease, to stretch and relax, and perhaps for a little while loosen the lacings of one's hauberk. But already the tension that rose every evening with the faint mists at sunset had begun to creep through the camp, so that men hitched at their sword-belts, and laughed much, but checked often in the midst of their laughter, to listen.

Close in among the roots of the ash-tree, one such knot of men-at-arms were playing knuckle-bones, almost at the feet of the gleeman who stood leaning against the silvery ash-trunk, tuning his harp, and watching the fall of the bones with an abstracted eye, while the boy who had come with him squatted at his side, burnishing the blade of a dirk.

They had been accepted without question, Frytha and Bjorn, for what they claimed to be, and the camp had seemed glad of their coming. Gilbert, Ranulf Le Meschin's Norman minstrel, kept all his skill for the knighthood and nobility, and was above singing for mere archers and men-at-arms; and even a gleeman with Saxon sagas and a few guard-room ditties in his store was much better than nothing at all. So they had come and gone freely about the camp, all these three days, seeing and hearing whatever there was to be seen and heard.

Frytha, her hands busy and all her mind seemingly on her work, was telling over the list to herself now. They knew how many thousand the Normans numbered in archers and men-at-arms, foot and mounted, knights and squires, and under whose banners and gonfalons they mustered. They knew the expected size of the band—the last band of all—that was due to come in in a few days' time under the banner of Ingram de Caen. They knew how the army stood for weapons and supplies, and that when it advanced, William would be remaining behind to keep the supply lines open. They knew that there was sickness among the horses, but that the men were in high heart; in higher heart, Frytha thought, than they could ever have been before. There was a feeling of confidence running through the camp, as though for the first time they felt that their leaders knew what they were about. It was a mood that was deadly dangerous to the men waiting under their raven banners among the fells.

Well, at least they would be forewarned. Only a few hours now, and they would have every detail of the odds against them; every detail save the actual timing of the Norman advance. No good waiting for that, because by the time it was settled, it would be too late, in all likelihood, to get word of it back to the Jarl. No, they must get out tonight, as they had planned, she and Bjorn, far enough ahead of the Normans for the tidings they carried to be of use to their own people. Somehow, they must get out tonight; the nearest of the War bands were close by among the woods and the fell fringes, she knew, though there had been no attack on the camp in the past three days; and once clear of the Norman defences, they could be with their own kind in three flights of an arrow.

But all at once it came to her quite clearly that they would not win free so simply as that. It was as though her heart knew what her head could not: that the matter of Bjorn's Firedrake could not be so lightly settled. Some pattern of Wyrd's weaving, whose beginning went far back beyond that ancient quarrel with Erland over the sword song, beyond Ari Knudson's death, to a curlew's mating flight on the high shoulder of Beacon Fell, would be left unfinished if they slipped out safely tonight between sentry and sentry in the dark.

She tried to shake off the sense of fate, telling herself that it was only because the time for getting free was so very near, but it clung about her, not a foreboding of evil, just the feeling of a pattern—closing in.

And then, across the evening sounds of the camp, she caught the nearing beat of a horse's hooves. Somebody riding hard.

Here and there among the groups around the ash-tree men broke off what they were doing, to turn and listen, but riders who came and went at speed were not strange in a war camp, and after a few moments they turned back to their pastimes.

Presently the nearest group showed signs of breaking up. One of the men-at-arms gathered up the knuckle-bones, tossing them into the air and catching them again, before he rattled them into his pouch.

'If I spend many more evenings casting the bones with you, Rafe lad, I shall have not a feather left to fly with!' he said cheerfully.

'Nay, man, your luck will change tomorrow of a surety,' said a tall young archer in a worn buff jerkin; and yawned until his head seemed to split wide open from ear to ear. 'Or the morrow after—or the morrow after that.'

'Plague take you, how many more morrows?' demanded a third. 'Twenty year I've been fighting this war, and there grows to be a sameness about it that eats into a man's bones!'

'Reckon we shall be on the move soon enough when de Caen comes in with his fellows,' said the first man. 'So make the most of the easy days while they last, say I, for I warrant they'll not last long.'

Even as he spoke, the jink of harness sounded close by, and the dull-edged clop of hooves on beaten turf; and out of the misty shadows that were beginning to gather, there loomed the figure of a man-at-arms leading a horse that was clearly spent with hard riding.

Someone on the fringe of the crowd called out to him, to know who the rider was, and what news he brought, and the man called back over his shoulder, as he plodded on toward the horselines, 'It's one of de Caen's men come on ahead. The rest will be in tomorrow.'

'*What?*' Several of the men-at-arms were afoot on the instant, and thronging round him. 'Are you sure? But they weren't looked for for three days yet. You've got it wrong, Hob!'

'A fool I may be, but I aren't all that of a fool. Ha'nt any

160

of you ever heard of forced marching?' said Hob disagreeably. 'Let be, lads; I've got to get this brute rubbed down, unless any of you cock-brained lot mean to do it for me.'

A burst of voices closed in over his words, and out of them, one voice was thrown up clear. 'Then there's one thing plain enough, lads: we'll be out of here the morn's morn, or I'm a Jew!'

Frytha stole a swift glance at Bjorn. The great bole of the ash-tree was taking on a moony, white-owl pallor in the dusk and the firelight, and the sky through the dipping branches was water green; and against sky and branches, Bjorn's bent head and his hands and the slender curves of the harp he held were little more than shapes cut out of tawny shadows. He was still tuning the Sweet-singer, plucking softly at one string after another, so softly that the notes were shadowy too. She could not see the look on his face, but she saw his right hand move quickly, and heard the tiny flight of notes that were nothing to do with tuning—notes that were like a small triumphant exclamation, a snap of the fingers, and she knew that Bjorn also had heard.

And then another figure loomed into the firelight, and she saw that it was one of the young squires.

He caught sight of Bjorn against the ash-bole, and came toward him, picking his way between tree-roots and men-at-arms. 'Brought to bay!' he said, laughing. 'I thought I should find you hereabout. My Lord bids you come and prove your skill up yonder, according to your bargain.' He jerked his head in the direction of the group of tents at the centre of the camp, rising darkly above the mist that was beginning to creep along the ground.

Bjorn, still leaning against the ash-bole, slowly lifted his gaze. 'Your Lord? You are Roger de Lacey's squire, if I mistake not?'

'Yes. Are you coming? My Lord likes not to be kept waiting.'

'Few of us do, but sometimes it is good for us to learn,' murmured Bjorn, listening to the pitch of his treble string. 'Yet

I will come in but one moment. . . .' He tossed the little white-bronze key to Frytha, and pushed off from the ash-trunk. 'I will come even now.'

Frytha sheathed her dirk, dropped the tuning-key into the harp-bag, and rose without a word to follow him. But suddenly there had come swooping back on her again, more strongly than before, that feeling of being caught and meshed in some pattern of Wyrd's Weaving; and the pattern—closing in.

## XIV

## THE FIRE-DRAKE

THE SQUIRE LED them not to the great pavilion, but to a smaller one set a little apart, which was for Ranulf Le Meschin's own especial use. The entrance was looped back, and a stain of light flowed out into the misty dusk to meet them, together with the greasy smell of food, and the faint sweetness of burning apple logs. And as Frytha checked an instant on the threshold, the scene within seemed to flash upon her, so that ever after she remembered every crowding detail.

Supper was over, and the trestle-boards had been carried away, but the few assembled knights still held their wine-cups on their knees, and their squires moved to and fro among them, carrying the wine-flasks, while camp curs foraged under the benches for the bones and gristle of the meal. Two more squires stood bored but patient against the canvas walls, holding torches, and by the mingled light of torch and fire,

Frytha saw the faces of men gathered there. Faces of old knights, who had helped to break the Saxon shield-wall at Hastings, and of young squires who had not yet blooded their swords; one or two of the faces were Saxon, for under King Henry the old division was growing blurred in the south. Faces of churchmen, too—there were many churchmen about the camp. All else seemed lost in shifting shadows, save where, here and there, the smoky light jinked on well-worn ring mail, or struck answering fire from the jewel in a dagger-hilt or the eyes of a hound crouching among the rushes.

And now she was walking forward at Bjorn's heels, into the midst of the scene.

'I have brought the gleeman, sir,' the squire was saying.

Roger de Lacey turned from his neighbour, quirking a thick eyebrow. 'Ah, thank you, Hugh.' Then to the man who sat in the high place, 'This is the harper of whom I spoke, Le Meschin.'

Frytha also looked at the man in the high place. He was clad in his hauberk, like all the rest, for in this camp men lived and slept in their mail with their swords belted on; but also like the rest, he had laid aside his helmet and loosed the mail coif under it, so that it fell on to his shoulders, and his face, which until now she had only seen rimmed with mail and barred by the nazal of his helmet, was bare to the torchlight. It was a tired face, pouchy under the worried blue eyes, scored with deep lines from the big nose to the corners of the weak mouth; the face of one living on a knife-edge and not liking it. Looking at him, this man who had spent half a lifetime in arms against her people, Frytha felt an odd stirring of pity. He was making a last throw of the dice that would redeem thirty wasted years or break him utterly, and he was not strong enough to live with the knowledge that it was so.

He nodded briefly at de Lacey's words, and stared at Bjorn, who stared levelly back.

'You have a way with horses, so Sir Roger here says,' he said at last. 'Show us now your way with a harp.'

'Very willingly,' Bjorn began, 'though I fear——'

But the other cut in testily, 'Fear! What do you fear? That my minstrel will grow jealous and lay you flat?'

Bjorn glanced toward the willowy young man who had risen from a stool nearby, and stood nursing a very beautiful little gilded harp and looking on with the expression of a sulking bairn. 'I do not think that he could,' Bjorn said, his lip twitching. 'Nay, My Lord of Carlisle, I do but fear that my stock of Norman minstrelsy is small. I was bred in Haverford, ar from the Norman kind, and trained by a song-smith of the old school; I can sing you the camp ditties that you may hear as well from any of your men-at-arms, but if you would have the High Music, minstrelsy that is worthy of the name, then it must be the minstrelsy of my world, not yours.'

Ranulf shrugged, and glanced about him. 'Nay, it is nothing to me. How say you, de Warrenne? My Lord Bishop?—How say you, William?'

'By all means,' said the little stout man with a scar under one eye, who sat beside him; and gave a soft chuckle. 'There is a certain—zest, in the choice of a Northman's saga for the evening's entertainment, and beside, it will annoy Gilbert, and it is always pleasant to annoy Gilbert.'

Sir Roger turned to Bjorn. 'Is your skill up to the song of Beowulf?'

'What part will you have?' Bjorn was already fingering his harp. 'There will scarce be time for the whole—if you would indeed be marching south the morn's morn.'

There was a burst of startled laughter, and men glanced at each other, as Le Meschin leaned forward, fists clenched on knees, demanding, 'Who told you that?'

'No man in particular,' Bjorn said coolly. 'It is all over the camp. Is it a false tale, then?'

There was an instant's silence, and then Le Meschin said harshly. 'Never trouble whether the tale be true or false. Choose your song, and sing.'

Bjorn bowed, and turned toward the low stool from which the minstrel Gilbert had lately risen. As he did so, Frytha close beside him, felt him stiffen. Her gaze flew to his face, and she saw his eyes widen on something, or someone—beyond her. Almost in the same instant, he had recovered himself, and with a foot on the low stool, was settling the Sweetsinger on his knee and into the curve of his shoulder. But Frytha, snatching a casual-seeming glance in the same direction, had seen sitting near the entrance a young knight, redeyed and dusty from hard riding, whose shield, propped against the bench beside him, showed the waspish glint of three golden flames on a black field. Black and gold, wasp colours, danger colours, all the world over, and as she settled herself in the rushes, her heart was thudding wildly. Bjorn had been only a boy when he brought back that other black shield with its three golden flames, that hung among the trophies in the Jarl's Hearth Hall; only a beardless boy, she told herself, and why should its owner know him again?

But something, deep within her, knew.

Bjorn had begun to draw his hand across the harp-strings. The single notes seemed to leap free and rise, fierce and shining like the sparks that rose from the spluttering torches, and under the wakening power of the harp-music, the whole company grew hushed to listen. Frytha dared not look again toward the knight by the entrance, lest she should draw his attention. She looked at a bishop with a long clerk's face; she looked at a young knight who sat elbows on knees, frowning into space, and an old knight with hooded eyes, who smiled into his wine-cup as though all life were rather a wry jest; she looked at the little stout man beside Le Meschin, who was his brother William; she watched a cur-dog scratching for fleas beside the fire.

Bjorn had begun to weave the notes together, into an intricate, shining braid of sound that was somehow kin to the sword-song that he had made in the Jarl's hall seven years ago. He was giving tongue now, half singing, half declaiming, chanting the fight at Finnsburg; weaving and interweaving verse and harpsong into the old epic word-patterning of his people.

The spell of it caught even Frytha from her sharp sense of

danger, or perhaps it was her sense of danger keying everything in her to a higher pitch that in some strange way made her more aware of this harping than she had ever been before.

Then it was over. Bjorn swept his hand across the harpstrings, and let it sink to his side. There was a moment's silence, while the last flight of notes thrummed away into the stillness. And then a ragged burst of applause. Bjorn stood quietly in its midst, until it too had died away; then, with a faint smile lifting the corners of his mouth, he turned to de Lacey, and challenged softly, 'Well?'

'Passing well,' said de Lacey, and he glanced about him. 'For myself, I have heard harping this night. How say you, my brothers?'

'For myself, I find such minstrelsy harsh,' said Le Meschin. 'None the less, it was good and fiery of its kind,' and delving into the pouch at his belt, he brought out a silver coin, and tossed it to Bjorn's feet.

Bjorn left it lying there. 'I did not come for My Lord of Carlisle's silver,' he said. 'I came because Sir Roger de Lacey bade me according to the bargain that was between him and me, to give proof of my skill with a harp.'

Le Meschin flushed, but said nothing. It was the minstrel Gilbert who broke the little silence. He had been angry that a strange gleeman should be given his place, even for so short a while, and now he was jealous, because in his heart he knew that, skilled musician though he was, he could not wake the fire that had woken under the gleeman's touch, and the knowledge hurt him. To ease the hurt, he must instantly make Bjorn seem less in all men's eyes, above all, in his—Gilbert's—own. So, laying down his own harp, he strolled out of his corner, rather unsteadily, for he was a little drunk, and set a hand on Bjorn's shoulder, saying with an air of kindly condescension that was an insult in itself, 'None so bad, none so bad at all, for a raw lad out of the wilderness. With teaching and much practice, you might make a passable minstrel, one day.'

'You do but seek to be kind,' Bjorn said.

The other missed the mockery in his tone. 'Nay, I speak as

I find. But mind you, nought comes without hard work; and you are but a homespun harper, very far from a minstrel as yet. . . . That seems a good harp you have—see now, I will show you what may be done with it by a skilled hand.'

He made to take the Sweet-singer, but with a quick 'By your leave, friend,' Bjorn side-stepped, so that Gilbert's hand slipped from his shoulder and he swayed and teetered before regaining his balance.

'Nay, I but seek to take the harp a moment.'

'I have not asked to touch that pretty gilded toy you laid down just now,' Bjorn said.

The other's eyes narrowed. 'So I am not good enough to touch this precious harp of yours, eh?' he demanded thickly.

'I did not say so,' Bjorn said.

But the very quietness of his tone seemed to enrage the minstrel. He made a sound like an angry cat, and next instant there was a dagger in his hand. Frytha cried a warning: and Bjorn flung up his free hand and caught the man's wrist. 'Don't be a fool,' he cried. 'The drink is in your head. Go you and sleep it off!'

But the other only struggled the harder to free his dagger hand for a stroke.

The thing had burst up with nightmare swiftness, before anyone was well aware what was happening, and almost in the same instant, Frytha, on her feet now, heard a sharp exclamation behind her, and snatching a glance over her shoulder as the sudden tumult rose, saw the knight of the black-and-gold shield leap up from the bench on which he had been sitting, his arm outstretched to point.

'My Lord! My Lord of Carlisle—if I mistake not, this gleeman of Sir Roger's is a spy of the Northmen!'

His cry, cutting across the uproar, sobered Gilbert. He loosed his hold on the dagger, and as Bjorn at the same moment released his wrist and swung round to face his accuser, the little weapon dropped into the rushes.

Ranulf in his high seat demanded, 'What is this that you say, Sir Fulke?'

'He is a spy of the Northmen,' repeated the knight. 'I have seen him before.' He made a sign to the two squires who stood nearest to Bjorn, and instantly they were upon him, pinioning his arms, while one whipped the dagger from his belt. He made no attempt to resist, but stood disarmed between them with the Sweet-singer lying at his feet, and gazed frowning a little as though in utter bewilderment at the knight of the black-and-gold shield, who had come striding forward to stare into his face.

Then he laughed, angrily. 'If this be a jest, Sir Knight, it is a sorry one, to my mind.'

'Nay, it is no jest,' said the knight. He kicked aside the fallen dagger and spoke over his shoulder to the crowding squires. 'Lay hold of the stripling.'

Frytha, her dirk drawn, was springing to Bjorn's side, even as he spoke, but a burly squire struck it from her hand, and she was caught and borne backward. She turned on Le Meschin's body-squire, who held her, fighting like a cornered vixen to break free; she saw the blue joy of battle in his eyes, and she tore one arm clear and with a furious cry, clawed his young round face, leaving four bleeding stripes on his cheek in the wake of her nails. He let out a yelp, and the light of battle turned to cold rage in his eyes. He grabbed her wrist and wrenched it down, almost breaking it. 'What a cursed woman's trick!' and then with a shout of discovery, 'Saints in Heaven! This one's a wench!'

She was aware of Bjorn wrenching half-free and knocking someone down, and the sudden uproar as a bench went over and a dog ran howling into the night. And then his arms had been twisted behind him again, and the knight Sir Fulke was saying without much interest, 'So? Stripling or wench, hold it for me until I need it, Tristram.' The uproar of a moment ago had dropped to utter stillness, as he continued to study Bjorn's face. 'Odd, that I should not have known you before,' he said at last.

Bjorn said levelly, 'I do not know what you mean. I have never seen you before. Since it seems you give orders to My

Lord of Carlisle's squire, bid him to let my kinswoman alone.'

Sir Fulke ignored both statement and demand. 'There is the beard, of course,' he said thoughtfully. 'You were only a boy when we last met.'

Ranulf Le Meschin crashed a fist on the bench beside him. 'What in Our Lady's name lies behind all this, Sir Fulke? Am I to sit here with riddles buzzing like wasps around my ears all night?'

Sir Fulke turned to him slowly. 'I crave your pardon, My Lord: the matter is simple enough. Six years ago, when we were encamped upon the Rafnglas road, and these mountain wolves harried us day and night, this—gleeman and I, both separated from our own kind, came upon each other in a certain dawn, and did each our best to kill the other. We fought breast to breast, his left hand gripping my dagger wrist; and the stone in the ring he wears caught the first sunlight and flashed green fire into my eyes. I did not know him again because he was a boy then, even as I said, and because my memory of him was asleep: but when that ring caught the torchlight but now, and he wrenching at Gilbert's dagger wrist as once he did at mine, my memory awoke, and I knew him.'

'You lie,' Bjorn said softly. 'I was in the South country six years ago. '

Ranulf's face had darkened as he listened, and the pouches under his eyes seemed to fill with angry blood. 'If you are right, Sir Fulke,' he said, 'by Our Lady, if you are right, he shall weep that he was ever born !'

'But are you right? That is the question,' de Lacey put in quietly. 'You could not be mistaken, Sir Fulke?'

'When once you have fought for your life with a man, breast to breast, you are little likely to be mistaken!' said Bjorn's accuser. 'But we can put the matter to a further test very simply—if it be as I suppose, the mark of my dagger is on his shoulder.'

Ranulf crashed up from his seat and came tramping to join them. 'Then in the Devil's name strip him and see!'

170

Sir Fulke himself twisted a hand in the neck of Bjorn's kirtle, and ripped it back from his shoulder with the sark beneath. The two torch-bearers had drawn closer, and heads were craned to look, those behind peering over the shoulders of those in front. The old wound had healed neat and cleanly under Storri Sitricson's leechcraft, but in the hollow of his shoulder the scar showed faint but unmistakable, a silvery seam on the brown skin. Frytha could not see what passed, for the heads in between, but she heard the hiss of breath, and the rising mutter, half angry, half excited; and the voice of Gilbert the minstrel, demanding, 'Did I not say he was no harper?' and breaking into high, unsteady laughter that seemed to go on—and on.

'It seems that you are in the right of it, Sir Fulke,' Ranulf said; and then savagely to Bjorn himself, 'So you thought to learn our secrets, did you? To ferret out our plans and carry them back with you to your mountain wolfpack?'

Bjorn said, 'Seems it not possible to you, My Lord of Carlisle, that in six years a man may change the pack he runs with?'

'There are men who may change it as many times as there are fingers on my two hands, and it may be that you are such a one; but I'll take no chances.' Ranulf's voice had sunk from its rather high pitch, to a tone of quiet and deadly purpose much more like that of his brother William. 'It is a fortunate coming, this of yours; for though you have doubtless learned our plans, you will not, I fear, be carrying them back to your rebel Earl; while we . . . it may be that there are matters we can learn from you, that shall stand us in good stead when we march south in the morn's morn.'

'I doubt it,' Bjorn said deliberately.

'Fire between the fingers has remarkable powers of persuasion,' Ranulf snapped; but it seemed that Bjorn's tone had flicked him on the raw, for his voice had shot up and grown ragged again.

'Bring the girl in closer so that she may have a better view,' suggested William Le Meschin, still lounging in his place, wine-cup in hand. The group swayed open, and Frytha was thrust through into the inner circle.

She could see Bjorn clearly now, and her first thought—an odd one for such a moment—was that she had never noticed before how tall he was. He had dropped all attempt to lie his way out of the mesh, and in doing so, seemed to have gained something that made him seem head and shoulders taller than the men around him.

She saw the humorous face of de Lacey, with all the humour gone from it; the minstrel Gilbert's, bright with malice; faces of churchmen and fighting men, and in none of them any mercy. But they had known, she and Bjorn, that there would be no mercy for them if they were caught. And somehow the faces did not greatly matter.

Ranulf had turned to one of the torch-bearing squires. 'Jehan, your torch here.'

Jehan stepped forward, and Bjorn looked once at the flaming brand he carried, and then turned his eyes away.

'Well, will you answer a few questions without more trouble?' Ranulf asked.

'No.' Bjorn spoke the word between shut teeth.

'You may regret that, in a while . . .' My Lord of Carlisle moved back a pace. 'Get to the work, then, Jehan.'

Bjorn's right arm was dragged out, and the squire Jehan brought the torch nearer. 'Hold it well below, so that he just catches the bite of it. Aye, that will serve to begin with,' Ranulf said: and then to Bjorn, 'How many fighting men has this Jarl of yours yet left to him?'

'I have not counted them.'

'How far into the fells is this hidden stronghold of which we have heard tales?'

No answer.

'So. A trifle closer, Jehan.'

Frytha had shut her eyes. She heard Bjorn catch his breath, and then the hateful voice again. 'Aye, that begins to bite, does it not. Answer my questions, if you would have Jehan take it away.'

There was a dead silence. The red torchlight seemed to beat like a drum on Frytha's closed lids.

'Closer, Jehan.'

Bjorn was gasping now, long shuddering gasps, with silence between, and there began to be a foul stink of burning flesh. Then came a shuffle and a low curse, as though one of the torturers had got scorched himself, and Le Meschin's voice again. 'Hold the flame steady, you fool.' Nothing else.

Standing helpless with her arms pinioned, Frytha fought down the clammy waves of sickness rising within her, and opened her eyes again.

How long it lasted, she never knew. It seemed to go on for a dark gulf of time that there was no measuring. The merciless, repeated questions, the searing torch-flame withdrawn a little, and brought close again, the long silences filled with the ghastly stench of burning, and again the questions—questions.

Bjorn was ashen grey to the lips, his face shining with sweat in the torchlight, and he drew his breath in long agonized gasps through flaring nostrils. But no other sound came from him.

And then quite suddenly he was drooping in the grip of his tormentors, so that but for their hold on him, he would have fallen.

Someone peered into his face, then gestured to Jehan to withdraw the torch. 'Give him a respite. You'll gain nothing if he goes out like a snuffed glim, with his mouth still shut.'

Ranulf cursed. 'Let be a while, then, and try the wench. Maybe that will loosen his tongue for him.'

Until that moment, Frytha had not thought of her own danger, because everything in her had been turned toward Bjorn; but now, as she was thrust forward into the centre of the group, the understanding broke over her in an icy wave. And then the wave ebbed, leaving her with an odd feeling of remoteness from all that was around her, from everything except Bjorn. Even then, it did not occur to her to wonder whether she herself would be able to endure and keep silent;

only that Bjorn must. And she cried out to him hoarsely, desperately, 'Bjorn—don't tell them anything.'

He raised his head, and looked at her, his eyes pale and bright in the torchlight. He had bitten his lower lip almost through, and a dark trickle of blood ran down from it into the darkness of his young beard, but there was a kind of shadowy triumph in his face. 'I was not going to,' he said.

And in a sudden flash of clear-seeing, Frytha knew with absolute certainty that whatever happened he would not speak, neither for his own sake, nor for hers.

Somebody drove the back of a hand across Bjorn's bleeding mouth; and Jehan looked inquiringly at Le Meschin, who nodded impatiently, hitching at his sword-belt. 'Get on with it, man.'

But even as he spoke, from somewhere in the misty darkness beyond the tent opening there rose a cry, cut off short— hideously short, almost before it was begun. And as the men about Frytha looked into each other's suddenly tensed faces, it was followed by a smother of voices and a rush of feet, and then the clear warning yelp of trumpets.

'The ravens are with us again,' said William Le Meschin composedly, rising to his feet and turning to take the nut-shaped helmet which his squire had caught up and was holding for him. All around Frytha was a swift buckling on of helmets and tightening of sword-belts, tramping footsteps and the ringing jar of mail, and quick cursing voices. All like a dream, everything like a dream, save Bjorn, suddenly straightening in his captive's grasp, as though the sound of the fighting were a draught of mead.

The hands gripping her were different now, and the squire Tristram was at his lord's side, helping him with helmet and shield. A bishop fell over a scavenging dog and cursed in most unbishoplike manner, and steadily, the noise outside grew louder, and more urgent.

'What are we to do with this pair of wild-fowl?' somebody was demanding.

'Truss them up and leave them,' Ranulf shouted over his

174

shoulder, already tramping toward the looped-back entrance. 'They'll keep safe enough until we have dealt with their friends.'

Frytha was flung down among the mailed feet of the last leavers. 'Here's a strap will serve for her ankles,' someone said: and someone was lashing her wrists behind her with a leather thong. The tent was emptying with bewildering swiftness, as squires caught up their weapons and ran out after their knights. Churchmen and minstrel were gone; torches were dashed out on the makeshift hearth-stone, and the dark came crowding in as the last man gave a final tug to the thong about Frytha's wrists, and springing to his feet, belted out after his fellows.

## XV

## THE SHIELD RING

IT HAD ALL happened so swiftly that Frytha seemed scarcely to have tensed herself to face the searing torch-flame, before she was lying bound in the deserted pavilion, listening to the thud of many running feet pounding away into the rising roar of the fighting.

It was very dark, for the night was warm and the fire had been allowed to sink low; and with the quenching of the torches, the outer world that had been deeply blue beyond the entrance, had faded to cobweb grey. Bjorn began to shift in the darkness to her right, gasping a little as he strained at his bonds. Neither of them spoke.

The roar of the fight seemed to ebb and flow, a formless smother of sound that threw up out of itself shouts and the sharp clash of weapons like the spray thrown up by rolling storm-water. It was torment to know that Gille and the War bands were out there, almost within a spear's throw, while they, with the gathered knowledge in them that might be life or death to their own kind, lay helpless, bound hand and foot here in the dark.

'Bjorn,' Frytha whispered, 'maybe they will break through,

176

Gille and the rest. Bjorn, do you not think they might break through?'

There was a little pause, and then Bjorn's voice came out of the dark, jerkily, like a man who has not yet quite got back his breath after being winded. 'They will—not be seeking to break through; not—right up here into the heart of the camp. Cost too many men. That is why we—must break out to them.'

'Break out?—Bjorn, how?'

Bjorn was already moving. Slowly and painfully, she heard him dragging himself over the rushes toward the hearth. 'There's still some life in the fire. If I can burn my wrists free—I can maybe untie yours and—then you can do the rest.'

'You'll never do it, Bjorn! Not with those embers!'

'Maybe not, but I've got to try. One of us at least has got— to get out—more than ever now that we know—how soon they march against us; and there's no other way.'

'Then let me try it!'

She heard him snatch his breath, and knew what the bonds must be doing to his right hand; but the movements went on unchecked. 'I'm nearer to the fire than you are, and I'm scorched already.'

With no thought but to get close to him, to help him some-how, she rolled over toward the sound, straining and wrench-ing at her own bonds, and her bound hands found something in the kicked-up rushes. Breath in check, she felt the cold sharpness of the thing, and let out a croak of triumph.

'Bjorn!—The dagger!'

'Dagger?' Bjorn said, and the rustle of his movements stopped abruptly.

'The minstrel's dagger that he dropped when it all started. Don't you remember? It must have got scuffled into the rushes and everybody forgot about it.' She was fumbling frantically as she spoke. 'I have it!'

Something between a sob and a laugh broke from Bjorn. 'Bide you where you are, then, lest you lose it again, and I'll come to you.'

177

The brushing sound began again, and in the gloom she could make out his dark shape, working like a wounded snake toward her. Then, close beside her, he spoke again. 'Roll over with your back to the fire, so that I can get what light there is to see by.'

She obeyed instantly, hearing him scuffle in the rushes behind her. There was a pause, and then he spoke again, soft and urgent. 'I shall have to hold it in my teeth, and I shall probably nick you, but there's no help for that. Pull your wrists apart as hard as you can.'

She felt his teeth against her fingers, and then the dagger was plucked away. Thankful that she had remembered to tighten the muscles of her wrists to make them as thick as possible, when they were bound, Fyrtha strained them apart until the thong bit like hot wires, and felt him set to work. Time seemed to crawl interminably, while every moment the minstrel, drunk though he was, might come back seeking his lost dagger. Again and again the blade stung like a hornet, but she barely noticed that in the agony of the slow crawling moments.

At last she felt something yield. 'Wait! I can break free now,' she whispered, jerking her wrists apart; and felt the bonds slacken and fall away. In an instant she was kneeling over Bjorn. 'Now you.'

He laid down the dagger, like a dog laying down a bone, and rolled on to his face. The glow of the dying fire was barely enough to show her where his hands were, and she had to feel for the tight-lashed cords with fingers that seemed made of wood. Almost sobbing in her haste, she sawed at them, feeling the strands part one by one, until with a little groaning catch of the breath he too jerked his hands apart, and rolled over. 'Ah! Now give me the dagger again.'

He had succeeded in freeing Frytha, and was hacking at the last strands about his own ankles, when her straining ears caught the sound that she had been dreading. Nearer and more menacing than the surf roar of the fighting; the pad of footsteps coming toward them.

Bjorn had stopped hacking at his bonds; there was an instant's frozen silence within the tent, and then his urgent whisper, 'Lie down as though you were still bound. Quick!'

He side-slipped away from her, and when the footsteps reached the entrance, he was lying where he had lain before, but with the dagger in his sound hand, hidden under his body.

Frytha saw a figure loom into the opening, swaying a little as it came inward. 'I mind me I've left a dagger hereabouts,' said the voice of Gilbert the minstrel; and there was a muffled crash as he stumbled against the overset bench and recovered himself swearing. 'Fiends and Furies! My poor shin! Ah, there you lie, nicely trussed, the pair of you, and I wouldn't be in your shoes, come the morning! Here's your harp—your precious harp that I wasn't good enough to touch. But the strings are torn out, and I don't want a harp anyway, I want my dagger.' He was scuffling about as he spoke. 'Should have brought a light,' he complained. 'Just about here I dropped it. You'd not be lying on it, would you? There's that ring, too, if no one else has got it already; might as well——'

He was bending over Bjorn. Frytha, lying rigid, could make out his dark crouching shadow in the gloom. She sensed rather than saw a swift movement that ended in a cracking sound, and the crouching shadow subsided with a surprised grunt.

Instantly she was up, half falling again as her cramped legs gave under her. 'Bjorn! Bjorn, are you all right?'

She heard a breath of a laugh in the darkness, as Bjorn crawled from under his fallen enemy. 'Neatly done, though I say it myself. Yes, I'm—well enough. Can you stand?'

'Give me a moment.' She got unsteadily to her feet, aware of Bjorn feeling about in the rushes. 'What is it? The dagger?'

'Safe in my belt. No, it is the Sweet-singer—strings or no. . . . Ah, here she is. Now we get out of here.'

As Frytha turned to the entrance, her foot touched against the yielding bulk of Gilbert the minstrel, lying where he had

179

fallen. 'Did you kill him?' she asked, not much caring because in her world killing was a small matter unless it were one's own kin.

'I think not. I only used the pummel in the back of his neck. He's no fighting man.'

They checked an instant in the tent opening, glancing to right and left. Faint mist lay over everything, blurring the dark shapes of tent and fodder-stack, creeping and wreathing along the ground like smoke; and out of the mist came the formless surf of sound that meant fighting: the clash of arms and the shouting of men, the frightened stamping and snorting of horses in the picket lines, the brazen tongues of Norman trumpets. A ring of fighting all round them, but here at the heart of the camp, nothing moving save the mist-wreaths.

From somewhere strength seemed to have come to Bjorn, like his second wind to a runner. He thrust the battered harp under his arm, and drew the minstrel's dagger from his belt left handed. 'Keep close,' he whispered. 'Now——'

They plunged out into the mist, running low, from tent to fodder-stack, from fodder-stack to cook-place, heading for the stockade and the clamour of the unseen combat. Once, as they crouched in the shelter of a wood-pile, a knight went past them at speed, his shield high on his arm, and they knew by his voice—for he was cursing—that it was Ranulf Le Meschin himself. Once they all but blundered into a party stumbling back with wounded from the breast-works. Torches flared in the mist, and figures brushed them by; but through all the swarming activity of the camp, they passed unchallenged in the confusion and the milky darkness.

Light was growing ahead of them, a rolling tawny smear in the murk; and then all at once, as it seemed, they were in the thick of the fighting, and the light was all about them. The Northmen had thrown in torches and bundles of flaming straw to make shooting light for their archers; and in places the gorse that was interwoven in the stockade and the grass, dry after the long spell of fine weather, was blazing up like heath-fire. Long curved ripples of flame were spreading among the defenders, sending up smoke that mingled with the gilded mist into a bright murk that set men choking; and the fierce light came and went, flaring on helmet and leaping blade, as Northmen and Norman battled for the stockade.

Frytha had the dagger by this time, for on the fringe of the fighting, Bjorn had stopped to twist the spear from the hand of a dead man-at-arms; and she grasped it ready for instant use as they thrust into the *mêlée*. But in the random hurly-burly of close fighting, no one had eyes to spare for them, and yelling with the rest, they drove on toward the fire-streaked stockade. Frytha, her head down close to Bjorn's shoulder, seemed engulfed in a roaring chaos of fire and faces and leaping blades, and realized vaguely that they were only just in time, for already the tide of Northmen was on the turn, falling back across the torn and blackened breastwork.

Then they were at the foot of the stockade bank, in the midst of a reeling press of fighters. Frytha caught an instant's sight in the rolling golden murk above her, of a winged Viking head and great up-swung pole axe, as Gille Butharson turned astride the wreck of the barricade, for a parting blow. She never saw where the great axe crashed down, for Bjorn had whirled about with a yell of triumph, and flung his spear into the crowd of the on-pressing Normans; and next instant they were scrambling together for dear life up the bank and across the tangled ruins of the stockade.

On the crest, Bjorn checked, full in the leaping flame-light, and gave the high, wolfine call that Aikin's sword-band used among themselves. Frytha, poised beside him, heard it rise above the tumult, long-drawn and eerie; and that moment, caught there between friend and foe, and an archer's mark for both, seemed to her the longest that she had ever known. Yet the wolf cry had scarcely died away before it rose again in answer and recognition from somewhere among the crowding shadows below.

'Jump!' Bjorn cried, and his sound arm was round her.

And she felt the thrumming wind of an arrow on her cheek, even as she leapt out and down.

They landed on the far edge of the ditch, and also, she judged from the grunt, on top of a warrior crouching there. She stumbled to her knees, picked herself up—or was dragged to her feet by Bjorn, she was not sure which—and plunged on into the kindly shelter of the mist and the darkness; into the midst of the shadowy wolf-pack shapes of their own kind, that were suddenly all about them.

. . . . . .

It was still early when Bjorn and Frytha came up from the landing-beach toward the Jarlstead, and the morning smoke was curling up from the roofs of the settlement.

The sudden reserve of strength that had come to Bjorn in the dark pavilion had carried him somehow through the night. The foregathering among the Northern glens, with the War bands whose attack on the camp that night had saved them both from a hideous death; the borrowed ponies and the wild ride south through the mountains, until, a little after dawn, they had come down to the lake-shore at Hawes Point, turned their spent mounts over to the men there, and taken one of the light boats on round the nab.

It was with him still, as he strode up toward the Hearth Hall, where the antlers high on the gable end caught the morning sunlight and shone as though every tine were tipped with flame. But he seemed only half aware of the others of his own kind, gathered before the door, who came pressing round him with an outcry of greeting and eager demands to know what news he brought. And as he checked an instant on the foreporch threshold, he put out his sound hand to the rowan-wood doorpost, fumblingly, almost as though he were blind. Then, shaking his fellows back like a tattered cloak, he walked forward into the Hearth Hall.

Frytha followed at a little distance. The morning meal of porridge and bannock was already over, but the hall was still crowded, and by the central hearth, where Haethcyn sat staring into the fire, somehow incomplete because his hands were empty to the Sweet-singer, the Jarl himself stood deep in counsel with some of his chieftains.

He turned as they came in, to see the cause of the stir, and seeing, shot up his heavy golden brows, his gaze searching from Bjorn to Frytha and back again. 'God's Greeting to you, Bjorn Bjornson. So she did go with you. We judged that to be the way of it.' Then, as Bjorn came to a halt before him, and he took in the young warrior's haggard face and bitten mouth, and kirtle torn off one shoulder, his tone changed and quickened. 'But you have run into trouble. Are you scathed?'

Bjorn flung up his head like a pony, shaking the wild dark hair out of his eyes. With the battered harp in one hand and the other hidden in the loose skirt-folds of his kirtle, he had no hand free to thrust it back with. 'God's Greeting to you, Lord Buthar. I am none so scathed that it cannot wait.'

'So. And the word that you bring me?'

'Firstly, that the Normans will be on the march south by this time tomorrow,' Bjorn said.

His words seemed to fall into a sudden hush, and then out of the hush the Jarl said, 'Are you sure?'

'Unless the plan be changed since last night, I am sure.'

Buthar had begun to finger his beard. 'And for the rest?' he demanded after a moment. 'Do you bring me the answers that Aan Olafson could not give to my questions?'

'Yes,' Bjorn said. 'I think that we have not overlooked any.' And while the Jarl, silent among his silent chieftains, listened, tugging at his beard, he made careful report of all that he and Frytha had learned in the Norman camp.

When the last detail had been told, and the tally of men and horses was complete, Jarl Buthar turned his frowning gaze from the young warrior before him to his assembled chieftains. 'This makes ill hearing, my brothers; for it seems that we are more heavily outnumbered even than we had bargained for. Well, at the least we have forewarning, thanks to the Bear-cub. And it is a long road from Cocur's Mouth to the foot of Rannardale.'

Hakon Wall-eye nodded, scratching delicately at the tip of one ear. 'A long road, and much may happen on it. It is in my mind that where the Dale runs narrow at Brackenthwaite would be the best place for it to happen. Given a day and a night, we could strengthen the defences there still further.'

'There is good cover for bowmen in the woods, down there,' put in a big man with a round innocent face and a thatch of sandy hair. 'Let me go with Aikin's band, and give me my pick of the archers to follow me, and Le Meschin's ranks may be something thinner before they break through.'

Jarl Buthar eyed him grimly. 'And how many of my finest archers think you that you will bring back to me for Rannardale afterward, Sigurd Strongbow?'

'They may be better spent in Brackenthwaite, in the long run,' said Sigurd Strongbow.

'I like it not. We had meant but to slow them awhile at Brackenthwaite. This way, we may thin them, of a surety, but the thinning may cost us dearer than we can afford,' the Jarl said. He hesitated, tugging at his beard as though he would tug it out by the roots. 'Yet thinned they must be, before they come to Rannardale.' And then the hesitation fell away like wrappings from a sword-blade. 'So be it, then; we'll gamble on it. And the old Gods have ever loved a good gambler!'

He swung round, his great voice full of confidence and purpose, rising to the rafters, as he called out this man and that from among his chieftains for the tasks made needful by the swift change of plans.

Amid the sudden buzz and stir that was spreading through the hall, Bjorn turned to his foster-father, and held out the battered object that had been the Sweet-singer. In the morning light, only one string shone intact, the rest hung tangled and loose from broken pegs, or were lacking altogether, and the faintly smiling face of the woman, where cross-tree and front stay met, was notched and scarred on cheek and forehead. 'I am sorry that I bring her back to you marred and voiceless, Haethcyn Fostri.'

Haethcyn's hands came out like a mother's for a hurt child, and his face was grievous. 'What have they done to you, my beauty, my Sweet-singer? So so so—here is sore damage indeed. Ah, but it may be set right in time, and she shall sing as sweetly as ever, by and by.' He looked up at Bjorn. 'Voiceless or no, you have brought her back to me.'

'Could I leave her to be restrung and played on by a Norman hand?' Bjorn asked.

'Na na, or you were no true fosterling of mine.' But even as he spoke, the old harper reached out and caught Bjorn's wrist; and voice and manner seemed to pounce, so that once again Frytha thought of an old hound—an old hound snapping after fleas. 'So ho! Here is something else beside torn harp-strings! Show me your hand.'

Bjorn smiled a little, and shaking his right hand free from the loose folds of his kirtle, turned it palm upwards for the old man to see.

The Jarl had swung round again. 'Thor's Hammer! So this was the scathe that could wait? How did it come about, Bjorn?'

There was a sudden press of men all round them, in the midst of which Bjorn stood at his most spear-straight. 'The Normans would fain have had the answers to some questions of their own,' he said clearly and deliberately. He glanced about him at his brothers of the Sword-band, with an odd, rather wavering smile; and then, quite suddenly coming to the end of his strength, staggered as though the ground had side-slipped under him.

Frytha sprang forward to steady him, but somebody was before her, and she saw that it was Aikin. She had not realized that Aikin was there, but everything was a little hazy. 'Steady now, so so—steady, my Bear-cub,' Aikin said; and then Bjorn was sitting on a nearby bench, his head hanging between his shoulders. Garm's grey inquiring muzzle was against his knee, and Aikin was beside him with an arm round his shoulders, holding to his teeth the mead horn that somebody had brought, bidding him drink. Frytha was aware of it all dimly, as something seen through a mist, voices and quickly moving figures, and then the women were there, and there was talk of salves and clean linen. But in the midst of it all, Bjorn struggled to his feet again. 'Surely this is a great stir for so small a matter!' he said impatiently. 'I will go to Storri Sitricson and have him salve the scorch; and after, I will come back for my morning porridge—and for my dirk that I left with you, Fostri.'

And then he was walking away down the Hearth Hall, carefully, like one that is a very little drunk, but quite steadily, looking neither to right nor left. For a moment, nobody moved, and then Jon and Ottar Edrikson slipped from their places and went after him.

Frytha made no attempt to follow them; she did not even watch them go. She subsided on to the nearest bench, and sat there suddenly overwhelmed with a great weariness and a great quiet. Someone must have burst the membrane over one of the high windows and there had been no leisure to mend it; a long sunbeam slanted through the hole, straight across the hearth, and where the thread of smoke curled upward through the sunspot it was as blue as wild hyacinths. It seemed to Frytha the most perfect thing she had ever seen; unbelievably perfect; the slow curls and eddies like fern-fronds made of jewel-blue air; no, like running water, water eddying among stones, like the Sell Beck above the mill dam. Suddenly she was remembering, across the years, little birch-bark long-ships on the Sell Beck, and Ari Knudson's voice came to her so clearly that he might have been speaking beside her. 'That is our Shield Ring, our last stronghold; not the barrier fells and the tottermoss between, but something in the hearts of men.'

Odd, that she should remember so clearly something that she had not truly understood at the time. . . .

Gerd was beside her, scolding and coaxing, talking of milk porridge, and sleep and coming away into the bower.

## XVI

## MORNING IN RANNARDALE

ALL ACROSS THE head of Rannardale the watch-fires
flamed in the luminous darkness of the summer night,
casting a fitful glare along the lift of the great turf-
banks that closed the Road to Nowhere, and flaring redly on
axe-blade and ring-mail and horned helm, as the Northmen
came and went about their camp.

Word had come in, two days since, that the Normans were
out from their camp at Cocur's Mouth, and on the march
south. But they had made slow marching, halting again and
again to scour the side glens and to post bodies of archers
along the way to keep the supply lines safe behind them. And
every mile of their road, the Northern War bands had clung
about them, skirmishing around their advance guard and
harassing their flanks and rear. And so it was only this morning that they had come up with the strengthened defences at

Brackenthwaite, where, in the wooded narrows that were like a gateway to Butharsdale, Aikin and Sigurd Strongbow waited to give them welcome.

After that word came in, there had been only silence, a crawling eternity of silence, for the waiting War Host in Rannardale, until a while after dark, the little weary bands of men, many of them wounded, began trickling back.

And now, in the doorway of the half-ruined house-place of Ragna's steading, where the Jarl had made his headquarters, Jarl Buthar himself stood face to face with his brother, who had been one of the last to come in.

Aikin leaned against the rowan wood door-post as though he were unutterably weary, one hand lax on the head of the old hound pressed against his thigh. 'Aye, we thinned their ranks before they drove us out,' he was saying. 'I watched them through the woods, making camp for the night as I—came away; and they are a great host still, but not the host that marched from Cocur's Mouth. The ravens will feed full gorge in Brackenthwaite tonight.'

'On Norse slain as well as Norman,' the Jarl said.

'Surely. Yet the Norse slain are few to the Norman's many, though Sigurd and upward of half my pack are among them.' Aikin flung up his head and laughed a little wildly. 'Did you not say that the Gods loved a gambler? We have gambled most nobly, and behold! the Gods have loved us—if at a price.'

Outside, Frytha came and went with the other women among the wounded. There were many women with the War Host that night: all those who were strong and without young bairns to drag at their skirts. The bairns and their mothers, the old and the sick, they had sent for safety into the hidden glens further south. The sheep and cattle, too, had gone out over the passes into Burgdale and Ennerdale. Kneeling with a man's head on her knees, while the Countess Tordis clipped away the matted hair to come at his wound, Frytha was remembering the stream of folk and beasts winding up towards the pass: scared and bleating sheep, round-eyed children, women who had taken leave of their man for what might well be the last time. Gerd with the bairn at her shoulder—and the mazelin. Until now, the mazelin had never seemed to take much account of the coming and going of the War-bands, but this time his poor bewildered brain had seemed to make out what was in the wind. Frytha had seen him set out with the sheep, and he had asked her again, piteously, his eyes wandering from her face to follow a knot of warriors as they passed. 'What is it that I cannot remember?' And then, as the sheep caught at his swerving attention, 'They will get over-heated, driven in this weather in so much wool. Why have we not had the sheep-shearing yet? It is past shearing time.'

'We shall have sheep-shearing very soon,' Frytha had told him; and watched him go with Grim and the flock, still glancing back toward the fighting men, with the air of a half-memory stirring and then lost again.

'There is no more that we can do,' the Countess said. 'Come away and get some sleep. Soon it will be morning.'

But Frytha was too restless to sleep. In a little, she would lie down—not just yet. Instead, she drifted over to the circle about the nearest of the great watch-fires. Old Haethcyn was there, seated against the turf bank, and tenderly at work on his Sweet-singer. Bjorn stood beside him, leaning on his spear and watching the work, his right hand muffled in rags and thrust into his breast. He glanced up when she joined them, and showed her a drawn, mocking face, and eyes as bright as the mazelin's own; then turned away to laugh at Jon, who, sitting on his haunches close by, had fallen to his usual pastime of trying to balance his dagger on the tip of one forefinger.

Haethcyn glanced up at the new war arrows Frytha carried thrust into her belt, and there was the grim shadow of a smile in his beard. 'Did I not say to you, once on a time, that sword or distaff side, the day might come when you would have your chance to stand forth with the War-bands at the ravens' gathering?'

189

*The Shield Ring*

Frytha nodded. 'Surely you must have spread your cloak and caught the Second Sight from old Unna in it.' She folded up beside the fire, and looked up at Bjorn in the red flame-light, making little vehement palm-down gestures to him. 'Sit! sit!'

But Bjorn remained stubbornly on his feet.

Someone else had turned aside in passing, to join the group about the fire, and she saw that it was Storri Sitricson. All night, and for other nights before, he had been at work among the wounded, and his plump face was mottled with weariness under his flaming and defiant tonsure. He saw Bjorn and scowled. 'And what is it that you do here, Bjorn Bjornson?'

'I wait for the morning, Pappa Storri,' Bjorn said.

'Meaning that you are still set on a share in the morning's hunting?'

'Surely.'

'You know what I think of you,' said Storri with deep meaning.

Bjorn laughed on a fierce, crowing note. 'I have not forgotten. Wait but a little, and I will suffer all your leechcraft. After tomorrow I will be your man awhile; but tomorrow I am Aikin's.'

'And what use is it that you think you will be to Aikin?—a one-handed fighter?'

'One hand is enough for spear or dirk,' Bjorn said, his nose suddenly in the air. 'Shield, I can do without.'

And then an odd thing happened; for on the far side of the fire somebody leaned forward into the light, saying quickly, 'No need for that. I will be your shield-bearer, this holm-ganging, Bjorn Bjornson,' and Frytha saw that of all people, it was Erland.

Bjorn had swung round, and across the flames the gaze of the two young warriors caught and held, and suddenly they were both grinning. 'One shield and two spears; say, then, what am I? I am Erland and Bjorn at the fight in Rannardale,' Bjorn said. 'That will be a fine riddle for somebody to ask by the winter fire a hundred years from now. '

Frytha was still thinking of the odd ways of men when a little later she found a quiet corner, and lay down for a while. She did not sleep; instead she lay watching the clouds that had begun to drift across the stars. Dark winged clouds that seemed to stoop low above the camp like gigantic ravens gathering to a kill, like the Shield Maidens that her people still half believed in, come to choose tomorrow's slain; so that, watching them, she thought again of old Unna, and the night the wild swans flew over Rannardale.

Presently the under sides of the clouds began to be touched with tawny, and the tawny strengthened to gold and amber; and dawn came under a high watered wild-fowl sky, tremendous steeps of sky, dappled and shining, that arched far, far above those drifting clouds. There was a great crying of curlews over the fells, and a smell of rain in the wind that stirred and rippled the Raven banners in the midst of the camp. A wild dawn, but a golden one.

High on the heathery ridge where Rannardale Knotts humped themselves like the knuckles of a gigantic fist against the sky, Jarl Buthar was already waiting with his runners and certain of his chiefs and captains around him, when word came in that the Normans had broken their last camp, and were once more advancing. Two years and more, the Road had waited; and now the waiting was almost done. At dale-foot and dale-head, and among the rocks and birches of the fell sides between, the men of the War Host were in their places. Njal Scar-arm had taken up the new Raven that he was to carry that day for Gille Butharson, and Jon from the Mill house, grave for once, and bright of eye, had taken up the other, the ancient Raven that would lead Aikin's following into battle. And the time was come for the last of the leaders to be going their separate ways.

Gille walked down through the little barley-fields at the edge of the camp with Aikin, and at the last they halted and faced each other.

'The All Father be with you, Aikin my kinsman,' Gille said.

'And with you, Gille.' Aikin had both hands on the

191

younger man's shoulders. 'And with you. It may be that we shall meet in the thick heart of things this day; but if we meet next in the high hall of Valhalla, I think that at the least we shall have a fine tale to tell each other over the mead horns—and Ari Knudson will have been most fully avenged.'

Gille flung his arms round his kinsman and held him fiercely close, as Aikin himself had once done to Ari Knudson in another dawn. 'Aikin, Aikin, my heart is sore within me that I stand not at your shoulder this day; that what remains of the Sword-band must be split asunder in this that will be the greatest fight of all the fights that we have shared together.'

'Mine also—for I never wanted your shoulder against mine as I shall this day. But a host that fights under two Ravens must have its two leaders, as surely as beck runs to dale.' Aikin dropped his hands and slipped free of the other's clasp, laughing. 'A perilous thing it is to be friend or kin of yours, Gille Butharson! Ach! my ribs are crushed. It is you that should have been called Bjorn, for it is a bear's grip you have!'

He swung on his heel, whistling cheerily to Garm, who stood sniffing at the wind close by, and went striding off down the dale as though he were setting out on a day's hunting.

Gille stood for a few moments, watching man and hound dwindle smaller on his sight, then turned back to his own men beyond the ancient steading.

There was a lark singing above the barley-fields, he noticed.

Meanwhile, among the sparse birchwoods of mid-dale, Bjorn and Frytha also had come to the place and time for going their separate ways; and stood looking at each other, and away again, finding nothing to say; while the rain-scented wind swooped over the neck of the ridge, and set the birch-woods hushing all about them.

Frytha saw the dark flush on Bjorn's cheek-bones, and the burning brilliance of his eyes that seemed overnight to have sunk back into his head like the eyes of an old man; and suddenly she was desperately afraid. She longed to beg him to lay down his spear and go back to Storri Sitricson, but she knew that not all her pleading would even reach him, let alone turn him back from the day's work.

He had been gazing away down the dale, but suddenly he turned his head and looked full at her. 'It is in my heart that now I ought to wish you safe away with Gerd and the cubling,' he said, 'but I think that I am glad you are not. It is as you said when you came after me on the road to Le Meschin's camp; we have always shared the hunting, you and I.'

Frytha nodded, looking away down the dale in her turn.

'I was glad, that day, because you came,' Bjorn said after a moment. 'I could not tell you then that I was glad. I can now, Fryth.'

And she knew that the odd silence that had been between them since the day that word of Ari Knudson's death had come to the Dale, was a thing that had mattered once, but did not matter any more.

He had been fumbling something from his sound hand as he spoke, and now he held it out to her. 'Wear it for me today, Fryth.'

For a moment she looked down at the battered ring, making no move to take it; then up at him, questioningly.

'It is all that I have of my own, save for my dirk, and I shall need that. Take it, Fryth,' he commanded. 'It is in my heart that we shall win this fight, but how many of us shall bear home our shields from the winning is another thing. If I am killed today, then it is for you to keep. And if it be— you, Fryth, then still it is for you to keep. And if it be neither of us—then give me back my ring at sunset.'

Frytha took the ring and slipped it on to her finger, where it hung warm and heavy; loose as it had been on Bjorn's when he first wore it. 'I will bind a blade of grass round it, that I lose it not before sunset,' she said.

Then he was gone, slipping away shadow-silent as a wolf among the birches, on his way to stand with Aikin at the dale-foot.

Frytha stood only an instant where he had left her, then set

off down through the dale-side woods toward the Road; and
finding a place for herself in a patch of rowan scrub, laid her
bow ready strung beside her, and settled herself to wait.

How quiet everything was! Only the rain-scented wind,
and somewhere above the head of the Dale, a lark singing. For
all the sound of human life there was, she might have been
alone in the birch-woods, instead of one of a hidden host. She
hunted about for a blade of grass, but it was all heather just
here; and at last she dragged a thread of wool from the skirt
of her kirtle, and began to bind it round the shaft of Bjorn's
ring so that she should not lose it. The green stone was cool
and dark in the rustling shade, with the secret depths of a
forest pool. A small, oddly potent thing to have come down so
far; all the way from the dark woman out of Wales—Frytha
always thought of her as dark, like Bjorn, with the same music
and the same faint fierce mockery about her—and all the way
back behind her, back and back into the unknown. . . .

Suddenly it seemed to her that the ancient, battered thing
in her hand stood for that queer half-guessed-at difference between Bjorn and his kind. But the difference did not matter
any more, just as the silence did not matter any more. Whatever happened now, between this and sunset, however the
battle went, Bjorn's greatest battle was already fought.

A distant stir of shouting stole up against the wind; and
Frytha was aware of a breath of movement among the trees
and undergrowth on all sides, as men and women slipped
home their bow-strings. She pushed the ring firmly on to her
finger, and taking the arrows from her belt, began to stick
them barb down in a row before her, for quick shooting when
the time came.

## XVII

## THE LAST BATTLE

To the Jarl on Rannardale Knotts, the whole scene
lay spread below as a game of chess set out upon the
board. The Norman Army was in full view now, advancing up the lake-side: a dark and glistening cloud, a
swarm. The soft thunder of hooves and marching feet, the
high challenge of the trumpets, came up faintly, swelling
moment by moment, as the host rolled nearer: a haze of dust
hung over their further ranks; a flying fringe of archers was
skirmishing before their advance guard, running, halting to
shoot, breaking and re-forming as they fell back. And a faint
smile narrowed the eyes of the Jarl as he saw how skilfully
the Northmen were drawing the enemy away from the lake-
shore and up toward the mouth of Rannardale.

They were almost at the dale-foot now, and the host rolled to a halt, and the sun, swinging out from behind a cloud at that moment, gave to the close-massed ranks a dark beetle-wing lustre, striking splinters of light from helmet and lance-head. They were a great army still, despite Brackenthwaite, far, far outnumbering the hidden Northmen who waited for them: yet still, the Jarl smiled. A strong party was breaking off from the rest, swinging right, along the shore toward Hawes Point. No trace now of the old road; sun, rain and wind, and the ever-encroaching wild had blotted out the traces. No sign from the lake-side of the men who crouched among the scrub and boulders, with arrow nocked to string or hand tensed on axe-pole or ashen spear-shaft, ready for instant action should the Normans try to pass that way. But there was small likelihood of their doing that, if the secret of the Road had not been betrayed.

Looking down on them almost as an eagle might do, Jarl Buthar could follow their movements and their findings as clearly as though he was one of them. Galled by the arrows of the archers who had fallen back to the foot of the ridge, they were spreading along the rocky nab to the very brink of the water: deep water right in to the rock wall, and no way round save by boat. They were casting in toward the main ridge: a black rock wall, boulder and heather tuft rising almost sheer from the lake-side levels, and no way over, surely, for either friend or foe. And clear before them, the track looping away up Rannardale, as though pointing the way to their goal.

In a little, they swung back to the main column; and the whole army was on the move again, spreading up Rannardale Beck, with their centre on the Road to Nowhere.

Jarl Buthar drew back from his vantage point, and slipped over the crest of the ridge and along it below the sky-line, running low; and a few moments later, crouching among the mountain juniper, was looking directly down into Rannardale. Away down-dale he saw the Norman vanguard narrow in on itself as the slopes on either side steepened. He could pick out Ranulf and his household knights by the banners in their midst, and his lips twisted under his beard, while his eyes, narrowing to slits, were the bleak bright blue of far Northern seas.

Without turning his head, he spoke to the first of the runners beside him, and the man drew back a little, and was gone, snaking down through the juniper and heather.

And now the Normans were up to the earthworks in the mouth of the Dale, and as one man, the defenders there rose to meet them, and the sudden surf-roar of battle burst up to the watching Jarl on Rannardale Ridge, as a sea-wave leaping up a sheer cliff-face. He was still smiling as he watched the fight begin to swing to and fro across the line of the earth-works; still smiling when, as though yesterday's work at Brackenthwaite had drained the heart out of them, his own men began to give way. And when at last they broke wide, and, roaring their triumph, the Normans poured through into Rannardale, the smile broadened slowly to a grin.

'So ho! that was finely done!' said the Jarl softly, between his teeth, to the men beside him. 'The Wolf's head is in the trap. It remains now for his tail to follow, and we shall have fine sport, neighbours.'

Frytha, crouching bow in hand among the hidden archers in the birch-woods, could see nothing of what passed at the dale foot, but the distant roar of battle sweeping up through the birches told her when Norman and Northman came to-gether, and she heard the rising yell of triumph as the enemy swept aside Aikin's men and came pouring through. She heard the sound surge toward her, swelling louder, louder yet, like a flood that has burst its dam; the shouting and the weapon-ring, the rolling thunder of horses' hooves, while ahead of it, a shiver, a kind of long breath of ended waiting ran through the dale-side woods.

Nearer and nearer yet; a flicker of movement, of weapons and colour, and the manes of horses showed far down through the trees to her right. And then the track below her that had been empty the moment before spilled full of men—a great tide of men and horses with the coloured flames of the pennons streaming over all.

Frytha leaned forward over her bent knee, and plucked the first of her arrows from the turf before her.

The tail of the Norman army was well into Rannardale when the vanguard began to glimpse banks and ditches across the way, and the glint of sunlight on axe-head and winged helm through the trees. Ranulf Le Meschin, suddenly anxious of eye, shouted to his trumpeter beside him, and drove his spurred heel into his horse's flanks, so that the grey plunged forward snorting, as the trumpets sounded for a charge.

And in that instant, as though the trumpets had been a signal, there rose a wild outcry from the rear.

Behind the Normans, Aikin and the flower of the Viking War Host had swarmed from hiding, as though the empty fell-side had burst into a sweat of berserkers. They were swinging down the sheer rocks on ropes of hide; they started from behind every boulder and bracken frond, while at their backs, more came charging up from the lake-shore, some from the grain-boats that had brought them round the Point, others naked and dripping lake-water, having swum the distance with their weapons in their teeth. From fell scarp and deep water they joined and turned inward, shoulder to shoulder, yelling as they ran.

They were a mere handful, numbered against Le Meschin's hordes, but surprise was with them. They flung themselves against the Norman rearguard, crushing it in upon the baggage train, so that men and pack-horses were flung into confusion. And while the whole tail of the Norman column was reeling from the blow, a wave of Northmen were out over the defences at the dale head and charging down upon their vanguard, with Gille Butharson, pole axe upswung, yelling like a fiend at their head, and swooping and hovering in their midst, the black Raven banner of the Viking kind.

The Normans, penned in the narrow dale, faced outward all ways against the onslaught that was upon them from every side; and for a while it looked as though their so much greater numbers might yet carry the day. Again and again their mailed ranks steadied and hurled away the yelling berserkers of the War Host; again and again, with superb courage, Le Meschin's household knights spurred their horses against the enemy, tearing great wounds in the Northmen's wave-sweep ranks. But it seemed that nothing in Heaven or Hell could stop the thin hosts of the fells, while the heavily armed Normans, close jammed as they were, clogged every man his comrade's sword arm, and made a target that could not be missed for the archers among the birch-woods.

And all the while, whether it looked like victory or whether it looked like defeat, the man on the crest of Rannardale Ridge looked down with the same face, the same twisted smile, the same narrowed eyes that glittered with the cold light of far Northern seas. He was on his feet now, for the time for concealment was over. And Ranulf Le Meschin, tipping a haggard face skyward as he fought to steady his reeling ranks and stay the confusion that was all too surely spreading among his men, might have seen at last, high, high above him, dark against the drifting sky, the bull's-horn-crested figure of the ancient enemy who had held Lake Land against him for thirty years.

But the hail of arrows was slackening now, and the time was come for the Jarl to throw in the last of his resources. The hollow boom of the War horn rang and re-echoed from fell to fell, and far down through the birch-woods, Frytha loosed her last arrow into the chaos that was beginning to spread below her, and flinging aside her useless bow, was up and running with the rest of the hidden archers, freeing her dirk as she ran, to hurl herself into the wild *mêlée* in the dale.

It was all round her now, a nightmare of yelling, blood-bedaubed faces, of leaping blades and trampling hooves, a shrieking tumult that seemed to wash to and fro between the steep walls of the fells that hemmed it in, bursting upward toward the ravens of the high crags that already swept and circled overhead. And over all rang the brazen yelping of the Norman trumpets sounding for retreat, and the wild note of the Viking War horn from the crest of the ridge.

Somewhere close to her, a horse screamed, and Frytha was aware of a man almost naked, slipping in past her, running low among the legs of the battle, and knew that Jarl Buthar had unleashed his final and most horrible weapon against the enemy.

From all sides the men slipped in under the horses, stabbing upward with their dirks at the poor brutes' breasts and bellies as they ran; and were away to the next horse before the last crashed down.

And now the screams of stricken horses rose above all else; and as final, blind panic swept through the Norman ranks, men turned everywhere to the mouth of the dale, trampling their own wounded underfoot, hacking their way through friend and foe alike in a wild struggle to reach open country.

Close before Frytha, a berserker dripping crimson from head to foot darted across, and a great grey destrier shrieked and went up in a rearing turn, scattering Northman and Norman with his lashing hooves, and then crashed down on to his side; and in the momentary clearing that he made in his fall, Frytha saw his rider stagger clear, and knew by the white distorted face he turned upward as his helmet fell off, that it was Le Meschin himself. In the same flash of time, the squire beside him had swung down from his roan, and then the battle closed over again, and a man-at-arms was making straight at Frytha, his sword up, and there was no more time for thinking of Ranulf Le Meschin.

The whole fight was moving down dale, as the desperate Normans flung themselves upon Aikin's barrier of men, struggling to break through. Bjorn, using his spear left-handed, had been close to Aikin since the battle first joined, in the close knot of warriors about the Raven. The fire of battle was in him, the cold bright fire of his Viking blood, mingling with another fire that seemed to spring from his maimed hand, so that he felt strong and tireless as all the heroes of Asgard rolled into one, filled with a high wind of exultancy that seemed to lift him up so that there was no weight in his body and no substance in the ground beneath his feet. He was vividly aware of Erland's shoulder against his, as they fought together under the one shield. All around him battled his brothers of the Sword-band. They were his shoulder-to-shoulder men, and he theirs, and as they braced their thin, close-knit ranks to hold the flood of yelling, half-crazed Normans that flung themselves upon them, he felt his bond with them as never before.

They were his shoulder-to-shoulder men, and he was theirs, and there was nothing else in life than the fierce and shining bond, and the fierce and shining moment. But slowly, surely, they were being forced back by sheer weight of numbers against them, back and back, killing as they went, until their blades were glutted. And now a new sound rose above the roar of battle. The Viking kind had begun to sing, as their forefathers had sung under the Ravens before them; man after man catching up the song from his neighbour and chanting wild staves of improvised verse that set their own hearts and the hearts of their comrades on fire.

'Now in Rannardale the ravens gather, and the stinging serpents of the Warstrife fly!' Erland caught up the chant. 'Now in Rannardale the wolves are waiting, and deeply do our spears drink blood!'

'A spear-welcome for a guest that comes with spears,' sang Bjorn, jibing. 'A red welcome to a fine feast of wolves! Would ye go forth from Rannardale, ye who came unbidden? Is it that ye find our welcome over warm?'

Back and back, across the dale-foot barriers, killing as they went, until the keen blades were blunted, and the arms that wielded sword and pole axe cramped and turned to lead, and many warriors were down. And now the dale-mouth was broadening with every backward stop, so that the Shield-line was drawn out thin and thinner yet, until it began to fray like a chafed rope, and a trickle of desperate Normans broke through; men who stumbled in their tracks and rolled over, others who ran on, not pursued save by a random arrow, for the Northmen had other things on hand than the running down of fugitives.

A terrified roan horse crashed by Bjorn, the rider clinging half out of the saddle, lacking helmet and with mail coif dragged back so that his head was bare. Bjorn had one swerving glimpse of the wild white face of Ranulf Le Meschin that cried curses shrilly like a woman, and then horse and rider were past and away at headlong gallop.

Aikin's voice rose above the uproar, yelling to his Sword-band to hold fast, to close the Shield wall. 'Remember Ari Knudson, brothers of mine, and stand strong!' But it was impossible to stand strong when the line was drawn out to a ravelling thread; they could only fall back, or thrust forward. And suddenly he was sweeping them forward again in one last reckless charge. 'Sa sa sa! On, my hearts! Follow up—follow me! follow me home!' Wave-flame flashed like the arc of Bifrost the Rainbow as he swung the great blade above his head; the snarling grey shadow that was Garm sprang forward beside him, straight into the jammed and frenzied mass of the enemy; and the valiant handful that were left of the Sword-band stormed at his heels.

Bjorn saw Jon stagger and go down to a flung spear, and the Raven with him. He cried a word to Erland, hurled his own spear from him into the Norman ranks, and stepping clear from the protection of the other's shield, he caught up the black banner before it had well gone down, and reared it again amid the reeling press.

Steadying the shaft one-handed, he was wading forward against the flood of the battle, in the bright and terrible wake of Wave-flame. Above him the great black wings seemed to spread for flight, bearing him up and on—on into the sunlight—into the fire, and the fierce and flashing heart of things. . . .

The sun was yet high when it was all over. The last great battle for Lake Land had been fought; and of the great army of Ranulf Le Meschin, that had marched out from the camp at Cocur's Mouth so short a time before, a desperate rabble had broken out through Aikin's Shield-wall, and were flying for their lives down the wide vale: and the rest lay out in

Rannardale mingled with the Viking dead about the Road that led to Nowhere.

And now, with the rain-wind strengthening, and the sky above the dale-foot flushing angry red behind cloud-bars of purple and furnace gold, men and women were moving among the birch-woods and through the wreckage of the little fields, seeking their own wounded, stripping the Norman dead, killing the Norman wounded as they killed their own before now, when need be.

Groups of men passed, carrying some fallen warrior among them; the women were busy at the old work of womenkind after the fighting is over, and here, there and in all places at once, seemingly, went Storri Sitricson, with his kirtle kilted to his knee and his tonsure like a crown of fire in the sunset light, priest and surgeon by turns.

They had found Aikin a while since where the dead were thickest, far up the dale where the last charge had carried him, lying with Jon and Erland and a goodly company about him; Wave-flame reddened to the hilt in his hand, and Garm, with his grey muzzle tilted skyward, howling beside his body.

Frytha heard the howling of the old dog still, a piercing note of wild, intolerable mourning that seemed to reach to the very sky, echoing like the voice of all the loss and heartbreak in the world, over the spent battle-field. Presently she would grieve for Aikin the Beloved, for freckled happy-go-lucky Jon, even for Erland; just now the only thing that mattered to her very nearly was that she had found Bjorn, standing amid the few—the very few—who were left of the Sword-band, around their dead leader, leaning on the shaft of the Raven Banner, as last night he had leaned on his spear, and with the dark folds of it trailing on to his shoulder, as he looked down.

She had said 'Bjorn,' because there was nothing else to say.

And he had raised his head slowly, as though it were very heavy, and looked at her across the distance between, and said, 'Fryth,' and she had noticed that the place where he had bitten through his lower lip was bleeding again.

Now they were carrying Aikin's body down toward the

lake-shore, to be loaded with the wounded into the grain-boats that would take them home. And Bjorn was with her, a little behind the rest, as she checked beside the body of a great grey destrier, whose dappled flank shone coppery in the westering light.

'That is Le Meschin's horse,' she said vaguely. 'I saw it go down. Has Le Meschin been found?'

Bjorn shook his head. 'He broke the Shield-wall and won clear away. He'll be back at Cocur's Mouth by this, if he hasn't foundered the poor brute he was riding.'

'What colour was it, the horse?'

'A roan,' Bjorn said, beyond surprise.

'That will have been his squire's horse—the squire he called Tristram.' Frytha stooped as she spoke, and as though she knew what she would find, lifted the pale tumble of the destrier's mane from the face of the man who lay almost beneath the great brute.

Bjorn looked down in silence a moment at the squire's young round face with the four stripes of Frytha's fingernails still showing on his cheek. 'So he gave up his own horse to Le Meschin,' he said at last. 'I think that I should not care to be Le Meschin tonight.'

He moved away, as Frytha let the destrier's mane flow back over the squire's face; and almost in the same instant she heard him call rather strangely, 'Fryth, come here.'

She turned swiftly, and found him half kneeling beside another fallen figure, the Raven propped in the crook of his right arm, his sound hand still under the man's shoulder, where he had just turned him over.

'Who is it?' she said, but even as she asked the question, she saw. It was the mazelin. The mazelin lying with a broken spear still clenched in his hand, among Le Meschin's household knights.

'I suppose he came back after a strayed sheep, or for some such reason; and when he heard the fighting—he must have remembered,' Bjorn said after a pause.

And suddenly her eyes stung with tears. 'We shall miss

him at the sheep-shearing, and when lambing time comes round.'

Bjorn nodded. 'I hope he has found his orchard again,' he said, with an odd gentleness. He let the mazelin sink back on to his face, and got slowly to his feet. 'Come you.'

So they left the mazelin lying with his own people, and went on, down toward the shore.

The beck broadened a little lower down, slowing its rush as though to gather itself before it plunged at last into Crumbeck Water, and Frytha looking down into the glassy swirl of it under the rocks and bog-myrtle of the bank, saw every ripple and eddy stained with crimson. She checked an instant with a little startled cry, pointing, 'Look, Bjorn—the Beck is running red! Old Unna said she saw Rannardale Beck running red!'

'It is only the sunset shining in the water,' Bjorn said. 'The reds are up. We shall have rain before morning.'

'The sunset?' She looked at him a moment in bewilderment, then turned her face up to the fiery sky, suddenly waking to the time of day, and the angry crimson spreading like a stain from the west that was one vast bonfire, to fade at last into dim rose-flecks far over beyond Beacon Fell. 'Yes, of course. It is sunset.' She pulled off the ancient ring, and unwound the thread of wool from its shaft, and held it out to Bjorn. 'Here is your ring again; I have not lost it.'

# XVIII

## A SONG OF NEW BEGINNINGS

THEY CARRIED AIKIN's body back to the Jarlstead,
and laid it in the Hearth Hall, on the skin of a black
bear that he had killed twenty winters ago; and re-
kindled the fire on the hearth from the peat that had been left
smouldering in its firepot. The old hound Garm had ceased
his howling, and crawling close, sank his chin on his lord's
feet, and fell asleep as though suddenly he was comforted.
They let him lie there, while those that were left of the
Sword-band kindled pine-knot torches at the waking fire, and
took their stand around their dead leader, to keep their last
watch with him.

That was when Bjorn, in his place among the rest, began to
sway on his feet, as though he stood on a heaving deck instead
of solid ground. He steadied himself, looked about him
questioningly, seeming not sure where he was, and crashed
down full length on to the ferny floor.

Ottar Edrikson, who stood nearest to him, caught up his torch as it sputtered among the green fern, and was kneeling beside him on the instant, even as Gille himself, giving his own torch to another man, came thrusting through the little knot of warriors. 'Is he scathed?' he demanded.

Ottar shook his head. 'I think not. It is fever; burning hot, he is.'

Gille, kneeling on Bjorn's other side, turned him over. 'It is his hand,' he said; and his voice was hoarse and heavy with his own grief. 'Young fool—young *fool!* Have there not been gaps enough torn in the Sword-band this day?' He lifted Bjorn as though he had been a child, and getting to his feet, carried him across to the skin-spread benches and laid him down there. 'Go one of you and find Storri Sitricson, and tell him there is work for him here.'

Storri Sitricson came, carrying the tools of his trade, and scolding like a hen-wife. 'Tch, tch! Did I not tell him? But no, he must gang his own wilful gate—as though I had not work enough already!'

And hard on his heels came Frytha with water and linen and salves; and the fear that had gone away when she found Bjorn again at sunset crowding cold upon her.

It seemed a very long time that she worked with Pappa Storri over Bjorn's motionless body, before at last the life seemed to wake again under their hands. But at last he opened his eyes, frowning into space, and muttered something unintelligible about a firedrake.

'Maybe thinks he is one,' said Storri with a snort that was half satisfied and half exasperated. 'He's hot enough.'

But Frytha, kneeling with an arm under Bjorn's head and trying to make him drink the herb brew in the bowl she had taken up, knew better. So it had seemed like that to him, too. 'The Firedrake is dead,' she said quietly. 'Do you not remember?'

He turned his head a little to look at her, but she did not think he really saw her; and suddenly his face was touched with the same shadowy triumph she had seen there four nights

207

ago. He said clearly and deliberately, 'I was not going to,' and closed his eyes again, and she knew that he was back in the hands of Le Meschin's torturers.

'There is nothing you can do but stay with him and give him the brew when he will drink,' said Storri, gathering his belongings together. 'I will come back presently.'

All through that night the torches came and went through the settlement. Some of those who had been sent out of the Dale for safety had returned, and there was the crying of tired and frightened children; more wounded were carried into the Hearth Hall, for Storri Sitricson's little hospice had long since overflowed, and Storri Sitricson himself strode ceaselessly between hall and hospice, about his work. Jarl Buthar was with his warriors outside, and it seemed to Frytha, kneeling beside Bjorn as the long hours dragged away, that every time she looked up, the Countess was either coming in or going out, the Countess with her hood fallen back from her pale hair, and her pale intense face more than ever a Valkyrie's in the torch-light.

The wind rose and wuthered against the deep thatch, making the flames of the torches jump so that one moment the hall would be plunged in shadow, and the next the light would leap upward, playing on the smoke-dimmed shields that hung from the house-beam and bringing the snarling mask of the ancient figure-head leaping forward out of obscurity; then sinking so that all the hall was lost again save for the flame-lit ring of warriors about their leader's body.

The rain came at last, fine rain that hushed and whispered against the stretched membrane of the windows, and came through the smoke-hole to fall hissing into the fire. All through the night, the proud and tattered handful who were left of the Sword-band kept their watch, each man with a torch in one hand and his drawn blade in the other. And all night Frytha knelt beside the bench on which Bjorn lay, listening to his half-conscious muttering. Only a short summer night, but it seemed to her longer than any winter one that she had ever known.

In the morning, when the torches grew bleak and pale, Garm still lay unmoving with his old grey muzzle on his Lord's feet. Ottar Edrikson stooped, half hesitating, to touch him, then looked up at the rest. 'Always he ran at Aikin's heel,' he said rather unsteadily, 'and he was too old to learn new ways, I reckon.'

Aikin Jarlson was not how-laid with the rest of the Norse dead, in the long how behind the Jarlstead; for as a Viking Chieftain it was fitting that he should lie apart and on high ground. And even before the Jarl gave the order, there seemed no question as to where the place should be. So when the time came, his sword companions laid him on a hurdle and carried him through the soft rain-swathes up the Sell Glen and away over the fells to the high place from which he had handled his hosts in Keskadale, two summers ago, the place that he had loved since he was a boy.

Storri Sitricson led the way, with his dark kirtle belted knee high; the few survivors of the Sword-band followed, carrying their dead leader in their midst; then came the Jarl and the Chiefs of the War Host, and last of all, a throng of ordinary folk, warriors and women and boys, Saxon and Northman, who had left whatever they were doing to follow Aikin the Beloved.

In their midst stalked Haethcyn, angrily refusing all offers of help, though his legs were no longer really up to the mountain work; and beside him, Frytha; the old harper and the girl drawn very close together by their sick anxiety for Bjorn, left behind them in the Hearth Hall. Frytha had not wanted to come, had not wanted to leave Bjorn—but Bjorn, in one of the moments when his senses returned somewhat to his hot head, had demanded that she should go with the how-laying party; urging her with a wild vehemence born of raging fever, 'The Sword-band is already thin enough; therefore you must go—you *shall* go—for both of us, Fryth; lest Aikin count me faithless. Promise me you will, Fryth, promise—or I swear by the White Kristni, I'll go myself!' And Frytha had promised.

So here she was with the rest, climbing steadily in the wake of the sword-band; up to the beck-head, under the dark mist-hung ramparts of Grismoor and Eel crag; out along the last ridge that blurred away all round them into the rain-mist.

So at last they reached the place that had been made ready, and set down their burden.

The silence of the high fells was all around them, a silence that the soft bluster of the wind seemed only to intensify. The rain-mist drove by them, blotting out the dale below and the fells around. There was rain in their hair and on their shoulders, and rain hanging like silver beads among the rough hairs of the bearskin on which Aikin lay; and some-where out of the greyness rose suddenly a great crying of the gulls above Derwent Water, so that it seemed to Frytha for a moment that this was no inland fell on which they stood, but a tall sea headland; and she fancied that the mist tasted salt on her lips. And then it was not a headland, but a great ship, a long Viking galley, riding out into a grey sea. ('I was a Sea-King in those days . . .').

They laid Aikin in the place that had been made ready for him, with Wave-flame in his hand. 'Nay, it was between him and Ari Knudson,' Gille had said, when the question of the sword's fate was mooted. 'I am an axe-man, and I have al-ready the sword that was his before Wave-flame came to him. This was a blade for giants and heroes, and the giants and heroes are all dead.' Now it was Gille, doing for Aikin the things which were for a son or a man's closest friend to do, who drew the dark folds of the bearskin close around him, and set his linden shield and his spear beside him, and laid the old hound Garm at his feet, where he had loved to sleep since he was a puppy.

Storri Sitricson was speaking Christian prayers in a tongue that he seemed to have half forgotten, and that meant nothing to his listeners; and then, as the warriors stooped to lay back the heathery sods over all, old Haethcyn stepped out of the grave-head, with the Sweet-singer, restrung now and tenderly made whole again, in his hands.

He shook back his badger-striped mane of hair, and drawing himself to his full splendid height, as he seldom did nowadays, began the lament that he had made for Aikin Jarlson. And the wild falling cadences found a kinship with the desolate fell-top scene, and an echo in the hearts of the gathered warriors, as the Latin prayers could not do.

'Where the ravens gathered    black-winged over Warstrife,'

sang Haethcyn,

'Where the blows fell thickest    and warriors crashed together,
Crashed and hurled together    like a stormy sea;
There stood forth Aikin    mightiest of warriors.
Dealing lightning death    above the linden shield.
Mightily he wielded    Wave-flame the destroyer,
When the foe came rushing on    swift he hurled them back;
Laughed against their lightnings    while the ravens screamed;
Sprang to meet the grey iron-tempest. . . .'

They were piling stones above the place now, the first stones of the great how that would rise presently, marking the skyline for all men to see and remember.

Haethcyn sang on :

'Fell at last among them
Pierced by many wounds,    Aikin the Beloved
Mightiest of warriors,    lovely with his weapons;
Deadlier in War strife    than grey boar of the Wildwood.
Truer to his hearth-friend    than thrice-tempered blade.'

So Aikin Jarlson was how-laid after the manner of his forefathers, as the Chieftains of the Viking kind had been how-laid on high place and sea headland wherever the wandering Northmen ran their keels ashore. And his Sword-brothers piled the stones high, and left him to the wind and the rain and the curlews calling.

Gille and the Jarl stood a while with bowed heads beside the how, then turned away, last of all to leave the spot. And Frytha, glancing back once as they made their way homeward, saw that Gille had moved close to his father, and the two were walking shoulder to shoulder, as though perhaps their grief for Aikin had drawn them toward each other. She had certainly never seen them do that before.

A few days later, Jarl Buthar marched to Amilside, drove

out the Norman garrison, and leaving them contemptuously alone to make their retreat over the moors to Kentdale, reduced the old Roman fort to a pile of stones.

'I think that Ranulf Le Meschin will have no more need of a burg in free Lake Land,' said the Jarl.

Bjorn was still desperately sick then. He had kept on his feet somehow, through all the time of supreme need, as a spent man who knows that if he goes down he will not be able to rise again. And then, when the supreme need was over, he had gone down. And the long fight that they fought to save both his life and his right hand was a thing that only Frytha and his foster-father and Storri Sitricson knew, and none of them would ever forget.

They saved both, but sheep-shearing and hay harvest were long over, and the stone how raised full height above Aikin's grave, by the time that Bjorn crawled out again to sit on the bench before the Hearth Hall door.

A fine day of late summer came, an evening when the little pale barley-fields shone like silk along the shores of the Crumbeck Water and the apples were turning yellow on the trees in the garth. And Frytha, coming down the Sell Glen with four wild raspberries in the palm of her hand, was humming softly to herself a tune that had been running in her head all evening, since she passed Gerd spinning at the Hearth Hall door and singing as she rocked with her foot the cradle in which the bairn lay round-eyed and obstinately wakeful.

'Hush thee, hush thee, bonnie and bold,
Thee shall have a bright sword,
A helm of red gold.
Let thee go to sleep now,
And never cry,
And thee shall go a-Viking
Down the Whale's Road, the Swan's Road
Thee shall go a-Viking, by and by.'

An old, old lullaby that had come west-over-seas with the dragon-keels from Norway, and been old, even then. It was running so strongly through Frytha's head that when the harp notes reached her, they seemed at first to be part of it. Then she realized that it must be Bjorn somewhere nearby, and turning aside a little, found him sitting among the birch scrub, with his back against the warm turf of the intake wall, and the long, delicate shadows of the birch leaves playing over the strings of the Sweet-singer on his knee.

He was steadying the harp as well as he could with his right hand, which was still heavily bandaged, and fingering the strings with the other, almost as lightly, it seemed, as the leaf-shadows could do. His face, turned down glen toward the three great birch-trees above the mill dam (odd, that there were still three of them, Frytha thought suddenly; there should have been only one now, standing lonely), was intent and absorbed; but he looked round as Frytha came toward him, his gaze mocking. 'You would think that with two things that seem as equal as a man's two hands, each could do the task of the other? I cannot play this thing left-handed. . . . Have you been up to see Grim?'

Frytha nodded, and sat down beside him. 'Look—wild raspberries, the very last of the summer; two for you and two for me. I found him up at the hut and told him that the puppy is ready to leave its dam.' After a moment she added wonderingly, 'It is so short a time since it happened, and—Aikin, and Jon and Erland and all the rest—and already it seems important to us that a sheepdog puppy is ready to leave its dam, and you and I sit here eating wild raspberries.'

'Grim still needs a sheepdog, and wild raspberries are still sweet.'

'They shouldn't be,' Frytha said rebelliously. 'It is faithless for everything to be just the same as it used to be. Anyway, this one isn't sweet. It is all pips.'

Bjorn laughed, watching the play of the long-fingered leaf-shadows over the strings of the Sweet-singer. Then the laughter went from him. 'Nothing will ever be quite the same as it used to be. For another summer, or two—or even three, we may harvest the dale fields; but presently Buthar will go back to Eskdale, and Gille with him, and we shall take our share of flocks and gear, and scatter by little and little, and the fire will die in the Hearth Hall, and the settlement will be no more than it was thirty years ago, a few herding huts for the men who tend the Jarl's sheep on the high summer pasture.'

Frytha looked down past the three great birches and the mill house toward the broom-thatched roofs that she could glimpse beyond the mouth of the glen. She could see the smoke rising from the Jarlstead, and people coming and going among the garths, but in the thickening honey-coloured light of evening it all looked a little remote, like something that is over. It had come into being for a purpose, and now it seemed that the purpose was served. 'It will be the end of the only life we know,' Bjorn had said, that day at Bjornsthwaite; and she had said, 'I suppose the new one will be an adventure too, in a way.' But it had not seemed so near then.

Bjorn said suddenly, 'It is in my mind that we shall have to carry fire round Bjornsthwaite, and make the land-take afresh, before we begin to clear the bracken. It is so long since the farm went back to the wild.'

Frytha looked round to him, not speaking at once. As it had begun with fire, this life of the Dale with its fierce background of danger that was the only life she knew, so it was to end with fire; not the pale flame of burning thatch, this time, but the warm red flame of mark fires reclaiming an old Land-take from the wild. Bjorn had not asked her to go with him, and she had not said that she would; but there was no need. There never had been any need since that first time of all, when he had caught her by the hem of her kirtle and said, 'Come you,' like as it might be the King of Norway, and she had come.

'Grim must come too,' she said at last. 'He isn't only a shepherd—he can do anything.'

'Surely. Haethcyn says the land used to carry the best sheep in Eskdale, in the old days; but it will be a while and a while after the bracken is cleared, before it does that again. It is in my heart that you must have a long wait for your amber ear-drops, Fryth.'

'I shall not mind,' Frytha said.

They sat for a while in silence, while the day faded over the fells and the clear northern twilight stole up the Sell Glen. Away below them firelight began to flicker in the doorway of the mill house. The faint rooty scent of bracken seemed to grow stronger, and the purling of the beck louder, as the dusk deepened; and a pale-winged night moth hovered past Frytha's face.

Bjorn returned to his tentative, faintly clumsy left-hand fingering of the harp-strings. It was no tune that Frytha knew, scarcely a tune at all, as yet.

'What is it that you make?' she asked at last.

'I make a song.'

'Not another Sword song?'

'No,' he said. 'A song of new beginnings.'

# GLOSSARY
## of place-names

| | |
|---|---|
| Alverdale | *Allerdale* |
| Amilside | *Ambleside* |
| Bassteinthwaite | *Bassenthwaite* |
| Blencathra | *Saddleback* |
| Burgdale | *Borrowdale* |
| Butharsmere | *Buttermere* |
| Cocur | *Cocker* |
| Coupland | *Copeland* |
| Crumbeck Water | *Crummock Water* |
| Grismere | *Grasmere* |
| Grismoor | *Grassmoor* |
| Kentdale | *Kendal* |
| Keswic | *Keswick* |
| Longdale | *Langdale* |
| Mulecaster | *Muncaster* |
| Rafnglas | *Ravenglass* |
| Ryedale | *Rydal* |
| Sell Beck | *Sail Beck* |
| The Winding Mere | *Windermere* |